Sloan looked up at him steadily, a world of gentle understanding in her eyes.

Brett was moving before he even realized it. It had been so long since he'd felt the urge, he didn't recognize it until his mouth was on hers.

He felt her little jump of surprise, and a tiny part of his mind suggested he should stop this before he regretted it. But that cause was lost the moment he felt her lips under his, and turned to ash the moment her mouth softened, the surprise fading.

She was kissing him back. Lighting a fire in him that made the one on the hearth seem no more than a flickering match.

She leaned into him, and a gentle, quiet sound came from her, almost a moan. Need exploded in him, unlike anything he'd felt in longer than he could remember.

It was hot, swift, consuming, and he wanted nothing more than to hit the floor and take this woman here and now.

***

Be sure to check out the rest of the books in this miniseries—Cutter's Code: A clever and mysterious canine helps a group of secret operatives crack the case.

***

If you're on Twitter, tell us what you think of Harlequin Romantic Suspense! #harlequinromsuspense

Dear Reader,

One of the things I love about writing connected books is how various secondary characters take shape and eventually demand to have stories of their own. I especially love it when one I never expected to write a full book about develops into such an appealing character I just have to find out more about them.

In the Cutter's Code series there is one of those characters. He began simply as a device of sorts, someone I knew this string of suspense stories was going to need: a friendly cop. And the more times this character appeared in the books, the more fascinated with him I became, until I knew he was going to have to have his own story.

That time has finally come. After all the times he has helped the Foxworth family, they now have a chance to repay the favors, and in the process realize that they've become his family, as well. Brett Dunbar is one of my favorite secondary characters I've ever written, and I'm delighted to give him the heroic woman he deserves. I hope you enjoy their story.

As always, happy reading. And woof!

Justine Davis

OPERATION
POWER PLAY

Justine Davis

HARLEQUIN® ROMANTIC SUSPENSE

Recycling programs
for this product may
not exist in your area.

ISBN-13: 978-0-373-27906-7

Operation Power Play

Copyright © 2015 by Janice Davis Smith

Printed in U.S.A.

Justine Davis lives on Puget Sound in Washington State, watching big ships and the occasional submarine go by and sharing the neighborhood with assorted wildlife, including a pair of bald eagles, deer, a bear or two and a tailless raccoon. In the few hours when she's not planning, plotting or writing her next book, her favorite things are photography, knitting her way through a huge yarn stash and driving her restored 1967 Corvette roadster—top down, of course.

Connect with Justine at her website, justinedavis.com, at twitter.com/justine_d_davis, or on Facebook at facebook.com/justinedaredavis.

I'm stealing this dedication spot back from my readers for this book. If you read the first Cutter's Code book, *Operation Midnight*, you might remember the dedication included a dog named Murphy, who was instrumental in bringing my own sweet girl into our lives. He was also my first grand-pup. We sadly lost Murphy a few weeks ago, and I'm turning this space over to his mom.

A little more than twelve years ago a silly, baby-faced chocolate Lab puppy came into my family's life. The name Murphy seemed to suit him. Deliciously adorable, he was a goofy, fun-loving Lab puppy, digging up plants in the garden, stealing raw chicken breasts on the kitchen counter and developing an addiction to tennis-ball retrieving. He was gentle and loving around the elderly, and incredibly patient with children. The ultimate host, he ensured you had a good night's sleep by keeping watch outside your door. Murphy greeted every friend at the door with a welcoming bark and a wagging tail...right before he dropped his ball in your lap to throw for him. A mere ninety-eight pounds, he was the master snuggler of lapdogs. He loved road trips from California to Washington, spending the majority of it standing on the center console while sticking his head out the sunroof. His exhuberance for play was unwavering—at the beach, at the park, at home—ball in mouth, he was ready ALL THE TIME. He provided a daily reminder that unconditional love and happiness can exist. His absence is greatly noticeable in our house, but heaven just got a little brighter because of him.

Chapter 1

Is this really worth it?

Brett Dunbar was at the stage of his morning run where he always doubted it. The stage when even the beauty of his surroundings as the trail paralleled an inlet of Puget Sound didn't help.

His new companion was no help either. He'd thought Cutter would be a distraction at least. That the dog might act as dogs do, slowing to sniff everything in sight, thus allowing him to give in to the urging of his body to slow down, enjoy the morning quiet, make this a nice leisurely stroll. But this dog was acting like a demanding trainer, pushing, prodding, running ahead and turning to wait, subtly implying that Dunbar was slacking off.

"Darned dog," he muttered.

That was what he got for somehow ending up dog-sitting while Quinn and Hayley Foxworth were on their honeymoon.

He kept going as he came out of the thick trees and saw the gleam of the water. Sunrise was coming, heralded by the lightening of the sky across the sound. He knew that he was almost past the tough part, that just about here the endorphins would kick in and he'd hit that pace that was perfect, that seemed as though he could keep going forever. But every time, he had to get through this part first, this section where his entire body screamed at him to stop.

People had told him once he hit forty it would get

harder. Now, with his forty-second birthday looming, he had to admit the change wasn't in his pace or his stamina but in the increase in mental discipline it took to keep going. And yet the bottom line never changed. He did this six days a week, rain or shine, for one simple reason. He was a cop, and one day his life could depend on it.

The radiance began to grow from behind the distant ridge of the Cascade Mountains. There were enough remnants remaining from yesterday's storm to give the sun lots of clouds to light up. He watched the show as he ran. Orange, pink and bright blue streaked across the sky, clouds turning from gray to bright white as the light grew stronger. Some clouds stayed darker, appearing like black puffs against the white clouds behind, a stark counterpoint to the brilliant display of sunrise.

Cutter stopped just ahead, where the trail curved away from the water to run below a small group of houses up the hill. The dog's head was up, and if he'd been looking toward the sunrise, Brett might have thought the clever dog was enjoying the view, as silly as that seemed. He'd seen this dog at work—literally—and it wouldn't have surprised him.

But instead Cutter was looking up toward the houses. Intently, his ears as focused as his eyes, not moving at all. His nose was twitching and his ribs moving as he took in deep breaths, no doubt tangy with whatever had caught his attention.

The dog looked at him then, and novice though he was with this, even Brett could see something had changed. He slowed to a stop. The dog was no longer that taunting, teasing physical trainer. Something intense and focused had come into those amber-flecked dark eyes, and Brett suddenly remembered all the times he'd heard the Foxworth people talk about the dog willing people to do something.

As if he'd been waiting to be sure he had Brett's attention, Cutter started up the side path. Brett's brow furrowed. He took that path some days, because it led up to those houses and a sidewalk that was better to run on when the rain was coming down hard. But he'd never taken it in the four days Cutter had been with him, so where had the dog gotten the idea?

He picked up the pace as the animal opened up a lead on him. It wouldn't do for Hayley and Quinn to come home and find out he'd lost their dog.

"Should have put the leash on," he muttered as he started up the hill.

The leash was mainly for other people. While he wasn't huge, Cutter wasn't a small dog. And he tended to draw attention with his striking coloring, black head and shoulders turning to a russet brown over his back and hindquarters. But it was more than just his looks—his very intensity drew people's eyes, and the reaction ranged anywhere from fascinated to wary.

If the dog had been a cop, Brett would have called it command presence. That might be the right term anyway.

The dog never slowed his steady trot even as the path headed up the rise. Brett had to kick up the pace to keep him in sight, and his body registered the hill with quickened breathing and an uptick in heart rate.

By the time he hit the sidewalk, Cutter was already crossing the street. There were only three houses in the little cluster, two on the water-view side of the narrow paved lane, one on the inland side. Brett could see two women in front of the single house where Cutter seemed to be headed. One older, one younger. He hoped neither of them would be frightened by the sudden appearance of a strange dog.

He realized the second woman was familiar. He'd seen her before on his runs that brought him up this way. After years as a cop the cataloging had been instinctive. She was about five-six, nicely female, with light brown hair past her shoulders. Long bangs pushed to one side fell over a brow and nearly covered her right eye. He liked the careless look of it. He'd never been close enough to see her eye color, but he was betting brown. Maybe green. Today she was dressed in jeans and a pale green sweater that hugged those curves nicely.

She was also the reason he'd once caught himself thinking of taking this route on a perfectly dry day, on the chance she might be out working in the garden again, since she did it even in the rain. And that bothered him enough to make sure he never did it. That way lay folly.

Right now she had her arm comfortingly around the older woman, who appeared to need that comforting.

Cutter bounded toward them. The younger woman turned just as the sun cleared the mountains and poured down over the sound, lighting everything in its path. Including the hair he'd thought was simply light brown but now saw was an amazing combination of tan, gleaming gold and a light reddish color that seemed to spark fire to it all. He'd never seen her in sunlight before, he realized, because he usually took this route only if it was raining.

He gave himself an internal shake as Cutter slowed to a walk about ten feet away from them, as if he somehow sensed a running approach might scare them. The older woman was watching the dog warily, so he supposed the dog could have read her body language.

But the younger one was smiling at the dog.

And she had a killer smile.

Cutter had halted a couple of feet in front of the women. He sat, almost primly, ears up, head cocked as if studying them. It was probably the most unthreatening pose he could have taken.

Brett caught up and stopped beside Cutter. The younger woman still had an arm around the older, who, judging by the traces of dampness on her cheeks, had been crying.

He felt an instant stab of wariness. He quashed it. No

matter what was going on, it wasn't, thankfully, his business. He wasn't on duty, and this wasn't his jurisdiction.

"Sorry," he said. "We were down on the trail and he got the idea to head up here. Weird, since I've never been up this way with him."

"I've seen you running," the older woman said, sounding relieved. "Every day, I go for my walk downtown." She was smiling now, which relieved him. "My husband likes the cream cheese cinnamon rolls from the bakery, even though they're bad for him."

Brett smiled back. "I like them, too. So I run."

He heard a laugh, a short, pleasant sound that warmed him as much as the winter sun was trying to do. He looked at the other woman then. Close up, that smile was even more potent.

And the eyes were indeed green. A light, clear green that made him think of the first leaves of the spring that wasn't far off.

"I've seen you up here, too," she said. "When it's really wet."

"Trail gets kind of slippery. I break something, my boss won't be happy."

The laugh again. He found himself wishing he were naturally funny, just to keep hearing it. And wondering why Cutter was just sitting there; usually his furry trainer would have been pushing him for a final burst of speed right about now.

"Your boss isn't an understanding sort?" she asked.

"She'd understand, but she's tough. I'd end up stuck behind a desk."

"What is it you do?" the older woman asked.

And there it was, he thought. The answer always made people react strongly. Differently, but they always reacted. Relaxed or became wary. The lines had always been pretty clear-cut: if they relaxed, they were on one side; if they were wary, the other. But the lines were getting blurrier by the day.

And he didn't want to admit to himself that if Green Eyes reacted the wrong way, he was going to be disappointed. Or worse.

Best to get it over with, he thought.

"I'm a detective with the sheriff's office."

To his surprise, it was the older woman who drew back slightly. Green Eyes merely said, "Tough work."

"Sometimes."

"Your dog take off on you often?" she asked, gesturing at Cutter.

He wondered if she was hiding a laugh at the idea a cop's dog wouldn't obey him. He quickly shook his head. "Not mine. Dogsitting."

"How nice of you," the older woman said, seeming to have recovered from whatever had made her react. Or perhaps he'd imagined it.

He didn't think this was the time to try to explain that he hadn't had much choice—the dog had decided. He wasn't sure quite how that had happened. After the wedding reception the dog, still wearing his bow tie as a member of the wedding—ring bearer, a role he had executed flawlessly—had trotted over to his car and simply refused to move.

"Oops," the bride had said. "I think there's been a change of plans."

"Looks that way," Quinn had agreed, with remarkable patience given the way he was looking at his wife, whom he was about to spirit off to parts unknown for a month of newlywed bliss. Bliss Brett had no doubt would last. You could feel it rolling off them.

Next thing he knew, Foxworth's Teague Johnson, who had been going to watch the dog while they were gone, was loading up dog stuff into Brett's car, grinning widely.

They all said it had been Cutter's idea. He'd laughed

that off until, after waiting politely, the dog had jumped into the car the moment he opened the door, wiggled into the backseat and settled in comfortably.

And so far, he couldn't deny he'd sort of enjoyed it.

"His owner must be a good friend," the older woman said.

"Yes," Brett said.

"I don't know," the younger woman said, watching Cutter, who was watching her in turn. "He seems quite the gentleman."

"He can be. He can also be the most stubborn critter on the planet. And that's a direct quote from his owner."

"It must be interesting, then," Green Eyes said.

He couldn't help smiling at that. "He's an interesting dog, all right." Then, not sure why, he added, "And more company than I expected."

It was nothing less than true. The dog had been a quiet but solid presence, and even he couldn't deny that the occasional nudge of the dark head or the warmth of the dog curled up beside him on the couch was…comforting. He didn't like admitting that he might need comforting, but there it was.

"May I?" Green Eyes asked, reaching toward Cutter. "Is he all right with strangers touching him?"

Brett looked at the dog, whose attention had never wavered. "I'd say you've passed muster," he said. "Or he wouldn't still be sitting there."

She laughed once more, and he was glad she was focused on the dog, because he couldn't help smiling at the sound of it. It took him a moment to realize that the strange tightness in his face was the result of smiling so much in the past few minutes, something he'd grown long unused to.

"Hello there, boy," she said, petting the dark head. "What's his name?"

"Cutter. At least, that's what his tag said when he showed up."

The woman looked at the boat-shaped blue name tag that hung from the dog's collar, then up at him. "He was lost?"

He nodded. "Hayley—his owner—tried for months to find where he belonged. And by then he'd made it pretty clear he intended to stay."

Green Eyes smiled as the older woman spoke. "Your girlfriend takes in strays, does she?"

"My—" He stopped short. *Girlfriend* was not a word he'd used in reference to himself for a very long time. "No. No, Hayley's not… She's on her honeymoon. That's why I'm dogsitting."

"Well," Green Eyes said, straightening up from her attentions to the dog, "congratulations to her. And her new husband."

"They deserve it. They're good people."

"I'm Connie Day," the older woman said abruptly. "And this is my niece, Sloan Burke."

"Dunbar," he said automatically, as if he were on duty after all. "Brett Dunbar," he amended awkwardly. Should he offer to shake hands? That was always iffy with some women. And if this was how out of it he was when it came to non-work-related contact with other people, he should probably give it up altogether.

"We should be on our way," he said, letting the fact that he was still a bit sweaty decide the shaking-hands question. Not to mention that he was going to start stiffening up here if he stood around in the chilly air much longer. "It was nice meeting you."

"You, too," Green Eyes—Sloan—said.

"Come on, Cutter. Get back to nagging me to pick up the pace."

She laughed once more, and Brett couldn't help smiling a last time. But maybe it wouldn't be the last. He'd be running this way the next time it rained hard, and this was the Pacific Northwest in winter, so that was never far off at any given time.

But when he turned to go, Cutter didn't move.

"Dog?"

Cutter turned his head to look at him, but his furry backside never left the grass he was sitting on.

"Cutter, let's go." He took a few more steps. Nothing.

He sighed. He dug into his pocket for the leash, tugging a length out from the reel.

"Who was it who said when you get to thinking you're important, try giving orders to someone else's dog?"

Brett's gaze snapped to her face. She was smiling again, widely. And he found himself grinning back. It felt even stranger than the smiling had. He reached out to snap the leash on Cutter's collar. "He's usually pretty good about it. He must just like you."

"But we've only just met."

"He's a quick study."

He couldn't believe himself. He sounded as though he was flirting with her. Not a talent of his at the best of times. He turned back to the dog. Cutter was staring at him intently. Intensely. In a way he never had in the time he'd stayed with him.

He tried to look away. Managed only a second. The dog was still staring at him. He remembered all the jokes that abounded at Foxworth about knowing how sheep felt.

Mesmerized was the word that came to mind.

And then other words popped into his head, spoken by almost everyone at Foxworth at one time or another.

He just gives us that "Fix it!" expression, and we know we're stuck.

It all came together in a rush, Cutter's sudden and unexpected course change, the older woman's tears, his refusal to leave and now That Look.

Uh-oh, Brett thought. Now what?

Chapter 2

Sloan Burke wasn't surprised to learn that the lean, rangy man she'd occasionally seen running was a cop. Or a deputy, to be more accurate, she thought, although detective probably superseded that. Jason had explained it once, back in the days when law enforcement had been his life plan, before a terrorist attack had sent him to the military, determined to defend the country he so loved.

There was a look, a demeanor about such men. Something that set them apart. In this man's case, as in her husband's, it wasn't bluster or swagger, just a quiet strength that required no bragging and a straight, level gaze that told you whatever the job was, he would get it done.

And yet the dog at her feet was apparently the one in charge at the moment.

"I should have known he was only letting me pretend I'm in charge."

She laughed, both at the man's wry tone and that he had chosen the words she had just thought. "At least you realize."

"I should have sooner. He's got quite the reputation, this one."

"For?"

"Finding trouble. And demanding his people fix it."

She started to laugh again, but something in his expression told her he was serious. "Detective Dunbar, why do

I think you don't mean typical dog trouble, like finding holes in fences or the cat next door to chase?"

He seemed to hesitate, as if he wasn't certain he should tell her, before he said, "Brett, please. And no. Last one was a kid with a messed-up family. Before that it was a kidnapping. Then a cold case, a long-lost brother. And those are just the ones I know about."

She stared at him. "Must really take away from their day job."

"That is their day job."

She drew back slightly. "You mean that's actually what they do?"

He nodded. "They help people. People who have nowhere else to turn."

"What are they, a charity?"

"Might as well be. They don't take any payment except the goodwill—and willingness to help them help someone else later—of the people they take on. They did it before Cutter came along, but now it's all they can do to keep up with what he finds for them. He's got a...sense about things. It's hard to explain."

"So he finds people who need help, and your friends, they follow his lead?"

He looked as if he half expected her to laugh. "It sounds crazy, I know."

"Which part?"

She hadn't meant it to sound sour, but it did. She saw it register in the slightest narrowing of his eyes. She didn't elucidate—she wasn't about to explain to a total stranger that while she could believe the dog would help people, she wasn't so sure about people helping people. Not anymore.

She glanced back at the dog. "Well, I can see I wasn't according you the proper respect. I thought you were just a pretty face."

Cutter's tail wagged as if he'd understood. He got to his

feet then and crossed the distance between them. Coming not to her but to Aunt Connie, nudging her hand with his nose.

Connie, who had been watching all this with interest—and, Sloan noted, without saying a word, which was unlike her—responded by petting the dog's head. "You are a beautiful boy," she cooed to him.

The dog stayed still for a moment. Then he turned around and sat once more, now facing his running partner. And gave him that look again.

It was odd, she thought. She'd seen intense dogs before. Jason's best friend in the service had been a canine handler, and his partner, Eddie, had been a bomb-seeking machine. And she'd seen police dogs and the agility competitors that held events in the park a few blocks away.

But this dog was different. The intensity was no less, but the focus was different. She couldn't explain it herself; she could only feel it, so no wonder he didn't even try.

She looked back at the man then. She'd always enjoyed the sight when she'd seen him running. That part of her might be dead and buried with Jason, but she could still appreciate a good-looking man, and Brett Dunbar was definitely that. She liked his tall, lean build, found the touch of gray at his temples attractive. She had little patience for unlined youth these days. Or sunny, carefree attitudes. She'd lost her affection for naïveté long ago, in the halls of Washington, DC.

And the impression in his gray eyes of dark things seen was all too familiar.

He sighed. Audibly. He looked at Connie, then the dog, then Connie again. "I'm guessing you're the one with the problem?"

Aunt Connie blinked. "What?" She glanced down at the dog now sitting at her feet staring up at Brett, then at the man himself. "You mean he knows?"

"I have a feeling that's why I'm here. Why he led me here."

Clearly startled, Connie put a hand to her throat. "Oh, dear. My problem isn't anything like that. No one's missing, and certainly not one of those cold-case things."

"She's having a problem with the county," Sloan explained. "A permit problem."

"We need to build a new house," Connie said, "a single-story, up the hill in back. My husband isn't well, and the stairs are too much for him now."

"So what's the problem?"

"They're saying we can't subdivide the acreage," she said.

He frowned. "You own the property?"

Connie nodded. "Twelve acres. And we can't afford to build unless we sell this house."

Brett turned to look at the tidy Craftsman-style two-story. "Beautiful, isn't it?" Sloan said. Uncle Chuck had maintained it immaculately, and the yard was a showplace cottage-style garden.

"Yes. You should have no trouble selling it."

"It will be sad," Connie said. "This was our dream house, but needs have changed."

Brett looked back at her. "Could you sell it all and build what you need somewhere else?"

Tears brimmed anew in Connie's eyes. "It's already breaking Chuck's heart that we have to move out of this house. It would just kill him if we had to leave this land altogether because of him. His family has owned it for five generations."

"I'd rent this house from them," Sloan said, "but that doesn't get them the money they'd need for building." She put her arm comfortingly around Connie's shoulders. "It's awful. She's dealt with so much since my uncle's heart attack. And they're just being ridiculous about it. The standard for this entire area is a minimum of two-

and-a-half-acre parcels. But she's suddenly not allowed to break up twelve?"

"What's their reason?" he asked.

"Some nonsense about the entire area being under study for possible changes, and everything is frozen in the meantime." She knew her voice was rising, but it was so unfair it just made her angry.

"Sounds typical," he said.

"Except," she snapped, "that they decided to study it only after my aunt and uncle put in their application. It's a specious technicality, at best. County bureaucrats."

She realized suddenly that the man she was talking to worked for that same county.

"Sorry," she said hastily. "I didn't mean anything personal."

He gave her a crooked smile that again reminded her of her thought when he'd first laughed: he looked like a man who didn't do it very often.

"I'm not one of them," he said. "And sometimes I get as angry at them as you are."

She felt even worse. "I didn't mean to imply you were. It's just that the whole thing is so unfair."

"It certainly doesn't seem right," he said. He glanced at his watch, a complicated-looking thing like the one Jason used to wear.

"I'm sorry—we've truly spoiled your run," she said quickly.

"I'm sure you have other, more important things to do than talk about my little problem," Connie added.

"It's not little to you," he said, and Sloan thought she could have hugged him for that. When she caught herself wondering what that would feel like, she nearly jerked back in shock.

"I was just checking the time to see how long before they'd be in at the county offices," he said. "I know somebody over there. Maybe I could make a call, find out more about what's going on."

Sloan stared at him. Connie took an audible breath and again put her hand to her throat.

"No promises," Brett said hurriedly. "I may only find out that what they told you is right."

"Of course," Connie said, "but that would be so helpful. They didn't want to explain much to me. I'm sure they just thought I was a nuisance of an old woman."

"Then they need to be slapped silly," Sloan said, her anger rising again.

Brett looked at her with an expression she couldn't read. Perhaps, being a cop, he was assessing her capability for such violence. *Oh, I'm capable,* she told him silently.

But he said only, "Or reminded that they'll also be there one day. If they're lucky."

She liked that. Liked that he'd said it. Liked that he'd looked at Connie so kindly when he'd said it.

Didn't like the pain that shadowed his eyes when he'd added, "If they're lucky."

"I'll call the first chance I get," he said. "But again, no promises."

"Thank you," Connie said fervently. Then she looked at Sloan. "Give him your number, will you, Sloan? I don't hear the phone half the time."

Sloan frowned. As far as she knew, Connie's hearing was fine. She glanced at Brett, realized he seemed taken aback himself. But after a moment he pulled a smartphone out of the pocket of his sweatpants, and she gave him the number.

And nearly laughed aloud when the dog, who had been sitting quietly through all this, got to his feet. As if he had somehow figured out they were done now.

"Told you," Brett said.

She looked up to see him shaking his head in amusement at his furry companion.

Somehow this made her like him even more. And that made her a little twitchy.

"Well, now," Connie said, watching as man and dog resumed their run, "wasn't he nice?"

"Yes," Sloan agreed, still a little bemused by it all but more fascinated by Brett Dunbar's long, easy stride.

"And nice looking," the older woman added archly. "Just the type I would have gone for at your age."

She couldn't deny that, since she'd thought it herself. But she knew where Connie was headed and didn't want to go there. Again.

"Please. You've been in love with Uncle Chuck since you were teenagers."

"Indeed I have. That's why I want the same for you."

"And so you want to set me up with the first good-looking guy who comes along?"

"He's hardly the first, but he is the first I've seen you react to."

Oh, Lord, had she been that obvious?

In the instant before she dodged away from her aunt's scrutiny, she saw something twinkle in the older woman's eyes. Her gaze snapped back to Connie's face.

"You hear perfectly well," she accused. "And you've never missed a call if you're home or your cell's got a signal."

"There's always a first time," Connie said sunnily. "I wonder if he's married."

Of course he is, Sloan thought. *Look at him.* But she focused on her aunt's deviousness. "I can't believe you… used that."

"It got him your phone number, didn't it?" Connie gave her a wry look. "Besides, honey, when you get to be this age, sometimes the only weapon you have is making people think you're less than you are."

For a long moment Sloan just stared at her. Then she laughed and hugged the woman who had been her anchor for so long. "Have I ever told you I want to be just like you?"

"I believe you have once or twice," Connie said. "And it makes me very proud."

"As well you should be."

"Good. Then you'll eat breakfast this morning without telling me it's too much."

Sloan laughed again. "You are shameless." But she walked back toward the house without protest.

And denied even to herself that she was glad the subject had veered away from their neighborhood jogger.

Chapter 3

Brett drummed his fingers on his desk as he considered his options. The physical action and the slight noise seemed to help him focus. Or at least reminded him to keep his mind on the matter at hand and not on the woman who had been such a pleasant interruption in his routine this morning.

Besides, for all he knew, she was married and had kids. She hadn't been wearing a ring—so sue him, he'd noticed—but that didn't always mean anything. Or it could mean she was divorced with those kids. Not that he had anything against kids; he just knew a little too much about the ways they could go wrong. They'd planned on kids, someday, he and Angie—

Damn. He hadn't strayed down that painful path in a long time. So much for focus, he thought, and stopped the steady drumming.

Just decide on the next step, he told himself.

Rick Alvarado, his friend over at the county zoning-and-permitting office, had seemed as puzzled as he was.

"What's odd," he'd said, "is that there's no record of a study being done or even asked for that I can find. For that matter, I can't find any record of the Days' application either. It's not in the approved, denied or pending files. We are a bit backlogged, though. I'll keep checking."

When he'd warned Connie Day that he couldn't promise anything, Brett hadn't expected that there would be absolutely nothing. He wondered if the person she'd talked to had just been covering their backside, making up something because the paperwork had been lost. It happened—it was the nature of bureaucracies, he thought. He—

"Hey, Dunbar!" The division clerk's shout shook him out of his thoughts. "Aren't you supposed to be giving a deposition this morning?"

Damn. The Lester case. He had forgotten, even though he'd looked over his notes last night to refresh his memory. He looked at the clock, realized he had about twenty minutes to make a half-hour drive.

"Thanks," he said as he got up, grabbed his jacket and his phone, and headed for the door.

He hit the button to wake up the phone and gave it a quick swipe with his thumb. The last screen he'd used popped into view, where he'd entered and saved Sloan Burke's number. The blank silhouette seemed to chide him for not taking a photo for it when he'd had the chance. Not that he needed a picture. He remembered what she looked like. Perfectly.

He pondered for a moment as he hit the button to unlock his car. He could call, tell her what he'd found.

Hi, Ms. Burke. I just called to say...nothing.

Yeah, that would go over well.

He brought up the number for the prosecutor he was doing the deposition for and hit Call. Told the paralegal who answered he was on his way but might be a few minutes late. He was doing this only as a witness, because it wasn't his jurisdiction and he had only happened to be outside the drugstore a few blocks from his place when the dispute that had preceded the assault had taken place. He hadn't even had to break up the argument. One of the teenagers had sped away in his car. Only when he'd seen the vehicle description in the news that night did he find out the kid had later gone back after the other guy and beaten him pretty severely.

So now he was on his way to the north end to officially give a statement on what he had seen. He hoped it would be enough. He didn't really want to end up having to testify in court to his small part in it. There were witnesses to the actual crime, so they shouldn't need him. But a cop's testimony, even if he'd been off duty, could carry more weight, and he understood the prosecutor wanting to be thorough. Always better to have evidence you don't need than not enough.

He spent an hour recounting what he'd heard and positively identifying the two involved parties—and wincing at the photos of the battered face and bruised body of the kid who had taken the beating. He felt a flash of guilt. Maybe he should have guessed at something like this, but at the time it had been verbal only, and you couldn't arrest somebody for what they just might do in the future. At least, not yet.

"Not your fault, Brett," the prosecutor said, reading him accurately. "Kid had no record of violence. No reason to expect this. But he went home, stewed about it, took a little taunting from a friend who threw some drugs into the mix, and voilà, we have assault and battery."

And a little more knowledge of how kids could go wrong, he thought.

"Thanks," he said.

On his way back to the car he had his phone out and had that new number on the screen before he truly realized what he was doing. He had thought, in the middle of his recounting, that he did really have a reason to call but didn't think he'd decided to do it. Except apparently some part of him had.

Probably the same part that completely forgot that reason when he heard her voice answering.

"Hello?" she said, in a tone that jarred him out of whatever cloud he'd slipped into; it was the tone of someone who had said it more than once. He realized he was standing next to his car and had yet to hit the button to unlock it. He shook his head sharply. Unlocked the car and answered simultaneously.

"Sorry. Ms. Burke, this is Brett Dunbar. We met this—"

"Of course," she said quickly. "I didn't expect to hear from you so soon."

"I'm afraid I don't have an answer, just a question or two that I should have asked before."

Except I was in a hurry to get away before I said or did something beyond stupid.

"Of course. Do you need Connie? I can get her."

"Maybe you can answer these," he said as he opened the door and got into the driver's seat. "Do you know when they filed the application?"

"October 15. Eleven in the morning."

His brows rose. "That's rather exact," he said.

"I drove her there," she said.

"That was…kind of you."

"I could taxi her all over forever and never make up for how she's looked out for me."

She said it so fervently it was all he could do not to ask why she'd needed looking out for. Or where the rest of her family had been.

"Good for her," he said inanely, belatedly reaching to pull his door closed as someone began to pull into the space next to him.

"What else?" she asked, her tone brisk, as if she'd regretted her outburst. "You said a question or two."

He shook his head sharply. "Yes. Do you know if she happened to keep a copy of the application?"

"Yes, she did. I made her." She sounded a bit embarrassed. "I'm kind of zealous when it comes to that. Learned the hard way."

"Never a bad idea." He wondered what that hard way had been.

"Do you need it?"

"No. Not yet, anyway. Just wanted to know if there was one."

The conversation ground to a halt, yet he couldn't quite bring himself to say goodbye. Beyond stupid, but there it was. And after a moment she spoke, saving him.

"How's Cutter?"

"Probably still snoozing. Unlike me, he gets to rest up after our run."

She laughed. It rippled over him. "How else will he keep you on your toes when you get home?"

"He's relentless. I've taken to going home for lunch and running him ragged some more," he said. "He'll chase a tennis ball until he drops."

He didn't add that that very doglike behavior was one of the few reasons he was reassured Cutter wasn't something spookily more than just a dog.

"Where's home? You must be local, unless you run a marathon every day."

For some reason he didn't want to analyze, he liked that she'd asked. But still he hesitated, with that innate caution all cops had. He didn't generally discuss where he lived with people he'd only just met.

"Just off Cedar View," he said, figuring she'd know the area, given where she lived. The small house he rented wasn't much, more of a cabin, but it was all he needed. And since Cutter had come to stay, he'd made full use of the near acre it sat on. "Top of the hill."

"Wow. That's still a good long way to us."

"Only five miles, out and back. But that last uphill bit is a killer."

"No wonder you—"

She stopped so suddenly he wondered if something had happened. "Ms. Burke?"

"Sloan, please." She sounded odd, he thought. A little like he had when he'd realized she'd said hello more than once.

"All right." He felt absurdly pleased that in less than a day they were on a first-name basis. In the same instant, he wasn't sure he should be glad that the formality of "Detective Dunbar" and "Ms. Burke" wasn't still between them. "I'll let you know what I find out, if anything."

"We appreciate that you're even bothering," Sloan assured him.

"No problem," he said.

As he ended the call, he wondered just how big a lie that was. Because Sloan Burke was already nibbling around the edges of his mind the way a tough case did, always present, never far away. And that could be a problem.

Chapter 4

Cutter was sitting by the door when he opened it.

This wasn't strange. The dog had been right there every day since he'd been here. It didn't matter what time he managed to break for lunch—the dog was ready and waiting. Brett supposed he must hear him coming.

But today the usually present yellow tennis ball was absent. And instead of greeting him with a tail wag and a happy yip, the dog bolted past him and ran toward the car parked in front of the house.

"You want a ride?" Brett said, puzzled.

Cutter sat next to the back driver's-side door. He looked back over his shoulder at Brett.

"Buddy, I'm on duty. I can't just take off for a leisurely jaunt."

Cutter just looked at him.

"Seriously, dog, I can't."

Cutter yipped, short and sharp. But didn't move.

Brett sighed. "I have a feeling I haven't had enough sympathy for the Foxworth crew."

The moment he spoke the name, Cutter jumped up, letting loose a staccato series of barks. He rose up and put his paws on the car door.

"I know you must miss them, but they're not home yet."

Brett realized with no small amount of amazement that he was carrying on a conversation with a dog. A conversation that should have been one-sided yet felt anything but.

Cutter stayed where he was, only now he was pawing at the door handle. With his luck, he'd probably put some scratches in the paint that Brett would have to answer for. It was a county car, after all, even if it was his for the duration.

He glanced at his watch. Because he'd already been at this end of the county for the deposition, he had a bit more time. With a sigh, he gave in. It was for only a little while longer, after all. Then Cutter would go home, and his life would go back to the normal, quiet thing it usually was off duty. He needed that, with the kind of job that took up his working hours.

Cutter leaped into the backseat the instant he opened the door. Once he was back in the driver's seat, he pondered where to go. Maybe the dog just wanted to visit home, make sure everything was all right while his people were gone.

He nearly laughed at his own thought. He was fairly certain that kind of thought process was beyond the average dog's capabilities.

But then, Cutter wasn't an average dog.

He decided it couldn't hurt and started the car. The dog sat quietly in the back until he reached the intersection where he had to turn to get to Hayley and Quinn's place. He'd been there only once. Actually, he hadn't been there; he'd been to the next house over, which had been destroyed in an apparent propane explosion. When the firefighters suspected there might be a body inside, it had been all hands on deck until they'd sifted through the smoking ruin and determined there hadn't been anyone inside after all. Once that was certain, the case had gone back to the fire department and their investigators.

It wasn't until much later, after he'd met Quinn and Hayley, that he'd gotten the full, dramatic story on that one. Hell of a way to start a relationship, he thought as he started to pull into the left-hand-turn lane to head toward their house.

Cutter erupted into furious barking.

The suddenness and the sheer volume nearly made him jump. He hit the brakes, thankful for being in a semirural area without much traffic. The dog stayed on his feet, apparently braced for the stop. The moment the car halted, the racket ceased.

"What the hell, dog?"

He turned to look into the backseat. Cutter was still on his feet, staring intently out the side window. The other side, facing the opposite direction. Away from home for the dog.

It took him a moment to realize what lay in that direction. The Foxworth building.

"There's nobody there either," he said. "Quinn gave everybody the time off while they're gone."

Cutter never moved. Never even looked at him when he spoke. Just stared in that same direction.

"Okay, okay, I get it. Hang on."

He looked around to be sure they were clear and made a right turn instead. Cutter immediately settled down once more, seemingly happy that his temporary custodian—or should that be servant?—had finally understood. Brett's mouth quirked as he shook his head at himself. At least there was that big clearing behind the building, he thought. He could run Cutter as well there as at home. There seemed to be no shortage of tennis balls in his car these days.

The dog stayed still until he made the last turn, onto the narrow road toward the secluded Foxworth location. Cutter got up then but remained quiet, eager, but satisfied Brett knew where they were going.

He was sure if he stopped to think about the fact that he had just skipped lunch, gotten back in his car, driven twelve miles and then changed his destination, all at the direction of a dog, it would seem ridiculous. Trying to explain it to anyone who had never met Cutter would be impossible. He knew trying to explain it to, say, one of his fellow detectives would result in jokes about psychiatric committal.

Yet here he was, about to turn down the curving gravel drive that led to the green three-story building hidden among tall trees that was Foxworth's Northwest headquarters. And utterly certain this was what the dog had wanted. That he was doing what a dog wanted was something he was just going to have to come to terms with.

Then again, doing what the dog wanted this morning had ended up with him on a first-name basis with Sloan Burke.

There was no sign of anyone around. There was only one car, a slightly battered silver coupe he'd seen here before parked at the far end of the gravel lot. It was still wet from last night's heavy mist, so it had been here at least overnight.

He parked in front of the building. Cutter was practically dancing in the backseat, so he opened the door quickly. The dog leaped out and started at a dead run, not toward the main building but toward the warehouse, where the silver car was parked. Halfway there he let out an oddly rhythmic sound, a short yip, a full-on bark, then another yip.

Seconds later the smaller door on the warehouse opened, and Rafer Crawford looked out. Brett saw him spot the dog, then him. Then he reached back into the warehouse as if he was putting something down. Knowing what he knew of the man, had it been a weapon, he wouldn't be surprised. He must have heard the car on the gravel long before Cutter's distinctive greeting.

Cutter raced toward Rafe, tail up, bounding with obvious joy. Even the taciturn former Marine couldn't help smiling at the dog's demeanor. Brett remembered that moment at the wedding when Hayley, more radiant than any bride he'd ever seen, had found the two of them together.

"You two smiling, and at the same time? My work here is done," she'd said with undisguised delight.

"We were just talking about how beautiful you are," Rafe had said, deflecting her into a blush neatly.

In fact, they actually had been talking earlier about how wonderful she looked, but at that moment they had been speaking of Foxworth itself. Rafe's smile had been quiet, proud of what they were doing, while Brett's had been amazed acknowledgment. Doing what he did, seeing what he saw every day, he sometimes found it hard to believe that there was a group of people dedicated to helping those who had nowhere else to turn, who had fought until they could not fight any longer and lost hope. Those who were abused by either the system or people who wielded it like a club, those who were collateral damage in backroom deals, or those simply caught in the grinding wheels of bureaucracy.

Like Sloan's aunt.

And there she was again, popping into his mind like a persistent earworm of a song that wouldn't let him be. Not the most flattering of comparisons, he thought wryly. Put that on the list of things never to say to her.

"He driving you crazy yet?" Rafe asked as Brett caught up to the dog and the man who was scratching that sweet spot behind his right ear.

"Nah. He's really a lot of company."

"I know." Something in the way he said it told Brett the man truly did. It was probably a good thing they'd had the wedding as distraction that day, or they could have ended up comparing a couple of empty lives.

Now, where the hell did that come from?

He wasn't usually morose about his life, most of the time successfully thought he liked it the way it was. His work was enough. At least, it always had been. Or maybe it had been too much, as Angie had always said.

He gave himself a mental shake, trying to rid himself of the odd mood.

"Didn't expect anyone to be here," he said. "Aren't you all supposed to be on vacation?"

Rafe shrugged. "Just catching up on things that never seem to get done with everyone around."

"Figured you'd be off to somewhere warm, like everyone else."

"No place I wanted to go," he said simply. "And it's nice and peaceful around here now. Thanks to you."

Brett laughed. "I didn't seem to have much choice about it."

"Nope, when this boy—" he ruffled the dog's fur as the animal leaned into him "—makes up his mind, he's pretty much unstoppable."

"He's…different."

"Hayley says to quit trying to put dog interpretations on his humanlike actions. To just accept he's unique, and then we'll all be happier."

The man wasn't usually this talkative, and Brett wondered for a moment if this was too much isolation even for him. If maybe that was why Cutter had wanted to come here, to make sure this particular person of his was all right.

He was, he thought, losing his mind. Cutter might be the cleverest dog he'd ever seen, in a very different way than the well-trained and smart police dogs he'd known, but he was, in the end, still a dog.

"He's got a way," he said.

"And a nose for trouble," Rafe said. "But so far, he's never been wrong. Sometimes he drags us kicking and screaming into something, but it's always somewhere we should be."

For a moment Brett wondered what it must be like to

work strictly toward justice for those who deserved it. So much of his time was spent dealing with scum that he had little left for the victims, who were his reason for being in the job in the first place. And so often when he had dealt with them, they got a slap on the wrist and were back destroying innocent lives all over again practically before he even got the paperwork done.

Cutter seemed finally satisfied that his friend was all right. He turned and sat at the man's feet, staring up at Brett much as he had this morning. And so Sloan and her aunt popped into his mind again. His brow furrowed.

"Something?" Rafe asked.

"Just…someone he led me to this morning," he said, indicating Cutter.

"Uh-oh," Rafe said. "He give you that look? The 'fix it' look?"

Brett sighed. "He did."

"What's the problem?"

"It's just a hang-up on a county thing." He explained briefly about the aunt and ended with "I've got a guy I know over there looking into it, but so far nothing."

"Anything I can do?"

"I don't think so," Brett said. He smothered a smile at the thought. A minor paperwork problem seemed a bit soft for the rugged former Marine, who looked as if he'd be more inclined to take on a herd of killers or an approaching army. Although he was Foxworth, and Brett knew he believed in the cause, and they took on some things that would seem insignificant to outsiders. "I'm hoping there'll be a simple answer."

Rafe's mouth quirked, and he looked down at Cutter. "Not likely, when this guy's involved."

"I was afraid of that," Brett said glumly.

"And he is one of us, so if he's involved, we are."

"You're on vacation."

"Boring," Rafe said with a one-shouldered shrug. "I hate not working."

Brett laughed. Then stopped when he realized he felt the same way. And that empty-lives thought came back to him.

"I'll keep that in mind if my guy comes up empty," he said quickly, quashing the unwelcome thoughts. "I'd likc to be able to help Sloan out."

He realized what he'd done the moment he'd said it, but somehow trying to correct it to *Sloan's aunt* seemed as if it would only make it worse.

"Sloan?" Rafe asked.

"Sloan Burke. The niece," he said, hoping the short answer would suffice.

Rafe went very still. Brett felt the change as much as saw it.

"Cutter led you to Sloan Burke? The Sloan Burke?"

Whatever was coming next, Brett didn't want to hear it. But he knew he had to ask. "*The* Sloan Burke?"

"Wife of Chief Petty Officer Jason Burke?"

Brett absorbed it like a punch to the gut. He'd been right. She was married. The involuntary and instantaneous recoil at the words told him just how foolish he'd gotten. And in such a short time it was almost embarrassing. What the hell was he thinking?

"I don't know," he managed.

It shouldn't have meant anything. She was a woman he'd spoken to for maybe fifteen minutes and seen a couple of times before. It meant nothing. He wasn't in the mood or the market for anything more, hadn't been since—

"About thirty-five now?"

"I... Yes."

As if he'd just remembered he had it, Rafe pulled out his phone and began to key in a search. After a moment he selected one of the results, tapped the screen again, expanded an item and finally held it up for Brett to see.

It was a photograph. Of Sloan. Sitting at a table, in front of a microphone, rows of people sitting behind her.

Something stirred inside him, not because she was lovely in that picture, because in fact she was not. Her hair was pulled into a severe knot at the back of her head, she looked pale, and above all she looked tired. Exhausted.

She looked fragile, and it made his stomach knot.

She's married, he told himself. It was none of his business. He scanned the other people in the photo, wondering if one of the men was her husband. And how he could have let her get to this point.

"What is this?" he asked finally.

"Sloan Burke," Rafe said, in a tone Brett could describe only as admiring, "is a crusader. Of the best kind. Ask anyone who's in the service or has been, and I'll bet he's heard of her. And if she needed help, anyone who's been in boots on the ground would come running."

Rafe glanced at the image again before he blacked out the home screen and slipped the phone back in his pocket.

"Quinn, Teague and me included," he said, then added, "She's exactly the kind of person Foxworth was founded for."

Brett told himself he would be better off not asking. Not knowing. He would just do this little thing, maybe help straighten out a paperwork glitch, and then slip back into his quiet, unrippled life. And Sloan would go back to hers, with her husband.

He asked anyway. "What's the story?"

Rafe fell silent. Studied Brett again, silently. At last he said, "You sure you want to know?"

I'm sure I'd be better off if I didn't. "Tell me."

One of Rafe's dark brows arched upward, and Brett knew he hadn't missed the indirectness of the answer. But after a moment he seemed to decide.

"All right. But come on inside. I'm going to need fuel. How do you feel about leftover pizza?"

"Like we're related," Brett said drily, then chuckled as Cutter jumped to his feet.

"So does he," Rafe said. "Let's go."

Brett followed the two toward the main Foxworth building, telling himself he still had time to change his mind, to run before he found out something about Sloan that would make it even harder to walk away.

How the hell had he gotten into such a tangle so fast?

Even as he thought it, Cutter looked back over his shoulder at him. He couldn't even blame the dog. Cutter had only led him there, after all. He was the one who had jumped in with both feet.

And apparently left his common sense behind.

Chapter 5

Brett slipped Cutter the last bite of pizza, more bread than anything. The dog took it delicately, glanced at the table as if to make sure there was none left, then settled down for a nap with a happy sigh.

"Got what you wanted, dog?" he asked with a wry grin.

"He's good at that," Rafe said.

"So he wanted me, and/or Foxworth, involved in this. Which means…what?"

"That it's likely more than it looks like on the surface."

Brett sighed. Somehow he'd known that would be the answer. Steeling himself, he finally asked.

"So what's her story?"

"Jason was a navy SEAL. Killed in action in Afghanistan a few years ago."

"He's…dead?" Brett hated that, after the shock, his first real feeling was relief. That it was followed instantly by pain for what Sloan must have gone through didn't ameliorate his first snap reaction. This was an American hero they were talking about, and it shamed him that this was his gut reaction, even if it was more about Sloan than her husband.

Rafe nodded. "Officials put out a report on what happened. Sloan knew it wasn't true."

"How?"

"Burke had told her what was really going on. They'd talked on Skype the night before, and she had the truth.

And had recorded the convo, as she always did. Just in case."

Just in case. Three words that made some marriages different than all others. Military marriages. And police marriages.

Brett sucked in a deep breath. "What did she do?"

"She did it right. Jumped through all the hoops, worked her way up the chain of command. But when she hit the top, the brass wouldn't budge from their official version. So she went to the politicians. Started here, all the way up to the governor. Got nothing."

"Why doesn't that surprise me?" Brett said with a grimace.

"I think she hoped the governor at least would listen. He was newly elected then but under a cloud, and she thought maybe he'd want to establish his legitimacy with something big."

Brett's brow knit. "I remember that. His opponent just gave up."

Rafe nodded. "Evans wasn't a professional politician, and Ogilvie's party machine came at him hard. Rumor was he had some sort of breakdown. He pulled out and just vanished. Left the state entirely."

Politics, Brett thought with a grimace.

"So…what happened?" he asked. "With Sloan, I mean."

Rafe studied him for a moment, and Brett wondered uncomfortably what he was seeing. "She widened her net. Figured it would take a politician to fight politicians. Finally found the right senator, one from Jason's home state who had served himself, to step in."

"Then that picture, that was at some sort of official hearing?"

"Very official. On Capitol Hill. Her testimony was the tipping point. She was like a force of nature. Every service guy I know was glued to it. They all knew she was fighting for the truth. For one of their own." Rafe let out a compressed breath. "She showed more nerve and courage under fire than all of those suits and most of those top-of-the-heap guys sitting there with ribbons on their chests."

"I remember hearing about this." He'd just transferred to detectives, had still been learning his relatively new turf, so he hadn't had much attention to spare. He knew only that it had been ugly, loud and figuratively bloody. "Didn't a senator and even some presidential staff go down?"

"Yes." Rafe wore an expression of grim satisfaction.

"What was the story?"

"The official version was that Burke's squad had crossed a boundary they'd been ordered not to. That they knew if they crossed it, they'd be on their own."

"But?"

Rafe's expression turned sour. "There was no written record of such an order or boundary. Or anyone actually in action who had ever heard it. All the rank and file and even most of command denied any knowledge."

"What finally happened?"

"In the end they were forced to release satellite imagery of the ambush and the surrounding territory. It showed not only that they weren't even past that real or imagined boundary but that there was help within easy reach. A team that could easily have taken out the small force of attackers, and a chopper for air support. Once that came out, it all fell apart. Guys spoke up about how they had been ordered to stand down. And shut up about it."

"Why was his squad there in the first place?"

"They were going to pull out one of their informants. The guy had given them info that had helped them round up several high-level targets. And twice he'd warned them of ambushes just like the one they drove into that day. But he'd been compromised and was about to be executed."

Brett leaned back against the sofa cushions. "So they had good reason."

"Not according to the powers that be. They were ordered not to go, thanks to that someone way higher up on the civilian power pole. Something about offending the local terrorists."

Brett blinked. "Offend the terrorists? So they were supposed to just let the guy who helped them die?"

"Exactly."

"But—"

"They went anyway." Rafe grimaced as he shifted position. Brett wondered if it was what he was remembering or that his leg was bothering him. "That's what the Skype call had been about. Jason wanted the truth in someone's hands before they headed out. Sloan said her husband couldn't have lived with himself if he'd just left the man to die. So instead they all died, because some hack who never had a uniform on in his life was covering his ass."

Brett sat silently for a long moment. He wasn't sure how this made him feel, that Sloan's dead husband had clearly been a good man, a true hero, a man he would probably have liked and admired. It would have been easier, he thought, if the guy had been a jerk.

Just what would have been easier, he didn't let himself think about.

"What was the final result?" he asked.

"She hammered at them for nearly two years. With all their stalling, it took that long for all the pieces to come together. In the end she brought down an area commander, that senator and his brother-in-law, who they'd been funneling rebuilding contracts to—that was what the informant had found out and was going to tell—and a couple of the staff who helped in the cover-up."

"And they let her husband and his men all die for that? Some crony contracts?" He couldn't help the outrage echoing in his voice, and approval flashed in Rafe's eyes.

"Yes. Now Sloan helps others in like situations through an organization she started. Even the governor has come around." Rafe snorted. "After she won, he pretended he was backing her all along."

"Good for her," he said softly.

"She was amazing."

She still is.

Brett barely managed to keep from saying it aloud.

"You want to leave him here, take a break?" Rafe asked when he at last got up to go, and Cutter popped to his feet.

Brett considered the dog, who was looking at him steadily. With a bemused look, he said, "I suppose I'll let him decide. Why change now?"

Rafe smiled. "A man who learns fast."

"He's pretty hard to ignore."

"You'll let me know if there's anything we can do? I'm not much help with bureaucrats and paperwork, but Ty isn't on vacation, and he's a whiz at working through computer forests."

"I will, if my guy can't—" He broke off as his cell phone rang. Pulled it out and glanced at the incoming number. "Speak of the devil," he muttered, and answered. "Rick? I'm with somebody interested in this, so I'm going to put you on speaker if that's okay."

"Sure."

Brett switched the audio over. "Go," he said.

"I found it," Alvarado said without preamble. "The application was in a file in my boss's office. Unprocessed."

"After nearly four months?"

"Yeah. That's so wrong. We're not that backlogged. No idea why it's in here. He doesn't usually get involved until things are processed and need his signature."

"Did you ask him?"

"He's out this morning at some big confab in Seattle, so not yet. But it's weird."

"That he has it?"

"And that it's nowhere else. Not even a computer record of it being entered in the system. It must have been misfiled or just caught up in the wrong stack of papers."

"And what about this supposed land-use study?"

"It doesn't exist, as far as I can tell. And there's nothing about that area that would warrant such a study. Not saying it couldn't be happening, but it's not done yet, because a copy would have hit my desk at some point."

"Can you find out?"

"Sure. But I'm thinking it all must have just been a goof."

So. There it was. He was safely out of it. "It happens," Brett said.

"Yeah. I'll talk to my boss as soon as I see him and get back to you. In the meantime, I'll get this entered and started on right away. It looks pretty cut-and-dried. Should be no problem."

"Thanks, Rick. I owe you."

"Hell no," the man said. "I owe you times a hundred. Caro is doing great at school. My girl's going to make it through college with honors."

"I'm glad to hear it."

"Wouldn't have happened if not for you. You really got through to her, like I never could."

"She's a good kid. She just got a little lost for a while."

Rafe was studying him anew as he ended the call. "His daughter?"

Brett nodded. "It was a close one. She nearly got sucked up into something really bad."

"Ever get to you?"

"All the time. It's a rough world for kids these days. For every Caroline Alvarado, there are three who don't make it. It wears on you."

Rafe looked at him consideringly. "You know Quinn would take you on here in an instant if you wanted."

Startled, Brett blinked. "What?"

"Only reason he hasn't mentioned it to you himself is he's pretty sure you wouldn't give up being a cop."

Recovering, Brett admitted, "I came close, once. But it's kind of in the blood."

Rafe nodded in understanding. "Figured. But thought it might be good to know there's another option." He smiled crookedly. "Assuming, of course, you could live with the fact that we don't always follow the book."

"What you do," Brett said, "is get results."

"There is that," Rafe said, and grinned. "Besides, you're kind of handy where you are."

He'd barely seen the man so much as crack a smile before, except at the wedding, so this was something.

"Thanks. I think." He shifted his gaze to Cutter. "So what do you want, dog? Go or stay?"

The dog looked up at Rafe. "Up to you, mutt," he said. "Nice of you to visit, but I'm good. You don't need to stay."

The dog reached out with his nose and nudged Rafe's hand. Then he turned and trotted over to Brett.

"Guess he's all yours for the duration," Rafe said. "Good luck."

"Thanks," he said wryly, thinking he might just need it.

He spent most of the drive back to his place wondering if he could spare the time to stop by Sloan's aunt's place and let her know what Rick had said. But he was still a little too ashamed at his reaction to learning about her husband to do it. Relief sparked by a good man's death was not something to be proud of, no matter the reason. And the thought of how much she must have loved her husband, to do what she'd done, and how much pain she had gone through made him feel worse than useless. He knew all too well no words could ease that kind of pain.

So instead he dropped Cutter off at the house, spent ten minutes throwing the tennis ball for him, ten minutes that barely took the edge off the dog's seemingly endless energy, promised him more tonight and headed back to work. He would call from there, he told himself. Safer.

And he would finally get around to marking out another running route. One that didn't pass the path that led to the big Craftsman house.

Chapter 6

Sloan put the last dishes in the dishwasher. She considered the meal a success. Uncle Chuck was under strict dietary restrictions and claimed she was the only one who could make those meals palatable. Sloan suspected that was as much to take some of the load off of his wife, but since that was her goal as well, she happily went along. And it didn't hurt that they were all eating a bit healthier, she supposed.

She stopped herself from looking at the clock again. It would be five minutes later than the last time, she told herself, just as it had been all evening. Instead she got her aunt and uncle settled in with a movie selected from her streaming service, a concept they had taken to with enthusiasm.

She'd take this time to check the website and catch up with email. Her inbox had been too full for too long. She needed to get back on track. Her compatriots across the country were good people and had stepped up when they'd learned of her uncle's ill health, but *Accountability Counts* was her baby, and she had neglected it for too long.

After her initial sort she had two updates on current situations, four inquiries she would refer to the appropriate military offices—no doubt after having to reassure each that most of the rank and file were honest and true—and three cases she would direct to regional coordinators, mostly concerning other family members affected in ways similar to her own. One more was local, so she would look into that herself. Then came the standard batch of praise and threats.

Thankfully, today the praise outnumbered the threats two to one. She filed the good ones to read when she had time or needed the lift and moved the threats to the library she'd created just for that. If nothing else, she'd learned that early on. Document, document, document, the mantra of anyone dealing with large entities. She read them only for tone, to see if anything unusual jumped out, anything to indicate the twisted psyche behind them would do more than just spew venom from behind the safety of an anonymous internet. It wasn't pleasant, but it was necessary. She had ruffled some lofty feathers, and some were on birds in a position to do her great harm in many ways.

The rest were spam, scams or phishing, and she deleted them unread. That chore done, she wrote a quick blog post on the updates, ending it with her usual encouragement.

"Don't give up," she wrote. "There are so many good people out there, steadfast and loyal. You just have to find them."

Before she even clicked on the publish button, her mind was back on Brett Dunbar. She told herself he kept popping into her thoughts because she was anxious for him to call and tell her if he'd found anything out on the application.

Okay, she admitted, also because he was one of the good guys. She didn't know why she was so certain— these days it usually took her a while before she trusted someone—but she was. Something about him, maybe the shadows that darkened his eyes, told her this was a man who understood.

It was not because he was, as Connie had said, nice looking. She would have put him a bit beyond that, but still, she wasn't in that market anymore. She doubted she ever would be.

On that thought her cell rang. She picked it up, already irritated at the way her mind had instantly jumped to wondering if it was him. As if it were spelled with a capital *H*.

But that was nothing compared to how her heart leaped when she saw the number she'd seen only once before.

"Sloan?"

The way he said her name when she answered sent a little shiver through her and made an image of him, tall, lean, with those eyes and that touch of gray in his hair, snap into sharp focus in her mind, which irritated her even more. She nearly let out an abrupt answer but bit it back. Still, she needed a little distance.

"Yes. Detective Dunbar, isn't it?"

There, that was formal enough. And she knew he'd gotten it, because there was a fractional hesitation before he spoke again.

"Am I...interrupting something?"

"I was catching up on a little work," she said, before she realized he might have meant something else entirely. Which somehow also grated on her nerves.

Boy, it doesn't take much for you today, does it, Miss Snarky McGrouch?

"I'm sorry. This will be quick. It seems that your aunt's application was simply lost. It never got logged in, and my contact found it in a stack of other papers in a file cabinet in his boss's office."

"Lost? For four months?"

"Your tax dollars at work," he said, his tone so wry she nearly smiled despite her mood. "Anyway, he logged it in personally and will walk it through himself. He said it looked cut-and-dried, and it shouldn't be long."

Sloan felt her outrage at the delay ebb away. Relief flooded her. She let out an audible sigh. "Thank you. Truly, I can't thank you enough, Brett."

And just like that she let down the wall she'd thrown back up when she'd answered the phone.

"You're welcome, Sloan."

And he'd caught it, she thought ruefully. And made a mental note not to underestimate this man. He was, after all, a detective; he wasn't likely to miss much. But she had the feeling that would be the case no matter what career he was in.

It wasn't until after they'd hung up that she realized that underestimating him wouldn't be a problem, because he had no reason to ever call again. He'd done a favor, generously, because he was a good guy. And now it was over. No need to ever talk to her again.

Unless he wanted to for other reasons, personal ones. She felt herself flush and shook her head sharply. No. Just no. That way lay idiocy. He was a cop, and on the don't-get-involved scale, that was barely a step below a serviceman.

Not, of course, that she had any reason to think he was even interested. Just because Aunt Connie was an inveterate matchmaker didn't mean the other party she'd chosen would be cooperative.

But she certainly couldn't fault her aunt's taste.

There was no reason for him to be doing this. The situation with the Day permit had been resolved, if not completely explained. But it would go through now, and probably quickly. They'd be in a hurry to make up for the screwup.

So there was no reason for him to see or even talk to Sloan Burke again. Unless it was on some rainy day when his run took him past her aunt's home. Which, if things went through, wouldn't be her aunt's house much longer.

It didn't matter. He was going to be running a different route anyway, as soon as he laid one out. It was a nonissue.

He looked back at the website on his screen. If they'd had any idea who they were dealing with, that application probably would have been done in a day, he thought.

Accountability Counts.

Catchy. To the point. Effective.

Cutter stirred at his feet, but only to change position and go back to sleep. Brett had thrown the ball—the glow-in-the-dark one, since it was dark by the time he got home this time of year—for a good hour and had at last surrendered to arm twinges and hunger. The dog had appeared barely winded and probably could have gone on for another hour, but he'd amenably followed him back inside. It had taken several towels to dry them both off enough to go past the mudroom, and he'd looked glumly at the small pile, thinking he'd never done this much laundry in his life.

Dinner for both had been a hurried, eaten-standing affair, leftover Chinese takeout for him, the usual for Cutter, from the supply Teague and Laney had laughingly stuffed in his trunk at the wedding. Those two wouldn't be long behind Hayley and Quinn. He was happy for them. Teague was a good guy, and Laney was a sweetheart.

His thoughts had been distraction enough that he'd done what he'd sworn not to do. He'd pulled his laptop over and done a search on Sloan Burke. Her website had been the first listing, but before he'd even gotten that far, the photo in the upper-right corner of the results page had snagged him. It was the same photo Rafe had shown him, from the hearing on Capitol Hill. He had clicked on it, enlarged it. And felt his stomach knot again at how weary she looked. But in this larger version he could also see the set of her delicate jaw, the determination in her posture, every line of her declaring she wasn't going to give up, ever.

And she hadn't. The website on his screen now was proof of that. *Accountability Counts* was an active site, with a forum he couldn't read because he wasn't registered, but he could still see many threads with different posters. He wondered how many crackpots it attracted.

Some, he guessed, just by its nature and the nature of the online world, too often a hiding place for predators and vicious cowards who would never have the nerve to confront anyone in real life.

But the list of successes on the front page was impressive. Red tape sliced through, reputations defended and restored, grieving friends and family given solace. In a way, he thought, she was running a very specialized sort of Foxworth operation.

For a moment he thought about what Rafe had said. *Quinn would take you on here in an instant if you wanted...*

Tempting, he thought. He'd always thought he would stay a cop forever. But Foxworth, free of the restraints he had to deal with, able to do the right thing even if it wasn't a police matter, willing to help people like the Days with something this simple just as much as they were willing to help Laney save her kidnapped friend, was indeed very tempting.

In his musing, he did the next thing he'd sworn he wouldn't do. He clicked on the About link and found himself reading the story of the beginnings of *Accountability Counts*. The story matched what Rafe had told him except that CPO Jason Burke, navy SEAL, came off as even more heroic.

As did Sloan. Just how long it had taken, how much controversy there had been and how far some people had gone to hide the true circumstances of the incident spoke of her courage in staying the course. Through it all Jason Burke's widow had been steadfast, persistent and determined to find the truth.

And the photographs were like another punch in the gut.

A young man, tall, strong, geared up, armed and ready, with eyes that looked as if they were seeing far beyond whatever was currently in their view. He looked like the kind of man who would charge into hell to save a friend or, as he had, someone he owed. A man with vision, who saw the big picture but could focus on the here and now and get the job done.

But it was the wedding picture that really hit him. That same man gazing upon the woman beside him as if he'd found all the treasure of the world. And that woman, dressed in a simple flowing white dress, looking up at him as if she'd been waiting for this moment—and him—all her days.

And he knew with utter certainty that had he lived, Mr. and Mrs. Jason Burke would have been together for life.

And that, he thought, *is the end of that.*

He closed the browser, powered down the laptop and put it on the table beside him. He went about the business of getting ready for bed mechanically, trying not to think. Let the dog out, waited for him to come back, all the while looking at the night sky, clearing now from the earlier rain. Dried the dog's feet, added another towel to the pile. Closed and locked the door. Brushed his teeth. Pulled off his clothes and again added to the laundry pile. Ignored the chill of the sheets as he got into bed.

And lay there for a very long time, staring into the dark.

Finally, he felt a bounce as Cutter jumped up on the bed. He was startled since the dog had never done it before. Not that he minded, really. Not as if he were displacing anyone, except maybe a sad memory.

A furry head came to rest on his shoulder, and he heard a quiet doggy sigh. It made him smile, and he lifted his other hand to stroke the dog's head. It felt oddly soothing, and when he finally slept, the dreams he'd been fearing didn't come.

Chapter 7

Sloan debated with herself for nearly an hour, all the time wondering when she had lost her usually sharp decision-making skills. She'd picked up and put down her phone at least three times, and the repeated action made her feel beyond foolish.

It wasn't that she didn't have reason to make the call; obviously she did. There was only one reason she hadn't already done it, and she didn't understand it. Yes, Brett Dunbar was six feet plus of very attractive male, but she'd run into that before—there was no shortage of those in the world. But too many of them were a lot smaller—and uglier—on the inside.

None of which mattered, she told herself firmly. This was a business call, in essence. It wasn't as if she were going to harass or constantly bother him. She just needed the name of the person he'd talked to.

She nearly laughed aloud at herself. She had called the chief of naval operations with less vacillation. She had called the chairman of the Joint Chiefs of Staff, for God's sake. And the White House. Yet she was worried about calling one sheriff's detective in a small county almost as far from DC as you could get short of Alaska or Hawaii?

She picked up the phone and hit the call button before she could change her mind again. Maybe she'd get his voice mail. That would be easier, wouldn't it? It would—

"Dunbar."

His voice was as deep and resonant as she remembered, but that was no excuse for the little leap her pulse took.

"Hello, Detective," she said after a too-long silence, realizing belatedly she should have decided how to address him before she had called. "This is Sloan Burke. I hope you don't mind that I used this number."

"That's fine, Mrs. Burke. What can I do for you?"

She supposed she had the formal tone coming after using his job title instead of his name. But then it hit her that he had said "Mrs.," not "Ms." as he had before. She frowned. She knew it had never come up in their conversations. But he was a cop. Maybe he checked on people as a matter of routine. It wasn't as if it were a secret; her story was out there for anyone to find. It was part of the price she'd paid. Unlike whatever nightmare put those shadows in Brett's eyes, hers were out there in public.

She pulled herself together. Distraction wasn't her norm, and it was starting to irritate her. "I wondered if I could have the name of the person you spoke to at the county," she said. "My aunt's application now seems to be among the missing."

There was a pause. Too long. That wasn't good—she'd learned that the hard way. Was it that hard for him to decide if he could trust her with a simple name? What was it about people in authority? Why did they always have to—?

"Sorry. I was driving. Missing?"

She was glad he couldn't see her, because she felt her cheeks heat. She'd made an assumption about his silence, that he was like all the others who had tried to fend her off, when in fact he'd merely been pulling over to talk safely.

"It's been a few days, so I thought I could at least find out where it was in the process. But I got the same person who told me it was frozen before. She said there was no application at all in my aunt's name."

"What? That's crazy. Rick had it in his hand when he called me back."

"That's your contact?"

"Yes. Rick Alvarado."

"You're sure he had it? He wouldn't…just say he did to cover losing it?"

"No. He wouldn't lie to me."

"Would Mr. Alvarado—or you—mind if I called him?"

"I'm sure he wouldn't. And why would I?"

"He's your contact."

"This isn't chain of command, Mrs. Burke. Feel free."

Was there an edge in his voice? And there it was again, that *Mrs. Burke*. And did that chain-of-command comment mean he truly had looked her up, knew she'd fought her way up that chain more than once? She sighed inwardly in exasperation. She hadn't spent this kind of time trying to guess at what someone wasn't saying since she'd had to deal with brass who wanted to help her but couldn't without damaging themselves.

"Been doing some research?" she asked.

"The joys of the internet," was all he said, but he sounded a bit embarrassed. "I'll call him again if you want," he said, quickly dodging any further questions on that subject.

"It's not your problem. You've already done enough." Purposely she added, "Thank you, Brett."

"You're welcome, Mrs. Burke," he said, and was gone, almost abruptly.

Mrs. Burke. Even when she'd called him Brett.

Obviously he had done that research. So he had to know her husband was dead. And how. And what had happened after. For some people, that put her in the too-uncomfortable-to-talk-to category. It seemed Brett Dunbar might be one of those.

That disappointed her.

And that, in turn, set off a warning bell in her mind.

With a stern self-directed lecture about foolishness, she ordered herself back to the task at hand and called the permit office once more.

Brett sat in the car where he'd pulled off to the side of the road, his phone still in his hand.

That, he thought, had been a disaster of a conversation.

No wonder she'd cowed half the top brass in a couple of military services. He had a feeling she would have eventually accomplished what she'd done even without the help of that battle-toughened senator. She was smart, determined and dedicated. She'd figured out he'd looked her up and tacitly, with her formal tone, acknowledged the distance he had put between them by using her married name. That didn't surprise him; he'd guessed as much.

What surprised him was how much it bothered him, that tone in her voice. It was what he'd wanted, wasn't it? He'd wanted that safe distance between them.

Well, he'd gotten it. And if he didn't like it, that was his problem.

He checked the highway, picked his spot and merged back into traffic. He made himself map out the rest of his afternoon so he wouldn't dwell on one Sloan Burke. Or how the more he'd read, the more he'd admired her. Or how he had, against his better judgment, called up online video of those hearings, had watched with a pained sort of raptness as she told the story of her husband's death and the cover-up it had revealed. Her testimony had been passionate, articulate and damning. She had never faltered, never let herself be diverted or intimidated. She had shamed them all with her courage, and in the end she had won.

And with each moment he'd watched, he'd envied a dead man more.

Chapter 8

Brett arrived back at the office to a slew of messages, paper, voice mail and emails. Some were the kind that ate at him, queries on cases where there was no progress. One was a break—the suspect in the case where he'd given the deposition had pled out, saving him from any potential trial appearance. The last two were information he'd asked for on other cases.

He sorted them out, prioritizing, making notes of requested details and happily deleting the one from the prosecutor freeing him. For once, the clerk didn't come by to gripe at him for not giving everyone he dealt with his cell number. He was pondering that miracle when that cell phone rang.

He recognized the number immediately. Stared at the small screen for a moment. Glanced around to see if anyone was within earshot, then grimaced at himself for doing it.

Finally, he answered.

"I'm sorry to bother you again," she said without preamble. "And I'm probably being horribly presumptuous, but…"

Her voice trailed off, and a dozen ways she might be presumptuous shot through his mind, most of which kicked his pulse up into territory it rarely visited unless he was running.

And running was just what he should do. Far away from Mrs. Sloan Burke.

"What is it?" He knew he sounded clipped, and with an effort, he added more evenly, "Do you need me to call Rick again after all?"

"That's just it. He isn't there."

He frowned. "He's not always. He has to visit sites sometimes. You might have to call him back later."

"No, I mean he's gone. As in no longer working there."

Brett went still. "What?"

"That's why I called you back. It didn't seem like you knew that."

"No, I didn't. Did they say why?"

"No. But they very pointedly didn't say why, with that tone people get when there's an unpleasant story behind it. You know what I mean?"

"Yes." He fought a sinking feeling. Rick had had that job for a long time, and he couldn't imagine why he would leave it. Not when he was working so hard to help his daughter stay straight. "I can't believe he'd just quit. He's got a daughter in college, and he's trying hard to keep her there, out of trouble."

"She was in trouble?"

"A few years ago," he said. "It was one of my cases."

It had been quite a mess Caro had gotten herself into, following some less-than-well-chosen friends into drugs and then into a small crime ring, stealing phones and tablets they would wipe and resell. He'd seen immediately she was in way over her head, scared, and had known there was a chance to save her. She'd just been reeling after the death of her mother. The girl had, with a little help, pulled herself free and turned her life around, he'd thought for good.

He hoped some major problem with her wasn't the reason Rick had left.

"You helped her, didn't you?" Sloan asked when he didn't go on. "That's why her father thinks he owes you."

She didn't miss much, he thought. And he shouldn't have said that about Caro getting into trouble. It wasn't anybody else's business. Not to mention she'd been a juvenile, not the kind of case he should be discussing with a civilian.

"She helped herself," he said. "I just gave her a little direction. That's all they said, no hint as to why?" he asked, fending off any other questions he couldn't or shouldn't answer.

"Nothing. But I'm a stranger. They'd probably tell you."

"I'll call." And after a moment's hesitation, he added, "Thank you, Sloan."

"Of course."

"I'll ask about your permit, too."

"That's all right. You need to deal with your friend's situation. I think we'll just forget it and start over. We'll go in this afternoon when the visiting caretaker is here for Uncle Chuck."

"That's generous of you."

"I've calmed down a bit," she said, her tone wry. "Sometimes you just have to cut your losses. And in the grand scheme of things, a lost application isn't much."

"I suppose not," he said. Not compared to what she'd been through before, he thought as they disconnected. Maybe he should just show them who they were dealing with. Perhaps a clip of that video from DC would help them realize they did not want this woman coming after them.

He found Rick's work number quickly, since he'd just called it. Instead of the usual businesslike recording of Rick's words, he got a mechanical voice telling him to leave a message at the tone. He left a brief, innocuous message asking him to call. He found the cell number and called it. It went straight to voice mail. Then he tried the home phone with the same result.

He debated for a moment over his next step. He didn't really want to call Rick's boss, an autocratic guy his friend had complained about more than once, but his gut was beginning to fire. He checked the county directory on the wall and got the number. As he listened to the ringing, it occurred to him that perhaps Rick might have had good reason for leaving. Maybe another job, one that paid more, would make things easier on both he and Caro. He hoped that was the case.

Another encounter with a recording, this one declaring rather importantly that Mr. Franklin was at a meeting with the county administrator. He didn't leave a message this time.

There was one other call he could make, he thought. Caro. He did call occasionally anyway to see how she was doing, offering support if she needed it. She was a success story in his book, even if his involvement was exactly the kind of thing some at LAPD had tried to grind out of him. "Finish the case and forget it" was a philosophy he'd never been able to adhere to very well.

He brought up Caro's number and hit the call button, expecting voice mail again. She wasn't as bad as some her age about texting only, but she often didn't answer right away. But she always checked messages, so he mentally ran through what he would say when the recording came on.

Instead he got a cheerful "Hey, you, what's up?"

"That's what I was calling to ask you. Everything all right?"

"I'm fine, for somebody on their way to statistics class," she said. "How are you?"

"Fine. Have you heard from your father?"

He heard the honest puzzlement in her voice as she

answered, "Not for a few days. But he knows I've been busy, and so has he. Why?"

"I just needed to talk to him about some paperwork thing," he said, "and he's not answering. And it was time to check in on you anyway."

"You worry too much," she said, but her voice held that note of appreciation he recognized by now. It warmed him. If he'd gotten an early start, he could have had a daughter her age by now. Normally that idea would have frightened him; now it just made him feel oddly wistful. "Anyway, Dad's probably at some site out in the sticks somewhere with no reception."

"Maybe." If Rick hadn't told her yet, he wasn't about to. Besides, maybe there was some mistake. Or maybe he was going to surprise her with some great news about a new, better job. "How's everything else? Any problems with anyone, friends or anything?"

"Not that I know of. What's going on? You sound weird. Like you're in cop mode or something."

"I guess I am," he said. "You'd better get to class."

She sighed audibly. "Unfortunately."

She had sounded fine, he thought after the call ended. No sign of stress beyond that of any normal college student. No reason to think she was hiding anything. But clearly she didn't know about her father and his job. Which worried him; if it had been a good thing, wouldn't Rick have shared it with her?

He tapped a finger on his desk, his brow furrowed. There could be such a simple explanation for it all. One that could easily turn out to be true. One he might have assumed would turn out to be true if it hadn't been for that instinct nagging at him. He couldn't explain it—he never had been able to—but it was there, it was real, and it was right most of the time, in one way or another.

Still mulling, he picked a black dog hair off his sleeve. He'd more or less given up worrying about the fur for the duration. At least half the hair blended with his usual dark suits.

He wondered idly if Cutter's bizarre instincts were anything like his own. Maybe he did what he did because his gut wouldn't leave him alone either. He shook his head sharply; he was starting to sound like Foxworth, attributing human traits to a dog.

He picked up the phone and redialed Rick's boss. Reacting to that instinct again, he used the main line to call out instead of his direct one. This time a harried-sounding voice answered. He asked for Rick, on the slight chance it was all a misunderstanding.

"Rick Alvarado?" the man said, as if he had several by that name working in his office. "Uh…he's not here."

"When will he be back?"

"He won't be." A bit of the overweening boss crept into the man's voice. "He no longer works in this office."

"Did he transfer to another department?"

"No. I can assure you he won't be working for the county in any capacity again."

Brett frowned. "Are you saying he was fired?"

The thought of Rick doing anything that could result in that was absurd. The man was a workaholic in the way only someone using his job to get through his grief could be. Brett knew a little something about that. It was probably why the man had gotten through the normal barrier between cop and citizen.

"Who is this?" Something sharper had come into the man's voice.

"I'm a friend of his," he answered.

"Then wouldn't you know?"

If the man had been a suspect in something, Brett would have said he was stonewalling.

"If I did, I wouldn't be asking you."

"How do I know you're really his friend? You could be anyone."

Brett sighed. "I'm with the sheriff's office, as you can see by the number I'm calling from. Now can I get an answer?"

There was a moment of stark silence. He couldn't even hear the man breathing, but he could almost sense his mind racing.

"So…is this an official inquiry?"

Brett had purposely not said he was a detective or given his name, all the while wondering if his own imagination was running wild for no good reason. But his gut was telling him to keep his identity as vague as possible, so he pushed to get past the point where it would be easily asked for. He took what Rick had told him about the guy and chose the approach that usually worked the best with those types.

"Make it official," he said sharply, "if that will get me an answer. Now. Unless you want me there in person, shoving my badge in your face in front of anyone in the vicinity." Not that he would. This wasn't really official, and he was already walking a fine line.

"He was terminated."

"Why?"

"I'm afraid I can't give you details. The investigation isn't completed yet."

Investigation? "Are you saying there was malfeasance involved?"

"I truly cannot discuss it. This is being kept completely in-house. For PR reasons, for the county. You understand, I'm sure."

Oily. The man sounded oily. Trying to establish a rapport as if they were colleagues. He told himself that not liking a man's attitude wasn't reason enough to be suspicious. But stonewalling was.

"What is he being accused of that he's been terminated rather than put on leave until your 'investigation' is finished?"

"I can't discuss that either. I assure you, it's no business of the sheriff's office. Unless you suspect him of something?"

He sounded almost hopeful. *I'd sooner suspect you*, Brett thought. "No. I told you, he's a friend."

He considered, as he ended the call, bringing up the permit situation despite Sloan's assurance it wasn't necessary. But something stopped him. He wasn't sure what it was.

The only thing he was sure of was that his gut was now screaming that something else was going on here.

Chapter 9

She was just being paranoid, Sloan thought. There were a million gold cars on the road, and this one was a frequently seen model. It was just her imagination working overtime, although you'd think it would have been worn-out by now, with all the imagining she'd been doing about Brett Dunbar.

She had herself convinced until the car, some distance back, took the same exit. But she tamped down the feeling again. They weren't being followed; it was simply that this was the way to the county offices and lots of people went there every day. And when she made the turn to go to those offices, the gold car slid past without even slowing, proving she'd been being silly.

That sense of foolishness vanished soon after they went inside. She didn't like the man running this place. He wasn't bad looking, although his hair looked a bit determinedly blond, and if he was any taller than her own five foot six, she'd be surprised. But he had the same sort of arrogance that so many of those she'd encountered back in DC had. As if they knew best, and you, the mere peon, should be grateful they deigned to even speak to you. She'd called it sit-down-and-shut-up syndrome.

When Sloan had asked the beleaguered-looking clerk about making copies of the application, the man had rudely butted in and told them the copy machine wasn't working, even though the clerk had been using the thing when they'd come in. And then he'd glared at the woman, as if warning her not to contradict him.

"I don't like the way he talks to that poor woman," Aunt Connie whispered.

"Me either," Sloan agreed, feeling a twinge of guilt that she'd thought so ill of the woman when obviously she was at least in part the way she was because she had a jerk for a boss. No wonder Brett's—Detective Dunbar's—friend had left. Jason had always said the tone was set by the leader, and that certainly seemed true here.

Her aunt went back to the form she was filling out. Sloan had brought the copy she'd made of the original because it had all the necessary details already filled in. She'd thought on the way here that had it been her alone, she would have just shown them the copy and demanded a better explanation than "We have no record of it." But Connie was in a fragile-enough state already. She'd decided this was not a battle to fight just now.

When it was done and signed, she took the form from her aunt and got out her phone. She began to take photos of the document.

"Excuse me—what do you think you're doing?"

The man burst out of his office, sounding as outraged as if she had started to climb over the counter and into his domain.

Since the answer to the literal question was obvious, Sloan didn't answer it. She took her last photo before she even looked at him. "Merely making a record for our own files, since your copy machine is broken," she said, keeping her voice even. "Surely you have no problem with that."

"You can't take photographs in here!"

She had started to slip her phone back into her purse, but something about the man made her decide to slide it into her jeans' front pocket instead. If he decided to come after it, he'd have a tougher time.

"Why not?" she asked, feigning mere curiosity.

"Because you can't," he said.

"Oh. You do realize that kind of answer makes you sound no better than a petty tyrant?" she asked with a sunny smile.

A bright red flush rose in the man's face. "You—"

Aunt Connie cut him off. "Young man, I've paid property taxes in this county for forty years," she said, giving the man the glare that had straightened up many a child during her years as a teacher. "Taxes that built this building and help pay your salary, I might add. I'll thank you for a little respect."

Sloan had to fight a smile, not so much for what her aunt had said but because she had roused with such spirit. It was the first sign she'd seen that Connie had some of her old fire left, and Sloan rejoiced in it. And quickly decided to let her run with it. Especially when the man glared at her but scuttled back to his office and pointedly shut the door without saying another word.

"I'll just get this entered right away," the beleaguered clerk said, taking the application. "We don't want another mix-up."

"Thank you, dear," Aunt Connie said. "I'm sure it wasn't *your* fault."

Sloan didn't think she'd mistaken the look of gratitude in the other woman's eyes or the spark of pleasure she'd seen when Connie had been chewing her boss out as if he were a fourth grader.

Still, she was glad to get out of there. As, apparently, was her aunt.

"What a smarmy little man," she said as they walked to the car, hurrying through the rain and holding their jackets closed against the wind. "'Because you can't.'" She mimicked his tone perfectly, and Sloan laughed.

"The typical nonreasoning answer of a despot, no matter how tiny his...domain," she said with a purposeful leer.

Connie burst out laughing. "You are so bad, Sloan Burke. And I love you for it."

"Where do you think I learned it?" she said, slipping her arm around the older woman's shoulders, so delighted to see her spirit returning that she put everything else out of her mind for now. "Come along, and let me buy you lunch. The tea shop, maybe? Surely you wouldn't turn down a nice hot cup of tea on a day like this? Then we can sneak down to the candy store in town and buy something evil."

Sloan saw her aunt's forehead crease slightly. "I should—"

"Ah-ah. Remember what Uncle Chuck said. You're not to worry about him and take some time for yourself."

"But—"

"He worries about you. This will make him feel better."

There couldn't have been a more persuasive argument, and her aunt surrendered graciously. They went off to the local tea shop, and once they were seated, Sloan allowed herself a mental pat on the back. She had been standing within mere yards of the sheriff's office building for nearly an hour and had thought of Detective Brett Dunbar only maybe three times.

The sergeant was out, so Brett walked over to Lieutenant Carter's office. She was on the phone and held up a finger to indicate it would be only a moment. He propped a shoulder on the doorjamb and waited standing up, indicating in turn he didn't expect this to take long.

From what she was saying, the conversation was about a prisoner over in the county lockup involved in some kind of scuffle. She was mostly listening. She looked more annoyed than concerned, so he deduced it wasn't anything serious.

He glanced at the three photos on the credenza behind her. To the left was the requisite formal family shot, she and her husband and the two kids, in the middle was her academy portrait, and on the right, rather whimsically, an amazingly detailed and ornate snow castle. He assumed her husband, an architect, was behind that one.

A happy family. He didn't begrudge her that; she was good people, just tough enough but not hardened. But he still felt a pang whenever he saw that array.

"Be glad you didn't take this job," she said as she hung up the phone.

"I was never in the running."

"Only because you didn't want to be. You could have had it easily."

"Too much desk time."

"Amen to that," she said rather fervently. "What's up?"

"Just wondering if you know anything about Al Franklin."

Her brow creased. "County guy?" At his nod her mouth quirked. "Honest opinion?"

Uh-oh. "Please."

"He's a bit of an ass," she said. "Full of himself. Match what you thought?"

"Yes."

"You run afoul of him?"

"He just wasn't much help on a query I made. But it was personal, so I didn't push too hard."

"Problem?"

"Don't know yet. Just wanted to know if my feel on him was right."

"Well, tread carefully. He's an ass, but he's an ass with connections. He's in tight with Harcourt Mead. And you know where that string leads."

He did know. Straight from Mead's county administrator office to the governor's office. The two men had gone to school together, and in some circles the phrase *thick as thieves* was pointedly used to refer to them. God, he hated politics.

"Thanks for the heads-up," he said as her phone rang again. She rolled her eyes at him as she reached for it. He left, glad once more he'd never even considered that job opening when it had come up.

He made a stop to talk to the victim of an armed robbery who was due to testify at the trial in a couple of weeks. Toby Markham was a feisty old guy, but Brett knew that often bravado broke down over time. He'd promised the man he would be there for him, and he'd meant it. After assuring himself the wiry war vet was fired up and ready, and drinking a cup of coffee he would swear could be used as lubrication for a jet engine, he excused himself.

A few minutes later he was outside Rick's house. The tidy small cottage appeared quiet, but he supposed Rick could be holed up inside, feeling miserable.

Or worse. That family had been through so much; Brett didn't like to think where his friend's mind might be right now. Losing his job and likely his ability to keep Caro in school, with her finally safe and finding her way, he couldn't be in a good place.

And apparently, he wasn't here. Or wasn't answering.

Brett walked around the house. There was no sign of lights on, despite the dark gray sky. He fixed the layout in his mind from the times he'd been here. He could see through the windows into several rooms, and all appeared normal, undisturbed. Only the back corner windows, where he thought the master bedroom was, were blocked with heavy drapes.

He headed for the garage and peered in through one of the rain-stained windows. Empty, except for a lawn mower, a bicycle and a workbench with some tools and what looked like an oil filter sitting out.

He wasn't sure if the empty garage made him feel better or worse. But at least it made it less likely Rick was lying dead inside. And for a moment he envied people who wouldn't even think of that, because such things never happened in their lives. He'd seen too much too often.

And once, it had happened in his own life.

He shook his head sharply. He was not going there. It was pointless.

He called Rick's cell again. And again it went to voice mail. He dug out a business card and wrote a note on the back. He stuck it above the doorknob on the back door. It was the closest to the garage, where he knew Rick usually came in from.

He walked slowly back toward the front of the house. He had a decision to make. He could play with what could turn into a nasty political football or opt out. Let it be. Wait and see. Maybe Rick would come back and there would be some mundane explanation. He didn't know the man so well that he knew every aspect of his life. Who knew what else might have come up? Or maybe he was out on job interviews.

He hoped Franklin wouldn't screw Rick over on that. But after the lieutenant had confirmed his assessment of the man, he didn't hold out much hope that he wouldn't enjoy twisting the knife. He wondered if Al Franklin was the type who couldn't stand to have an honest, decent man around.

"Too much contrast," he muttered.

Pushing this could land him in hot water. But he'd been in hot water before, and dropping it went against every instinct he'd developed over the years. His gut was insisting there was more to this, and anytime he'd ignored this kind of insistence in the past, he'd regretted it.

He's an ass with connections...

Connections.

It occurred to him then there was a third option. He grabbed his phone and made the call.

Again with the voice mail, he thought as Quinn Foxworth's voice spoke. No identifying remarks, not even a name, just a brusque "Message, please."

"Rafe, this is Brett Dunbar. If you're there, I need some discreet Foxworth help after all. I can't explain why, but I think—"

He heard a click, then Rafe's voice. "No explanation needed."

"Thanks. Because my gut's saying my friend Rick's in trouble."

"Good enough. Give me what you've got."

He did, and when he'd hung up, he marveled a little at the faith he'd gained in Foxworth in such a short time. And they in him, for that matter.

Maybe, one day when it all became too much, he might talk to Quinn about making that offer.

Chapter 10

"What are you, living here?" Brett asked, noticing the plate and glass set to one side on an end table. He'd been surprised when Rafe had called him back that same evening, then told himself he'd seen Foxworth in action before—he shouldn't be surprised that he had news already. He'd loaded up Cutter for the visit and headed out.

Now Rafe gave him a one-shouldered shrug. "Pretty much. Hayley's not around to nag me to go home."

Brett wondered where home actually was for the man. He had a feeling it was perhaps even less impressive than his own small place. Which in turn was less impressive and not quite as comfortable as the living quarters here at Foxworth. He remembered that Quinn had been living here, before Cutter literally dragged Hayley into his life.

As if he'd heard his name in Brett's thoughts, the dog lifted his head. He was almost getting used to it, that uncanny timing the animal had.

It was a cold, windy, rainy evening, and they'd tacitly agreed the living area in front of the fireplace would do nicely. The laptop open on the table before them chimed an incoming message. Rafe leaned forward and hit a key, held it, then tapped another, and an image popped up on the flat-screen monitor on the wall in the same instant the small webcam above it looking back at them went live. Brett saw a young man, thin, with sandy hair that looked a bit rumpled. He had a small patch of beard below the center of his lower lip. And looked quite awake and alert, given it was two hours later where he was.

"Have you two met?" Rafer asked.

"No," Brett said, "but I assume you're the famous Tyler Hewitt?"

The young man grinned. "That's me. And you're Detective Dunbar, right?"

Brett nodded. "You do some impressive work."

"I'll take that as a compliment."

"That's how it was meant."

"Some cops don't appreciate some of the things I do."

"I appreciate the job getting done and no damage being done in the process." One corner of his mouth quirked upward. "But I'm probably better off not knowing exactly how you do it."

Tyler laughed. "Hey, I like him," he said, shifting his gaze to Rafe.

"We all do," Rafe said quietly. And Brett felt an odd sort of warmth at that. These were good people, the best, and their good opinion meant more to him than he would have ever thought.

"What did you find out?" Rafe asked.

"There's no record of any flight reservation in the name of Rick Alvarado and no charges to any airline on either of his credit cards, at least not in the last three months."

"Any uptick in gasoline purchases?" Rafe asked. "Or anything else?"

"No. No unusual purchases at all, based on the pattern I can see."

Yes, he was definitely better off not knowing how Tyler got information that it would often take him a week and a warrant to manage, Brett thought. If he hadn't trusted Foxworth completely to be on the side of the angels, he'd have had a problem with it. But they'd never put a foot wrong, in his view, and he did trust them. How completely he hadn't realized until this moment.

"You want me to check airline manifests?" Tyler asked, as if it were no more complicated than a web search. And perhaps for this guy it wasn't. But still…

"No," he said. That was federal territory he didn't want to tread on unless he absolutely had to. "Not yet, anyway."

"Okay. There's also no significant activity recently on his checking account. In fact," Tyler added, "there hasn't been any financial activity at all."

Brett drew his brows together. "What was the last transaction?"

Tyler looked to his right, apparently at another screen. "A debit for $9.27 at something called The Mug. Coffee place, I guess?"

Brett nodded. "A chain. Rick's a regular."

"Must have been for two, or food," Rafe observed. "Even they're not that expensive."

"What time was it? It'd be like him to grab something quick for lunch there."

Tyler looked, then nodded. "Processed at twelve thirty-two."

"What day?"

"Tuesday."

Brett went very still. No explanation. No contact with his daughter. Empty house. Car gone. No record of a flight or even a reservation. No financial activity.

And the last trace of Rick was the day after Brett had asked him to look for the Days' paperwork. Coincidence? Or connection?

He had been a cop too long to believe much in coincidence.

Every step of his run so far this Saturday morning had been spent wondering where to look next. There had still been no word from Rick. Tyler was still monitoring his bank account and credit cards for activity, but there had been nothing. The barista at the espresso stand had remembered Rick from that day—he'd bought a muffin with his usual latte—but said he hadn't stopped by since. His neighbors hadn't seen him. It had been four days now.

A woman with one of those small fluffy dogs was walking toward them on the trail. She grabbed up the white puffball and looked warily at Cutter. There was no leash law in this unincorporated area, but some people got huffy anyway.

"He's fine," Brett called out, hoping he wasn't lying.

Cutter didn't even look at the dog, or the woman, just kept up the steady pace. The woman relaxed, nodded but waited until they passed to put her dog down again.

"Thanks, buddy," he said to Cutter when they were out of earshot.

He went back to his pondering. Yes, Rick's car was not in the garage at his house. But nothing else looked amiss there—he'd inspected as thoroughly as he could without breaking in. And yes, Rick was an adult and free to drop out of sight if he wanted. But he would never do it without telling Caro. He just wouldn't. He'd nearly lost the girl once and wouldn't do anything to jeopardize the good relationship they had now.

And Brett couldn't stop thinking that Rick was the perfect sad case. No family except a daughter across the state, and the man had been so focused on saving her that he'd had little energy for anything else in life, such as friends or other activities. And now to lose his job—he hated to think of how he must be feeling. Cut adrift. Lost.

Brett knew the feeling himself. Because in fact, Rick had more than he did.

He dodged the root from a big cedar tree that had started to grow across the surface of the trail. A walker headed the other way nodded at him. He nodded back as he passed.

Once more he ran that last conversation he'd had with Rick through his mind, looking for any sign something was up with him. Other than being puzzled at the misplaced application, he'd sounded perfectly normal.

Basic logic said there was no reason to assume there was a connection, to link Rick's disappearance with the discovery of the explainable missing application just because they had both happened at about the same time.

But his gut had never been very good at logic, and his brain didn't like coincidences.

He was going to have to do it soon if nothing turned up. He was going to have to call Caro and tell her and suggest she should file a missing-person report. And he dreaded that idea in a way he hadn't dreaded anything in a while. The girl was doing well now, but he wasn't sure how solid it was. Or how solid it would stay if she lost her dad. Losing her mother was what had sent her on that spiral downward in the first place.

He swore under his breath. Cutter, his usual distance ahead, looked back at him.

"What are you now, the language police?" he complained.

The dog woofed, then resumed trotting ahead.

It was, he thought as he tried to regain his rhythm, a double-edged sword. A report would make it official, but it would also take it out of his purview. Rick lived in one of the towns in the county that had their own police department. And while effective, it was also small and lacked the county's resources. But he knew a couple of guys there. They'd probably let him consult, at least, if they knew his interest was personal as well as professional.

He supposed he could argue Rick was so far last known to be in county territory, at the espresso stand, and get the case moved in-house. Of course, technically it still wouldn't be his. He didn't normally work missing persons unless it was a high-risk or child situation where all hands were called in.

He'd have to—

Damn. Cutter had turned up the hill.

He opened his mouth to call the dog back, realized the absurdity of thinking he would come and shut it again.

"Should have put you on the leash anyway," he muttered.

But he knew deep down that if he'd really wanted to avoid this, he would have followed through on his vow to measure out another route and taken it. But he liked this one. He hadn't gotten bored with it yet, and it was the perfect combination of distance, terrain and variation.

But he'd sworn he would never again take this detour.

Right. Too bad Cutter had other plans.

The hill was still a challenge, at least to maintain his steady pace. He focused on that, telling himself it was unlikely Sloan would be there, or if she was, she wouldn't be outside. Then again, it was one of those rare severely clear winter days that taunted with the promise of spring and generally drew everyone in the Northwest out to bask in that infrequent visitor, the sun. There had been more people out on the trail than he'd seen in a month.

So maybe Sloan Burke would be outside, maybe pruning those roses of her aunt's or something. Or did you do that this time of year? He knew next to nothing about gardening. He could tell an apple tree from an evergreen, but that was about it. Flowers were beyond him, except for the purple crocuses that were the first harbinger of spring and were even now beginning to pop up in some protected areas. But once you got past those and roses and daisies, he was reduced to colors. And according to Angie, he'd been helpless at that, too. Women had more names for colors than there were colors, he thought. They—

Cutter burst into a run, tail up and bouncing happily. In seconds he'd rounded the corner and was out of sight.

Brett knew long before he made it to the corner himself. She was there.

She was sitting on the front steps, lacing up a pair of

lightweight boots, as Cutter raced up to her. Brett picked up his pace, kept his eyes focused on her as she greeted the dog. When she straightened up, her bangs had fallen forward, nearly masking her right eye behind a red-gold curtain. He found it oddly appealing, sexy somehow. Not that she needed that to make her sexy.

She had looked unhappy until she'd seen the dog, he thought. He hoped nothing else had gone wrong.

A smile curved her mouth as she reached out to pet the dog.

Lucky dog.

Damn. Where had that come from?

By the time he caught up, Cutter was fairly wiggling with obvious delight at her touch. And Brett was thinking he didn't blame the dog one bit.

She stood up as he came to a halt.

"He got that wild hair again," he said. "Sorry."

"Don't be. I think I needed a bit of doggy cheer this morning."

So he'd been right about her unhappy expression.

"Problem?"

She gave a one-shouldered shrug as she shook her head. "Nothing to bother you with. You've already done enough. Did you talk to your friend?"

"Not yet. He's lying low, apparently." He didn't expand. It really wasn't his place to broadcast Rick's personal problems. "And his boss wasn't much help."

"If he's the same guy we ran afoul of, I'm not surprised."

"Is that it? The application?" he guessed.

"It was denied."

"Why?"

She gave him a sideways look. "Trust me—you don't want to get me started on that absurdity."

Cutter made a small sound that drew his gaze. The dog was giving him that look again. Apparently he did want to get her started. Brett sighed inwardly. This was the most insane thing. Letting the dog choose their route was one thing; letting him control conversations and actions was...well, crazy.

And yet he said it. "Tell me."

She gestured up the hill behind the house. "They said there's a wetland area up there. And that is, pardon the word, bu...unk."

He nearly laughed at her asking pardon for the innocent word until he realized the hesitation and shift midword meant she had been about to say something else less socially acceptable. Then he did laugh.

"So there's no wetland?"

"I grew up in this house. I know every inch of that land up there because I played there almost every day. There has never been anything even remotely close to the proper definition of a wetland."

He glanced at her feet. "I gather you're about to head up there?"

"With my camera." She gestured at a small digital camera on the top step next to where she'd been sitting. "I want video proof there's no such thing before I take them on."

Cutter turned and sat down at her side, waiting.

That she would indeed take them on was something Brett didn't doubt for a moment. "I'm sure a small county official seems like nothing compared to the entire federal government and the armed forces."

She didn't look at him. "I just did what anybody would have done."

"No," he said. "Not everybody would have. Many would have given up, thought the fight too big."

She let out a compressed breath. "If they'd only told the truth, I would have been angry, but I would have eventually let it go. But they lied, then lied about the lies, then about those lies. So I kept on. I owed Jason that much. *They* owed him."

She picked up the camera from the steps. Cutter got to his feet. The dog was stuck to her like a barnacle. She glanced down at him, stroked his head, then looked at Brett.

"I think he wants to go with you," he said, his mouth quirking. "So I guess I do, too."

"You always let him decide?"

"I've been told it's best to just agree and cooperate," he said wryly. "He's a very unique dog."

"Obviously. Come on, then. I want to get this done before the sun decides to disappear again."

She started walking along the side of the house, headed toward the hill behind. Cutter trotted beside her, not even looking back, apparently confident he would follow.

And why not? Brett thought. All his people followed his lead; why shouldn't the dog think that he would, too?

He started after them, wondering how boring his runs would be once Hayley and Quinn Foxworth got back and repossessed their uncanny canine.

Chapter 11

"That's it?" Brett asked. "They're calling that a wetland?"

Sloan shook her head as she stared at the small puddle. All of a foot and a half across, it couldn't constitute a "wetland" in any sane person's mind.

"Absurd as that is, it's not the point," she said.

"What is?"

"It's never been here before. Ever. Not in thirty years, not in the rainiest of rainy seasons. And I would know."

She looked around at the landscape that was as familiar to her as her reflection in the mirror. She heard a rustling and looked back the way they'd come. Caught a glimpse of Cutter ranging through the woods below them on the hill.

"He'll be along," Brett said. She looked back, caught him studying her rather intently. Something in that steady gaze unsettled her.

Face it, the man unsettles you, she silently admitted. But then, Brett Dunbar could unsettle any woman with a pulse.

"You really grew up here? With your aunt and uncle?"

She nodded. "My parents were killed when I was seven. They took me in."

"I'm sorry. That was good of them."

She grimaced. "If you'd known my grandmother, who wanted to take me, you'd know it was more than good—it was lifesaving."

"Not the warm, fuzzy type, I gather?"

"Hardly. I swear, she was the source of the phrase the *evil eye*."

He lifted a brow. "And I thought mine was bad."

She realized abruptly that she knew very little about him, that when they'd talked, it had been mostly about her. She wondered if that was because of the circumstances or his nature. Or maybe because of his job, he was used to always asking the questions.

"Was she?" she asked, thinking it about time she turned those tables. Besides, she was curious. And, she told herself firmly, her curiosity had nothing to do with the fact that she seemed to go on hyperalert around him.

"She was…a bit stiff. And appalled at me. She'd had only girls. And they were all very…" He stopped, looking a bit awkward.

"Very what?" she asked, realizing with surprise that she was enjoying this.

"Girlie," he said, as if he'd searched for another word and failed.

She laughed. "Some are, I'm told."

"Not you?"

"Not since I was seven."

She saw him put it together. "Your parents' deaths changed that?"

"My mother wanted one of those girlie girls. I wasn't one by nature and rebelled. Lord, I hated those frilly dresses!"

He looked as if he couldn't picture her, even as a child, in frills.

"Don't get me wrong—I loved her, but she wanted me to have her childhood over again. My aunt didn't care as long as I was happy. Although I'm sure some people would think she let me run a little too wild."

"Your grandmother?"

"Oh, she was the font of dire predictions for my eventual fate."

And there she was, talking about herself again. What was it about this guy? If he got suspects to spill the way he'd gotten her to jabber, it was no wonder he was good at his job.

"I'm glad you didn't end up with her, then."

"As am I," she said fervently.

Cutter trotted over to them. He had a few dead leaves clinging to his coat, and Brett brushed them off as he spoke to the dog.

"Find anything interesting?"

Cutter let out a soft whuff, then lowered his nose to sniff at the small puddle of water.

"Not sure you should drink that, if that's what you're thinking," Brett said. "Not if we don't know where it came from or why it's here."

"You always talk to him like that? Instead of just saying 'No'?"

"It works," he said, gesturing to the dog, who was not drinking but sniffing around the perimeter of the puddle as if looking for a better spot.

"He does seem to understand."

"Frightening amounts," he agreed.

He watched the dog for a moment longer, then began to walk around the puddle himself. With each circuit he moved farther away from the water, always looking down at the ground. She could hear the faint rustle of the nylon running pants he wore today, wondered idly if he switched to shorts in the summer. Which led her to other thoughts she was better off not having racketing around in her mind.

"Looking for something?" she asked.

"A source. If it's never been here before, there must be a reason it's here now."

"I admit, it's been a couple of weeks since I've been up here, but—"

He stopped walking, looked straight at her. "You were up here that recently?"

She nodded. "Looking at possible building sites. I came right through here and that—" she nodded toward the puddle "—was not here."

"Hmm."

What was that supposed to mean? He didn't believe her? "It wasn't," she insisted.

He drew back slightly. "I'm not doubting you. If you say it wasn't here, it wasn't here."

"Oh." She sounded as abashed as she felt.

He looked at her steadily for a moment. "I'm not one of them, Sloan."

She realized then she had reacted as if he were one of those overstuffed shirts back in DC. And that he knew it.

"Just how much research on me have you done?"

"Enough to come to admire you as I do few people."

Well, that neatly took the wind out of her sails. And now she didn't know why she'd hoisted them in the first place.

Cutter barked, short, sharp and sounding oddly commanding. Only then did she realize he was heading up the hill at a steady trot, his nose still to the ground.

"Where's he wandering off to?" she wondered aloud.

"I don't think he's wandering," Brett said. "That's full intent."

"And so you follow?" she asked as he started after the dog.

"I'm going to have to go get him anyway," he said. Then, with a grimace, he added, "But based on his reputation, who knows what he's on to?"

She had to pick up her pace to stay even with his long strides. But she liked that he didn't slow them for her, just took it for granted that she could keep up.

"So how did a dog convince a detective that he's worth following?"

"Results," he said. Then he smiled. "Well, that and the fact that none of us are entirely convinced he's just a dog."

She laughed at that bit of unexpected whimsy from this man. And also unexpectedly, it made her feel good to know that despite the shadows that darkened his eyes, he could still find amusement in life. She remembered the first time she had laughed after Jason had been killed. It had shocked her, felt so foreign, and then filled her with guilt, as if it were a kind of betrayal of him to even be able to laugh. It had taken her a long time to get past that feeling.

They caught up with Cutter when he stopped just below the road that ran along the top of the hill through a tract of large, expensive houses. He was nosing around again, and she wondered what creature had gone through here that was so fascinating to the dog.

"Is this still their property?"

"We're right at the edge," she said, pointing out the property peg a few yards away. "That's the corner marker."

"Doesn't seem like twelve acres."

She pointed to the west. "It goes that way from here. It's an odd sort of L shape."

Cutter seemed to have settled on one spot to sniff, where the dirt looked less solid, as if some animal had already been digging around. That must be what had his attention, she thought.

Brett looked up at the large house on the road. She followed his glance.

"They wanted to buy this land when they were building those homes, but Uncle Chuck wouldn't sell," she told him.

He looked back at her then, his brow furrowed. "Just how badly did they want it?"

"Badly," she said. "They actually offered a fair price for all of it except the acre their house sits on."

"No problem breaking it up, then?"

She grimaced. "Not at all. Makes you wonder, doesn't it? But Uncle Chuck didn't want to break it up then and didn't need to. But I've wondered if—"

She stopped. The theory that had occurred to her late one night was a bit out there.

"You're thinking there's a connection between your uncle's refusal to sell then and the refusal to allow him to divide the property now?"

"I know it's silly. That was a long time ago, at least five years. And it was the builder who wanted it, not the county, so why would the county care?"

"Why indeed?" he said, looking back up at the house above.

A sudden sharp bark made them both look at the dog. He was digging now, swiftly, front paws tossing dirt behind him. And all over him.

"Uh-oh. He's going to be a mess," she said.

The hole Cutter was working on was getting deep enough that the dirt at the top was starting to fall back in. The dog growled in obvious frustration, then stopped and looked at Brett.

"Hey, this is your entertainment, not mine," he said.

Cutter barked sharply. He stared at Brett, then into the hole he'd excavated.

"No way. It's bad enough you're a muddy mess. I'm not—" He broke off midsentence. "Muddy," he muttered, and covered the three feet between them and the hole in one long stride.

It took her a moment to get there. The dog was muddy now. And she realized suddenly that the dirt he'd been digging up had gotten muddier the farther he'd gone. Wetter.

Water.

Brett was kneeling beside the hole. And contrary to his declaration, he began to shove some of the dirt to the side to keep it from falling back into the hole. The moment he'd done that, Cutter dived back into the hole and began digging again. The cycle happened once more, Brett clearing, the dog digging, until they were down at least two feet.

And in the hole water was streaming, underground, headed directly downhill.

Sloan turned to look downhill. They were a straight line up from the previously nonexistent puddle.

"Son of a—"

Her head snapped back around. Brett was truly muddy now, but he didn't seem to care. He was staring sideways into the hole, and she realized Cutter had uncovered something else.

A water pipe. The kind she'd often seen piled on city or county trucks.

Only this one was leaking. Streaming, actually.

"That's it!" she exclaimed. "I knew there was something really wrong. This isn't any natural wetland. That's why it was never there before."

"So it appears," Brett said from his rather contorted position on the edge of the hole. He was still staring at the pipe and then reached out to touch it, clearing mud away from the spot the water seemed to be coming from.

She grabbed her camera. "Oh, I'm going to like telling them it's their own broken pipe causing this. I hope they feel stupid."

"Hang on, Sloan."

"Oh, I know, I have to wait until Monday, but I'm still going to love it."

"I didn't mean that." Brett straightened up then. Lord, he was as muddy as the dog. She should offer him a chance to clean up. An image, sudden and vivid, of Brett Dunbar naked in her shower sent a shot of heat through her that nearly made her knees buckle.

...he is the first I've seen you react to.

React? she thought as Aunt Connie's words echoed in her mind. More like combust. Spontaneously.

It had been so long she was stunned at herself. She couldn't even look at him, for fear it would show in her face. And she already knew he didn't miss much, trained detective that he was.

Belatedly she noticed he hadn't spoken again. She struggled to remember what he'd said last, before that vivid picture had fried her circuits.

"What did you mean?" she finally got out.

"I meant this isn't just a broken water line."

"What?"

"There's a hole. A neat, perfectly round hole."

She frowned. "What are you saying?"

"I'm saying this line didn't break—it was drilled. Somebody meant for this to happen. And I'd really like to know why. And who."

Chapter 12

"It was on purpose?" Sloan exclaimed. "To send that leakage downhill onto their property?"

"It's the perfect place to cause exactly that result." Reluctantly, he added, "But the on-purpose part would be hard to prove."

"You can't believe this is coincidence!"

"Coincidence and I are longtime adversaries," he said. "I'm just saying it would be hard to prove it was to intentionally create a fake pond, as it might have eventually become, on your aunt and uncle's property."

"What else could it be?"

He shrugged. "Hole could have been there and gone unnoticed."

"They lay water pipe, to carry water, and don't notice it has a hole you could put your thumb through?"

"Easy. I'm just saying they could claim that."

"Then why hasn't it shown up until now?"

"Maybe it only leaked enough to surface now."

He saw the anger spark again, but this time she fought it down. "I'm assuming you're playing devil's advocate here."

Relieved, he said, "Exactly. I just know what they might say. I've dealt with them enough."

"So what do I do? I'll fight them tooth and nail, but I have to have something to fight with."

He knew she would. In those videos of the hearings

he'd seen her do it, against a much bigger entity than the local government of a sparsely populated county. But when she'd gone up against the feds, she'd had documents and compelling audio and video evidence proving her case. And she'd been fearless, he thought, remembering the moments when one particularly nasty questioner had tried to beat her down. She'd quietly yet determinedly stood up to him, angering him, and in the process made him look like the malicious bully he was, berating a grief-stricken widow and accusing her of lying.

He'd felt a ridiculous urge, even after all this time, to go hunt that bully down and give him a taste of what he'd put her through. For his own peace of mind, not for Sloan's sake. She was tough; she didn't need his protection.

He wished she did.

Even as he thought it, near panic seized him. *Back off, back off, back off.* It clanged at him like an alarm on a fire engine in reverse.

"I think," he said, desperately grabbing for an answer, "it may be time for you to meet Cutter's people."

The dog, who had been standing quietly aside, seemingly satisfied he'd done his job, barked as if in agreement.

You, Brett thought, *are going out of your mind. He's. A. Dog.*

And she was dangerous. To him, anyway. Because she was making him think about things he'd given up on long ago.

He'd been scrupulously polite as they'd organized the logistics, Sloan thought. Almost as if he was using good manners to keep distance between them, in the same way he'd called her Mrs. Burke after they'd progressed to Sloan.

He'd made a temporary repair on the pipe to stop the water flow, while she'd done her best to clean up the muddy dog. He'd cut short his run and headed home for a quick shower—and she sternly ordered her mind not to dwell on that, wondering when she'd developed this fascination with male hygiene—then come back in his car to pick her up.

It had taken Sloan a few moments to get over the oddity of riding in a car with a large radio/computer installed in the console, discreet red and blue flashing lights aimed out the windshield, and a shotgun in a rack above her head. It brought rather fiercely home the reminder that this man was a cop, and all that entailed. Especially the danger and the knowledge that any day on the job could be his last. She would already feel bad enough if anything happened to him. He was a nice guy, and one of the good guys. As Jason had been.

Good thing she had no intention of this going anywhere, she thought. *And what was it the road to hell was paved with?*

She tried to shut up that pesky part of her mind that seemed to have slipped the leash. Yes, he was a very attractive man. She wasn't in the market. Period.

After a few miles of silence, she finally spoke. "Should I report that leak?"

He shook his head. "Let's wait until we find out what all we're dealing with. I think that plug will hold for a while."

More silence. She couldn't tell if he was lost in thought or if he simply didn't talk much. Finally, as they turned onto a narrow lane, he began to tell her a bit more about Cutter's people. She listened, fascinated by the very idea of Foxworth. And liking the way he sounded when he spoke of them. She liked a man who cared about his friends.

Stop it! she ordered herself.

"Who's left here?" Sloan asked as he slowed to take a gravel driveway that wound its way through thick tall trees. "If the two at the top are on their honeymoon, and the one who was going to dogsit is off with his girlfriend, and another back home in Texas, how many are left?"

"Here? Just one." His mouth curved upward. "But if you needed an army, Rafe would be a good start."

"So he's all spit and polish?"

Brett laughed. "Hardly. He left all that behind years ago when he left the Marine Corps. He's a tough one to figure, though. Don't know where he'd be if not for Foxworth. He believes in what they do. And he respects Quinn, when I don't think he respects many anymore."

"I know that feeling," she said, her tone a bit sour.

She wasn't sure what she had expected after that, but the tall, rangy man who stepped out of the warehouse that sat just beyond the plain green three-story building wasn't it. He was wearing jeans and a long-sleeve pullover, and his dark hair was a bit long. Even as she thought it, he shoved it back with one hand.

Cutter had taken off the moment Brett had opened the door for him, barking an odd combination of long and short barks as he headed for the man. In the few steps the man took before he stopped to greet the dog, she noticed a slight limp, as if his left leg was a little stiff.

Cutter danced around him, spinning, woofing happily, looking more goofy than she would have thought the rather imperious dog ever could. Clearly this Rafe held a special place in the dog's life. After a moment a small smile curved his mouth and the dog settled, as if that smile had been his goal.

They were only a few feet away when the man finally glanced up at them. He nodded at Brett, then shifted his gaze to her. For a moment he simply looked. Brett stayed oddly silent as the other man came to stand in front of her. She was about to introduce herself when he moved, straightening up as if he was snapping to attention. Slowly, he raised his right hand to his forehead.

Saluting. He was saluting her. Color flooded her face.

"It's an honor, Mrs. Burke."

I don't think he respects many anymore.

Brett's words echoed in her head. It would not do to brush this off by saying it wasn't necessary. Not with this kind of man.

"I... Thank you," she finally managed. Usually she wasn't easily flustered, but she hadn't anticipated this. "I should be thanking you. For your service."

"When you stood for one of us, you stood for all of us," he said softly.

"I only did what Jason would have wanted."

"With as much courage as he showed trying to save his men."

"I wasn't under fire."

"Weren't you?" Brett said, speaking for the first time since they'd gotten out of the car.

Rafe shifted his gaze to Brett and, after a moment, nodded. "Truth. And by some who'd as soon shoot you in the back."

She couldn't argue that. She'd been cornered, bullied, and they'd tried to intimidate her so many times she had come to expect it before it was over. She was convinced the stress of it had brought on her uncle's heart attack, since he'd been there with her every step of the way after the first time she'd been isolated in a back room by a bully threatening her with public humiliation or worse, much worse, if she didn't back off and quit talking about how his boss had refused to help her.

The rain picked up, changing the moment, and they headed for the green building. There were no markings, so when Brett had told her Foxworth didn't advertise, he'd apparently meant not even a sign with their name.

"You guys really do go incognito," she said. "How do people find you?"

"Word of mouth, mostly. Or," Rafe added with a glance at Brett, "from friends who know what we do." He stopped walking, turned to face her straight on despite the increasing rain. "We would have helped you, for instance."

"I could have used some help keeping some of those thugs off my back," she said.

Brett said something under his breath, something she thought might have been "Bastards." The fervency of it warmed her.

And then she was distracted by Cutter, who had trotted up to the door of the building and now rose up on his hind legs and batted at something with a front paw. She realized it was a handicapped entry trigger when the door started to slowly swing open. She found herself grinning.

"Quinn's idea," Rafe said.

"How long did it take to teach him to use it?" she asked.

"About seven seconds," Rafe said. "He showed him once. That's all it took."

"Wow." Cutter had vanished inside before the door finished opening.

Next on the list of things she hadn't expected was the warm, homey effect of the downstairs room of the utilitarian-looking building. There was a gas fireplace with a comfortable-looking leather couch and a couple of chairs arranged in front of it. A large colorful area rug marked off the seating area. She noticed a couple of books and a coffee mug on the low table. A knitted throw was tangled around a pillow at one end of the sofa, as if someone had been sleeping there. Restlessly.

Cutter never even slowed but headed up the stairs at the back of the room.

"I guess we're using the meeting room," Rafe said drily. He glanced at Brett. "I assume this is a business visit?"

"Yes," he answered as they went up the stairs. "I'm in about as far as I can go unofficially."

Rafe nodded. "That's why we're here."

Sloan hadn't thought about that, that Brett might get into trouble poking around on her behalf. It must be strange to not even be able to ask simple questions if people knew who you were, because even questions about a silly bit of paperwork could be construed as having the weight of the badge behind them.

They sat at a table next to a set of large windows that looked out over the clearing behind the building. On the other side of the clearing the ubiquitous evergreen trees were thick, broken only by a couple of red-barked madrones and a huge maple.

"Go," Rafe said without preamble.

"It may not all be connected," Brett warned. "You want it by issue or chronological?"

"Chronological. The way you came across it all. How'd it start?"

"Sloan's aunt applied to divide their twelve acres so they could sell their current home to finance building a new one more suited to her husband's medical situation on the separate parcel."

He went on as Sloan listened. She let him tell it—he knew this man and she didn't. Rafe stayed silent, listening intently, until Brett finished. Then he leaned back in his chair, tapping his right index finger on the table. Trigger finger, Sloan thought suddenly, remembering Brett had said the man had been a top-ranked Marine Corps sniper.

"Let me make sure I got all this," Rafe said. "First they say the application was denied because of a freeze due to a pending zoning study. But nobody seems to know anything about this study. Then they say there's no record of the application at all. But your guy finds it buried in some obscure place. Then he gets fired and disappears without a word to anyone, not even his only family, his daughter. Then the replacement application is denied for a totally different reason, a supposed wetland that was in fact caused by a leak in a water pipe that may have been intentional, below a housing development that wanted to buy that same land in the first place. And sitting on top of the whole thing is the fact that your missing friend's boss is in tight with a guy who's in the pocket of the governor. Is that about right?"

It all sounded much worse laid out that way, Sloan thought. When he talked about his friend, her shoulders had begun to knot. And now her stomach was churning with an echo of the feeling she'd had when she'd heard the official version of what had happened to Jason. A version she knew was a complete lie.

"Most I've ever heard you say at one time," Brett said to the other man.

Rafe grimaced; clearly he either wasn't used to talking that much at once or didn't like it. "On the other side, we don't know if your absent friend's situation actually has anything to do with the rest of it, or if the water leak has anything to do with any of it or is accidental, or in fact possibly intentional and perhaps or perhaps not connected to the housing development or the application."

"Exactly. It could all be connected, or none of it," Brett said.

"And if we proceed assuming either way, we could miss something proving the other."

Rafe went silent, obviously thinking. He absently rubbed at his left leg just above the knee. She wondered if that spot was the cause of the limp. Almost as she thought it, Cutter got up from where he'd been snoozing on the floor and walked over to him. The dog laid his head on the very spot Rafe had been rubbing. Snapped out of his thoughtfulness, the man looked at the dog. A smile more gentle than she would have thought the harsh-looking man capable of curved his mouth, and he began to stroke the dog's head instead.

"Thanks, buddy," he said softly.

He looked up then, caught her looking at him. He seemed embarrassed. "Can't explain it, Mrs. Burke, but it helps."

"Please, call me Sloan. And I'm not sure anything about that dog would surprise me at this point."

He smiled at her, and it changed the harsh, graven planes of his face. She realized then that in a very different way than Brett, this was—or could be—an attractive man.

"He is one of a kind." He looked back to Brett. "Since you have the in and the reason, why don't you take your friend's disappearance? Can you get his daughter to make it official?"

"Yes. I've been putting off calling her, but I will. I can make a case for us handling it since he was last seen in our jurisdiction, and the detective who'd handle it is a friend, so I'd have an in there."

"What about the daughter?" Sloan asked. "Can't she… demand that you handle it? She should have some say. And she trusts you."

"Should doesn't mean will," Rafe said wryly. "That's half the reason we exist."

"I'll work it out," Brett said.

"I figured," Rafe said. "Tyler's still monitoring his financials. Checking for the car, too. I'll have him poke around for anything of interest on the county people. Something might pop."

"You get him some help yet?"

"He says he doesn't need it," Rafe said. Then one corner of his mouth lifted upward. "But I think he's just afraid Charlie will step in."

"I can see where that would be terrifying," Brett said.

"Yeah," Rafe muttered.

Odd undertone in his voice, she thought. Although the thought of the CEO of something as big as Foxworth must be stepping in and "helping" you with your job would certainly scare her.

"I'll look into the housing development," Rafe said. "Drew Kiley might be helpful there."

Brett nodded. Obviously the name was familiar to him. "How are they doing?"

A smile flickered across Rafe's face. "Alyssa's pregnant, so I'd say okay."

"Thanks to Foxworth."

"And you," Rafe said.

So it wasn't always one way, Sloan thought. He helped them, too, it seemed.

"The other big question is, why?" Rafe said.

"Yes," Brett agreed. "Once you accept that this is intentional, you have to wonder why keeping Sloan's family from getting that land divided is so important."

"If it is connected to those houses, maybe they just want to keep them from building at all," Sloan said. "Maybe they promised the buyers no one would."

Brett studied her for a moment before saying, "You said you had a bit of an incident with Franklin at the office."

"Yes. He's one of those," she said. "Arrogant, wielding what little power he has like a club. He must be horrible to work for. I ended up feeling sorry for the woman I was upset with for being so unhelpful."

"What set him off?" Rafe asked.

"Well, he was already being horrid to the poor woman when we got there. But it got worse." She explained about the supposedly broken copy machine. "So I pulled out my phone to take photos of it for documentation, and he reacted as if I were a spy copying nuclear secrets or something."

Rafe looked at Brett. "Sounds like somebody who didn't want a record made."

Brett nodded. "Harder to claim it's lost when there are copies."

"What does your gut say?" Rafe asked.

"That a string of coincidences that would reach from here to the Space Needle is not just a string of coincidences."

"Once is happenstance," Rafe agreed.

Sloan's breath caught. It hit her solidly then that this had turned into more than just a misplaced piece of paperwork. Because she knew that aphorism. She'd heard Jason quote it often enough.

Once is happenstance.

Twice is coincidence.

And three times is enemy action.

Chapter 13

"What about me?" Sloan asked. "I can't just sit on the sidelines while you guys do all the work."

The two men exchanged glances. If either of them told her to just go home and wait, she wasn't sure what she'd do.

"Just how did you react to the little tyrant's arrogance?" Rafe asked.

She grimaced. "Not well. I might have even called him something similar to that."

Rafe smiled. "Then keep doing it. Keep the pressure on. Don't let them think you've gone away quietly. Do what you would do if we weren't here."

"And?" she asked, wondering what his point was.

"And while they're dealing with you, we'll sneak in behind them."

"So I'm a diversion?"

"I can understand why you'd think that beneath you," Brett said.

She waved that off. "Everybody has a job to do in a battle."

"Yes," Rafe said softly.

"Can you make some noise?" Brett asked.

"Of course. My aunt and uncle have a lot of friends, and there are some others in the area who might help if I asked."

"I have a feeling there are a lot more than you might

think," Rafe said. "And Foxworth can probably rally a few. What do you have in mind?"

"Protesters in front of the offices. Speakers at public meetings—I'll have to check the schedule. Make every hearing about this, even if it's not on the agenda. Every speech by a county official, the higher, the better. Every public appearance, even if it's only a ribbon cutting for a supermarket. Get the media's attention. Get it out there beyond local. Maybe even get the Americans with Disabilities Act invoked. That would take it national."

Brett looked as if he was stifling a grin. "Wow. I don't envy them."

"You have to make them listen. Especially when they've forgotten who they work for."

Brett walked her to the door of the house despite the suddenly heavier rain, because it seemed like the thing to do.

"Where do you live when you're not staying here?" he asked. He hadn't meant to. He'd intended to stay strictly away from prying questions. Details about her personal life were none of his business.

And yet here he was, asking anyway.

"I gave up my apartment," she said. "Uncle Chuck's cardiac rehab is going to take a long time, and I didn't want Aunt Connie to end up sick, as well. So I'm here for the duration."

"That's good of you." He meant it. Sloan was good people. Maybe he was just off balance because he hadn't run into any of those in a while. Yeah, that was it.

"I told you," she said as they hurried up the walk, "they're my family."

He didn't point out what he knew too well from his job, that too often family were the last ones to truly help in a crisis.

"Did you give up a job, too?" he asked as they went up the steps onto the covered porch.

"*Accountability Counts* is my job these days. Fortunately, my parents had insurance, my uncle invested it wisely, and along with Jason planning ahead, I'm okay, so I can afford it."

He looked around as Sloan isolated her house key on the ring and put it in the lock. From up here they had a sliver of view of the bay below, framed by tall evergreens. He'd hate to leave this spot, too. Her uncle must feel awful about it. He'd only ever thought of his running regimen as necessary for his work, but maybe it was time to start thinking about it as health insurance, too.

Sloan's aunt opened the door before Sloan even turned the key, clearly stirred up.

"Aunt Connie, what is it?" Sloan asked.

"Come in, come in," the older woman said, gesturing to them both. "It's pouring out there."

Brett was used to assessing his surroundings quickly. It was second nature, done so automatically he didn't even think about it. The inside of this home was as tidy and well kept as the outside. The furnishings were a bit flowery and ornate for his taste but nicely arranged and looked comfortable. There were photographs here and there, some he recognized of Connie and a man he assumed was her ailing husband in younger days and one collage in particular that was a progression of Sloan growing up that made him smile inwardly. Whatever losing her parents had done to her, she had blossomed under the loving care of these people, going from a scared-looking child to a confident, glowing teen to the woman she was now.

The woman who had his mind racing full tilt in directions he'd walled off long ago.

"What is it?" Sloan asked again. "Is Uncle Chuck all right?"

"Oh, yes, he's fine. Well, he's getting a touch of cabin

fever, I'm afraid. He thought he saw someone out in back a bit ago. I looked, but there was no one there."

"You're sure?" Brett asked with reflexive concern.

"Oh, yes. I think he's just grouchy that the broadcast of his basketball game was delayed by the governor's speech. I swear, that man never stops campaigning." That, Brett thought, explained the faint sounds coming from the back of the house. A television. "No, I got a phone call."

"From who?"

"She didn't say, wouldn't say, rather, but I'm certain it was that poor woman from the county office."

Brett had been staring, a bit unwillingly, at the photo that hung on the wall above the sofa. It was a wedding picture. *The* wedding picture, the same one he'd seen on the website. It hit him even harder here, in this setting and full-size. How did she do it? he wondered. How did she face that every day? He had stashed away every reminder, unable to even look at them. Sloan was obviously made of sterner stuff.

Or maybe it was that she still loved him, that man in the photograph. It was certainly believable given the way she was looking at him in that frozen image. And everything he'd found out about the man indicated he was worthy of such devotion.

He was glad when her aunt gestured to him to sit on the sofa, which put his back to the image. She sat in a big chair next to a basket that appeared to hold several items of clothing. Mending? he wondered. Did anybody do that anymore? Sloan stayed with her aunt, sitting on the arm of the big chair.

Better than sitting next to you.

He dragged his focus back to the conversation.

"She called you? On a Saturday?" he asked.

"That's why it was so odd."

"What did she say?" Sloan asked.

"She said I should know something about the first denial, the one before this wetland silliness. That it came on a personal direct order of the county administrator."

"Mead? How did she know that?" Brett asked.

"She said she overheard a conversation. I assume it involved that vile little man she works for, poor thing. I think she appreciated what we did, and that's why she called."

"You're the one who chewed him out like he'd thrown a spitball in your classroom," Sloan said, hugging the woman.

"Well, he deserved it," Connie said with a sniff of disdain. "She said she couldn't say any more, or she'd get in real trouble."

Brett's mind was racing. Why on earth would someone like the county administrator bother with something on this level? He'd met Harcourt Mead once, and he was far too consumed with his own importance. Why would he care about keeping an elderly couple, one of them ill, from building an accessible home on their own property?

He didn't know. What he did know was that his gut was still screaming at him, his every instinct telling him this went much deeper than it appeared.

Or much higher.

Sloan looked at him then. "This county guy, is he essentially your boss's boss?"

"Not really. The sheriff answers directly to the people. But the county admin's got a lot of pull with him."

"Then you can't go digging in that pile," she said.

"I could," he said. "And I would. But I'm not sure it would be wise at this point. Whatever's going on, it might be best if they don't know I'm involved in this. As far as your caller's boss knows, I was only looking for a friend."

"A friend?" Connie asked.

"He has a friend who worked there."

Connie frowned. "The woman said something else, that that man, Mead, got someone there fired. That's why she was afraid to say any more. She's afraid she'd lose her job, too."

Sloan looked at him. "Do you think it's connected?"

"At this point, I don't know anything," Brett said. *About anything.*

He shook off the inner voice and was almost grateful when a burly man with a fringe of gray hair appeared in the doorway. An oxygen line ran up to a cannula beneath his nose from the little tank he was towing behind him on a small dolly.

Brett stood up instinctively. He noticed Connie start to rise, but Sloan put a hand on her shoulder and started to get up herself. Saving them both the effort, he introduced himself.

"Brett Dunbar, Mr. Day," he said, crossing to hold his hand out to the older man. He took it, but it didn't stop him from looking Brett up and down. His grip was strong enough, and his eyes were sharp and alert.

"You're that sheriff."

"I work for the sheriff, yes," he said, deciding now was not the time to explain the fine points of differentiation between the police, sheriff and deputies. Some guys got snarky about it, but he'd given up worrying about it long ago. It didn't matter to most people. Especially when they were in a situation requiring law enforcement.

"The one Sloan likes," her uncle added.

It wasn't really a question, which was a good thing because he was having trouble finding breath to speak after that.

"Uncle Chuck," Sloan exclaimed, sounding embarrassed. "I just said he was nice."

The older man turned his head to look at his niece. "You mean you don't like him?"

"I... Of course I do. He's...nice," she said again, this time sounding as if she knew exactly how awkward that had come out.

He should rescue her, Brett thought. Would have by now if he hadn't wanted to hear what she'd say. So when her uncle shifted his gaze back to him, he smiled.

"For a cop," he said, "that's high praise."

"Hmm."

Brett had the feeling he was being assessed thoroughly and rather astutely. He'd never asked what her uncle had done before he'd had his heart attack. Perhaps he should have. And belatedly he realized he'd seen the man before. Not in person, and not as gray, but he'd been in several of the pictures and videos he'd seen of Sloan's appearances on Capitol Hill. So he'd been there for her, he thought, glad.

"I may be an old man," Chuck Day said, "but I still look out for her."

"Good," Brett said, hoping his expression was even. It was clearly a warning, and he tried not to think of what might have made the man think it was necessary.

Tried not to think about what would make it necessary for real.

He heard the change in sound from the back of the house; the game was back on.

"I should leave you to the rest of your Saturday," he said, since he was up on his feet anyway. "And I have a dog waiting in the car."

"That dog," her aunt said, rising now, "is an... interesting animal."

"Interesting isn't the half of it," Brett said drily.

Almost as interesting as his life had become. And that made him think about an old Chinese curse about living in interesting times. He'd considered it merely amusing before.

He wasn't amused anymore.

Chapter 14

Brett noticed the rain had eased up slightly as Sloan walked with him to the front door. Her aunt and uncle had headed for the back of the house and the game. Arm in arm. Leaning on each other. It moved him, that simple sight, in ways he didn't care to think about just now.

"Sorry about that," Sloan said. "He's a little—"

"It's all right," he said quickly, before things got even more embarrassing. Chuck Day had looked at him as if he were some sort of predator with designs on his niece. Whatever the man suspected, it was clear he wouldn't take kindly to Sloan being hurt. In any way. For that matter, neither would he himself. "You want me to look around outside?"

It took her a moment, as if she'd forgotten what her uncle had thought he'd seen.

"That's all right. Aunt Connie was probably right. He's very tired of being housebound."

"He was with you in DC."

If she was surprised, she didn't show it. "Yes, he was. Every step of the way. I doubt I would have made it without him."

Brett doubted that, but he said nothing as she glanced toward the back of the house, her expression going soft, worried.

"He loved Jason, too. They both did. The whole thing put incredible stress on both of them."

"You think it caused his heart attack?" He didn't want to think about how that must feel. He had a close association, too close, with that kind of guilt, and he didn't like to think of her living in that dark place, too.

"It didn't help." Sadness shadowed her eyes. "And it killed Jason's dad. Jason was all he had left in the world. Losing him was bad enough, but losing him like that, and then the lies, the cover-up, it was too much."

"So you kept going for him, too."

She lowered her gaze. "I kept going," she said quietly, "because there was no other choice I could live with."

Those last words echoed in his head all the way back to his place. And he wondered how many people were left in the world who would do what she had done, simply because it was the only acceptable choice. Most he encountered would have, if faced with a similar situation, turned back, decided that a choice they'd thought unacceptable, the choice to not fight, was something they could live with after all.

But not Sloan Burke.

"You were a lucky man when you were here, Jason Burke," he said to the air.

And from the backseat, a dog let out a very heavy sigh.

"I'm sorry, Brett," Shari Shannon said. "I know he's a friend."

Brett grimaced. He'd put it off as long as he could, knowing Caro would panic, but he'd finally had to follow through. He'd called and told her her father hadn't been seen or heard from since the day he'd talked to him. She'd been distraught, wanted to get on the first flight home, but he'd persuaded her to wait, told her who to call to make sure the case ended up at least in his office.

And then he'd corralled the missing-persons detective himself.

"He became a friend, yes." He gave her a sideways look. "No lecture on how that's against policy?"

"Friends are friends, regardless of how you meet them. And they're not so thick on the trees that you can ignore one that happens to fall in your path through your work."

He lifted an eyebrow at her. "Feeling philosophical this morning?"

She smiled. "Me? Never happen—you know me."

Shari was one of the most reality-based people he'd ever met. But she knew human nature, what motivated people, which was what made her a good detective. Unexpectedly, she had married an artist, a local wood-carver, a couple of years ago. To Brett it seemed like the proverbial odd couple, but it clearly worked for them. Maybe they balanced each other out.

Speaking of philosophical, he muttered inwardly, he'd been doing way too much of this mental wandering. Time to snap out of it and pay attention.

"What can you tell me?" she asked briskly.

He told her what he knew, kept it strictly about Rick and didn't give her any of the speculation that had been running through his mind. He told her about where he'd been last heard from, about checking the house, his car being gone and no sign of any struggle or forced entry. And by way of personal warning, he mentioned Rick's boss's close ties with the county administrator.

"Great," she muttered. "Can't imagine having to work for a friend of the governor's pocket pet."

Brett smothered a laugh that probably would have been more of a snicker at the image.

"The house. You didn't go in?"

He shook his head. "It was more curiosity at that point. And no legal standing."

"So he could be…inside."

He knew what she was suggesting as well as she did. That Rick could be lying injured or dead inside the house.

He shook his head. "I don't think so. Most rooms were visible through the windows. And it just didn't have that feel."

"All right. But it needs to be checked off the list."

He nodded. Shari was nothing if not thorough and her next question proved it.

"What did you call him about in the first place?"

He explained again but mentioned only Connie and Chuck, keeping Sloan to himself. And Cutter. There was no explanation for that dog he could give the practical-minded Shari and not get laughed out of the office.

Even so, by the time he finished, Shari was grinning at him. "You really are a big softy under all that tough exterior, aren't you, Dunbar?"

He grimaced. "I made a phone call." True, it had gone way beyond that now, but that didn't need to be shared.

"Right," Shari said archly, but quickly turned back to business. "And that was the last time you talked with him? When he called you back about that inquiry you made?"

"Yes."

"So," she said when he'd finished, "we know he was here, just down the street at The Mug, that Tuesday at twelve thirty-two. But that's the last he's been seen or heard from?"

"That we know of."

"The daughter said she gave you permission to break into the house if you had to. And vehemently only you."

"She knows me. Trusts me."

"Then I guess we're off to do a little B and E. One car?"

He shook his head. "I've got something else to do in the north end after."

"All right."

"I'll go sign out."

"Sign me out, too. And on the way to the parking lot, you can explain."

"Explain what?" he asked warily.

"Why all of a sudden you have dog hair all over you every day."

Chapter 15

"Detective Dunbar, good to see you!"

The hearty, jovial voice of Harcourt Mead boomed out across the room. Brett sighed inwardly. He was in no mood. The search at Rick's house yesterday had turned up nothing. No notes left, no sign of anything disturbed, nothing but the normal day-to-day things like a magazine here, a book there and the TV remote left on the arm of a chair. He knew nothing more than he'd known before about where Rick had gone. Caro might have to come home after all. She was the only one who might be able to tell them if there was anything unusual or missing.

And now he had to deal with this guy. Normally he would do whatever he had to, make up a meeting, fake a hot case, anything to avoid the man. Especially this time of day, when he was about to grab some lunch. But Mead was the reason he'd instead made a point of taking the case file he'd just completed straight to the sergeant, which meant walking past the lieutenant's office.

He'd met him only once, but the man bragged often enough about his knack for remembering faces and names. County administrator was an appointed position, but he acted like a campaigning politician anyway. Just by the way he acted, Brett was sure the man had designs on elected office someday.

He was also the man who, according to the harried woman in the county office, had personally denied the

Days' first application, even though it was not in his direct purview.

"I was just talking to your boss here about that big drug arrest the task force made this morning. Well done!"

The office had been buzzing about it. The lieutenant also oversaw the county's contingent assigned to the statewide narcotics task force, and one of their own had played a key part in today's closing down of a string of meth labs across the western part of the state. It was big news. And where there was big news, politicians tended to gather. The governor had already taken up more TV time, along with the law enforcement leaders whose departments were involved. The actual detectives who broke the case all shunned the spotlight. Too often they had to work undercover, so aside from one officer assigned to public information, they avoided the kind of limelight men like the governor—and Harcourt Mead—seemed to crave.

"Yes," Brett said when it became clear some sort of response from him was expected. "Those guys do good work."

"Since our sheriff is tied up in the capitol, I'm heading outside to speak to the local press right now, make sure our people get full credit."

Figured he wouldn't wait until the sheriff was back from the just-completed statewide press gaggle. He'd want his own face in front, at least locally, and wouldn't want to wait ninety minutes just to share the spotlight.

"Local media's already here?" Brett asked.

"Assembling on the front steps of the campus," he said, referring to the complex that housed the county offices, the sheriff's office and the county jail. "They'll want that hometown touch, you know."

I'll be going out the back, then.

"In fact," Mead went on, "I was trying to convince Lieutenant Carter to come out with me, but she has an unavoidable appointment."

Smart woman.

He glanced at the lieutenant, whose expression was unreadable. If she had an opinion about the guy inserting himself into a story he had no part in, it didn't show. Given the man's close ties with the governor himself—and his tendency to exploit those ties—hers was probably the wisest course.

"Sir?" A harried-looking young man appeared at Mead's elbow. Unlike Mead, he wore a visitor's badge. Brett wondered if the man refused to wear one, because of course everyone knew who he was.

"What is it, Perkins?" He didn't bother to introduce the newcomer.

"It's that woman again."

Mead frowned. "What woman?"

"The one who was outside your office yesterday, protesting. She's out in front trying to get the media to talk to her."

Brett's breath stopped. Sloan.

She had done what she'd promised, and she'd started immediately. In two days she'd already shown up at a hearing about a proposed new commercial district and a speech given by a port commissioner, and she'd rallied at least thirty people on short notice to protest outside the very office where Harcourt Mead fancied himself a czar. Her next target would be the upcoming county commissioner's meeting. That would really chap Mead's hide.

"That bitch," Mead muttered under his breath, so low that Brett doubted the lieutenant, still at her desk, could have heard it. And so viciously it sent a chill through him.

His gut instincts, lulled by a couple of hours full of paperwork, roared to life. He had no proof of anything—logic told him not to assume connections where there probably weren't any—but there were facts he couldn't deny. This man had personally interfered in something he technically had no authority over. The man Brett had asked to look into that something had been fired, apparently on his order. And that man was now missing.

And now Sloan was causing problems for him. Suddenly this diversion tactic didn't seem like such a good idea.

"Trouble?" he asked, keeping his voice level even as his mind raced.

"Just some fool who thinks she can fight city hall," Mead answered. It sounded dismissive, but something glinted in the man's eyes that made him even more uneasy.

"Want me to give you a hand clearing her out?" Mead looked startled at the offer. "Might look better than calling for uniforms."

Mead eyed him more closely then, taking in his dress shirt and suit. Brett half expected the guy to ask him to put on a tie, but after a moment he put that wide smile back on his face.

"That is an excellent point, Detective."

Lieutenant Carter was frowning. He gave her a sideways glance. She was no doubt wondering what had possessed him, he who would normally have avoided this like a black-tie dinner. But thankfully, she said nothing, probably eager just to get this clown out of her office.

When they arrived at the front of the complex, he took in the situation quickly. There was indeed a small cluster of media, cameras, recorders, some of the smaller local outlets using smartphones for both.

And there she was.

His eyes widened at the sight of her. He'd never seen this Sloan before. The videos online, shot from across a hearing room, hadn't come close to this. Her hair was upswept in a tidy knot, and he could see every delicate line of her face. Instead of her usual jeans and sweater, she was wearing a trim tailored suit in a shade of dark green that made her eyes look even more vivid. The skirt was slim, the jacket nipped in at the waist. *Legs*, he thought almost numbly. She had on a pair of heels that were almost the color of her skin, and her long legs were curved and... She was... She looked...

He couldn't think of a word that wouldn't get him in trouble. Most of them seemed to involve tasting, like *luscious, delicious.* But this was also the woman who'd gone to Washington, DC, and made a difference. She looked the part, sharp, smart, strong, and he felt a bit of the awe that had made the taciturn, hard-to-impress Rafe Crawford salute her.

She was still speaking, and as she did, she touched a gold pin on one lapel of her jacket.

"...belongs to my aunt. She gave it to me to wear in her stead because she couldn't be here, because my uncle is too ill, too weak to be left alone. She cannot fight anymore, so I'm here to fight for her. Just as any of you would do for your parents, I'm sure."

She was good, he thought. Really good. She had them listening to something completely different than what they were here for.

"That's her," Mead hissed in his ear. "Stop her."

There was little he liked less than facing down the media, but he couldn't shake the feeling that he had to get her out of there. And if it got him in good with Mead, that could only help.

He strode forward through the gathered group. He took Sloan's elbow, taking advantage of her surprise at seeing him. He hoped the media would interpret it as simple, not specific, surprise.

"Excuse us. Mr. Mead has seen to it the lady now has an appointment with someone to address her grievance," he said without looking at the crowd. Then, lowering his voice to a whisper only she could hear, he said, "Go with it. Make Mead really like me."

He felt her second's hesitation, wondered if she was doubting him. Given who she'd been up against in the past, he couldn't blame her. But after that brief moment she went without protest, smiling as if she'd believed what he'd said.

He glanced back. Harcourt Mead was nodding at him approvingly. And then the media cluster closed in, and out came the big smile once more.

"Yes, that's what I'm here for, to take care of the people of my county," he boomed out.

Brett was thankful his back was to the man as the cameras were raised once more.

"You think he'll tell you anything?"

Brett glanced at her. "I don't know. But I think he's more likely to now than he would have been before."

"Point taken," she said, sounding weary.

They were sitting in her car, a small black SUV parked down the street and out of sight of the county offices. The first thing she'd done when she'd opened the door was kick off the heels. Even her feet were beautiful, he thought with an inward sigh. Small, slender, with high arches, they seemed to draw his eyes up to delicate ankles and those legs...

Determinedly, he kept his mouth shut. He hadn't been this physically aware of a woman in a very long time, and he not only didn't know how to deal anymore, he didn't know if he liked it at all. He'd had that part of his life nicely and safely nailed away and had assumed it would stay that way. The occasional indulgence with a willing partner, a short-term hookup, was the most he ever wanted.

And Sloan Burke was so very much not the type for that. No, this was a woman who came with strings. The kind of strings he wasn't ever going to risk again. So he'd damned well better keep his eyes and his thoughts under control.

"How's Cutter?"

The question—and non sequitur—came abruptly.

"I… He's fine. I assume. He's at home. Of course." *Well, now, there was a cogent sentence.*

"I've missed him the last couple of mornings."

She'd noticed. He'd finally mapped out that other route for running. He'd half expected the dog to refuse the change, but he'd gone along with apparent unconcern. In a way it reassured him that he indeed was only a dog.

But it did nothing to change the fact that the entire distance, he was thinking of where he wasn't going instead of where he was.

"I was hoping everything was all right—you weren't hurt or something," she said when he didn't speak. She was studying her hands as they rested on the lower arc of the steering wheel.

"No. I'm fine. He's fine. I'm going to head out to Foxworth with him as soon as I get home."

That made her look up at him. "Did they find something?"

"No. I'm just wondering if they turned up anything on Franklin and Mead yet, so I thought I'd stop by. Give Cutter a chance to see Rafe, too."

"I should go, too, then," she said.

No. For my sake, no.

Obviously she was free of the problems he was having, of keeping himself at arm's length. And that alone should have been helping him maintain that distance. Clearly she wasn't interested, even if he was fool enough to pursue it.

"I'll drive," she said, "since we're already in my car. I'll bring you back to get yours."

"I can manage that without you having to come all the way back here," he said, not even realizing until he said it that he'd just agreed to her coming. But she did have a point, he told himself. And it would save him from hav-ing to tell her anything he learned later.

More important, it would save him from having that battle with himself over it.

Chapter 16

"Your girl is causing quite a ruckus."

Brett grimaced but decided it better to address the substance of what Rafe had said rather than the possessive terminology. The fact that he liked the sound of it made him even more determined not to react. It was a close thing, given she was in the bathroom inside changing out of that sexy suit into other clothes she'd had in her car, and he was having enough trouble keeping that out of his mind already. He was thankful she hadn't asked to do it at his place. He doubted he would be able to keep those imaginings out of his head anytime he went in to shower or shave. In fact, he was glad she hadn't even gone inside. He wasn't sure he could take images of her there haunting him.

"She's stirring things up," he agreed as he tossed the tennis ball again, keeping his voice as level as he could manage and his eyes on Cutter as the dog raced across the Foxworth meadow.

He'd just have Sloan drop him off at home, he thought. Or better—and safer—yet, he'd ask Rafe for a ride. Then he'd call for a deputy going off duty to run him back into the office in the morning so he could pick up his car.

He should have grabbed running gear at the house; then he could have just run home. Hey, it was fewer than fifteen miles. So what if it would be dark by then, and he'd be running on unlit narrow roads with no shoulder. What could go wrong? At least he'd be so tired he could sleep, maybe not even remember the dreams in the morning.

"Your friend's daughter make that missing-person report?" Rafe asked.

"Yes." That quickly got his mind straight. "It's official now. She's obviously pretty upset and very worried."

Cutter raced back, dropped the ball at his feet. He wondered briefly if the dog wasn't giving it to Rafe because he had a ripe sucker already in his paws.

"And you're worried about her," Rafe said.

He threw the yellow ball again. Cutter raced after it again. "She took a nosedive when her mother died six years ago. She pulled herself out of it, and she's doing great in school, got a scholarship from a local tech company, but…"

"Is that what she's studying?"

"Computer science, yeah. She's always had a knack."

Rafe lifted a brow at him. "She's good?"

"Seems like it to me. But I'm just your basic end user, so anything deeper than that seems impressive to me. Your Tyler is scary, for instance."

Rafe's mouth quirked. "He is that."

Brett took the ball Cutter brought back at a dead run once more. "We run five miles every freaking day, I spent half of Sunday doing this with him, and he's still got this much juice. Has anybody ever outlasted this guy?"

"Not that I know of," Rafe said. "Although I think Luke Kiley wore him out a bit."

Brett grimaced as he threw yet again. "Great. So it takes the energy of a six-year-old boy to keep up."

Cutter halted in front of them. Brett was reaching for the ball, mentally calculating how much more of this his own shoulder could take, when the dog suddenly dropped it. His head turned, ears up, toward the building. And then he trotted off toward the door. There was no automatic opener on this side, so he looked back over his shoulder at them and barked.

"I guess we're done," Brett said.

As he spoke, he heard an alert tone. Rafe pulled his phone out of his pocket and looked at an incoming text.

"Tyler," he said. "He's got something."

Brett looked at Cutter. So that was it. How the hell had the dog known?

"It's either magic or he heard the alert from inside," Rafe said with a wry grin as he pulled the door open. "Take your pick."

Brett chuckled, shaking his head. He stopped when he spotted Sloan sitting on the sofa close to the fireplace. She was now dressed in jeans—the same delightfully snug ones he'd seen before?—and a soft-looking sweater the same color her suit had been. He was sure there was some fancier name for the deep green color, but all he knew was what it did to her eyes.

He had to remind himself to breathe as he sat down a careful distance from her.

Rafe went to the laptop and opened the teleconferencing program. He sent it to the monitor, and the screen and cam on the wall came on. Tyler Hewitt's face filled the frame. Rafe briefly introduced Sloan, then got down to business.

"What have you got, Ty?"

The young man wasted no time. "I got a hit on Alvarado's car."

Brett sat up straighter. He'd thought it would be something about Franklin or Mead.

"Where?" Rafe asked.

"Somebody reported it to the rangers in Olympic National Park this morning. Parked at the—" he glanced down at something "—Storm King visitors center, near

Lake Crescent. Looks like it's been there overnight, at least."

Rafe looked at Brett. "Ring any bells?"

"Sort of. Rick used to take his daughter to the park a lot."

"This lake?"

"Not sure. It's a huge park. I know there's a photo on his wall of both of them in front of a waterfall. From when Caro was a little girl. He said it was a place in the park she loved to go."

"Waterfall?" Tyler glanced at the other screen and quickly typed something, still talking as he did so. "That center is really a ranger station. It's some historic old log cabin. But it's not staffed until summer." Tyler shifted his gaze back to his webcam, grinning. "No heat except a fireplace. Chickens."

"Say that again when one of those rangers takes down the bear coming after you," Brett said mildly.

"Bear? No, thanks. I'm a city boy." He turned his attention back to the screen to his right. "Anyway, the rangers haven't had a chance to get over there yet—they've got a search-and-rescue thing going on. I didn't know you guys got hurricanes there."

Brett blinked. Rafe drew back slightly. But Sloan laughed.

"Hurricane Ridge," she said.

"Yeah," Ty said, grinning at her from the monitor, apparently liking that she got his quirky humor. "I guess they got some unexpected snow up there last night, and some hikers got lost."

"Snow is never unexpected up there," Rafe said drily.

"Hang on," Ty said, waiting for something to appear on his other screen. "There," he said with satisfaction. "That ranger station the car is at is also at the base of the trail to something called Marymere Falls."

"I've been there," Sloan said. "It's beautiful. A nice, easy hike, and close to the highway. It would be great for kids, even little ones."

Brett tried to rein in his suddenly recalcitrant mind, telling himself it was no business of his if she'd gone there with her husband.

"Got a picture?" he asked Tyler.

"Yep. Coming at you."

An image popped up on the wall monitor. A tall waterfall, narrow at the top, widening as it hit rocks toward the bottom and spread out and flowed downward.

The waterfall Rick and Caro had posed in front of years ago, when she was indeed that kid.

"That's it," he said.

"Nice work, Ty," Rafe said. Cutter woofed as if in matching approval.

"Thanks," Ty said with a laugh. "Both of you. But there's more. On that Mead guy."

"Go."

"It's not much, just something interesting. He was on the visitors log at the governor's office in the capitol thirty-two times in the last year alone."

"Two hundred miles round trip nearly three times a month is a bit much even for a best friend," Brett said.

"And one more thing," Ty said. "A dozen of those times, that other guy you mentioned, Franklin, was with him."

Brett stifled a groan. He did not like the way this was heading.

"Thanks, Ty," Rafe said.

"Sure. I'll be in touch if anything new drops."

"Well, now," Rafe said after he'd signed off and the monitor went dark. "What business would a small-county department manager have that would take him to the governor's office every month?"

"Good question," Brett said. "I kind of doubt Mead took him along just for the company."

"You said the county administrator is an old friend of the governor?" Sloan asked.

Brett nodded. "College. So he has reason to be there. But Franklin?"

"Maybe his business was building his profile," Sloan said.

"Becoming known in the halls of power?" Rafe mused aloud.

"A certain kind of man, that's addicting," she said. "Or maybe he's got future plans."

And she would know, Brett thought. Smart as she was, she'd probably learned very quickly to tell honest public servants from those who just wanted the power when she'd been neck deep in that political swamp.

"But that's not important now," Sloan said. "Your friend is. I don't like that his car is there but he's not."

Brett had an odd tangle of reactions to her words. He was warmed that she was putting Rick first even though she'd never met the man but chilled at the implication of her words, even though he'd already thought what she was likely thinking herself.

But there it was. Rick's situation was bleak—he had seemingly vanished, and now his car turned up empty at a remote place where he and his daughter were once happy? It had all the hallmarks of an ugly possibility.

"We should go there," she said. "Look for him."

Brett opened his mouth to speak, but no words came. We?

"Good idea," Rafe said. "Sounds like it will be a while before the rangers can get there."

"It's about an hour-and-a-half drive, depending on the weather. The lake's a lot lower elevation than Hurricane

Ridge, so it should be okay, but I'll check." She pulled out her phone and tapped an icon.

"Damn. If Quinn or Teague were here, they could fly you in," Rafe said. "You'd have more daylight."

"If we leave right away, we should still have a couple of hours. I'll drive, since my car's here." Sloan looked up from her phone. "And it looks like no snow there, just rainy."

"I'd go with you," Rafe said, "but I'm meeting with Drew Kiley in an hour to pick his brain on that builder."

Brett's gaze went from one to the other as they took over the planning like a practiced advance team.

"We'll have Cutter," Sloan said. "I'm sure he'll be helpful."

Rafe nodded. "He's a good tracker. Let him sniff around the car, then be ready."

Both of them suddenly seemed to realize he hadn't said a word and turned to look at him.

"Don't mind me," he muttered. *Well, that sounded childish.*

"I didn't mean to take over—" Sloan began, stopping when he waved a hand.

"I just need to make a call," he said.

He dialed Lieutenant Carter, who answered on the first ring.

"Whatever you did, Mead loves you now," she said.

"My life's goal," he said drily, then got right to it. "That personal thing I mentioned? I'm going to need some time for it."

"Wow, here's a first. Brett Dunbar, the guy who never even takes a vacation day, asking for personal time?"

"It's getting complicated."

"Anything major on your desk?"

"Nothing that won't keep for a couple of days. Or Will can handle it."

"All right. You've certainly got the time coming. Take what you need."

And that easily, he'd locked himself into a road trip. With Sloan Burke at the wheel and a too-clever canine in the backseat.

Somewhere along the line, he'd lost control. And he didn't know whether to be worried or delighted.

Chapter 17

"Jason thought about going for submarine duty," Sloan said as they hit midspan on the bridge crossing the canal that led to the submarine base several miles to the south.

She didn't know why she'd said that. Except that she'd been thinking a lot about Jason lately. Probably because this thing with Aunt Connie and the county felt like the same kind of fight, on a much tinier scale.

It certainly had nothing to do with the man sitting in the passenger seat. She was wondering why she'd done that, too. She drove on, noticing that today, as was often the case, the water on one side of the floating bridge was smooth and glassy, while the other side was choppy. Sort of like her life, before and after this had all started. She'd finally achieved that calm, that internal quiet she'd been striving for since Jason's death, and then it all got torn apart. Beginning when a man and a dog had literally run into her world.

She glanced at him. "You would have done this anyway, right? Gone to look for him?"

"Yes."

That much was a relief.

"I'm sorry I inserted myself into—"

"Don't be."

"You don't mind me driving?"

He shrugged. "Your car, and you've been where we're going. I haven't."

So he wasn't a control freak, she thought, filing that bit of knowledge away even as she refused to admit why.

Since she was driving—carefully, because it was raining and they were floating mere feet above the chilly water of the canal—she couldn't study him as she'd like. But his tone was at odds with his reassurance; he sounded…not angry, but tense. No, that wasn't right either.

"You're worried," she said finally, glancing once more.

"Yes," he said, and she liked that he didn't try to deny it.

"You're wearing the same expression Uncle Chuck always had when things got particularly nasty."

There was a moment of silence again, and she had just decided she wouldn't be the one to break it when he spoke.

"Just how nasty did it get?"

"At first, just warnings. Our governor's personal bodyguard didn't like me much, and he made it rather nastily clear."

"Personal bodyguard? The state people aren't enough for him?"

"He doesn't own them. And by comparison he was fairly mild. Once we got to the upper DC level came the rape, death and dismemberment threats, a couple of actual burglaries to our hotel room, lots of stalking. Those who weren't threatening me were hitting on me, with my husband barely six months gone. Nice town."

She thought she heard him say something vicious under his breath. Cutter made a low sound from the back that sounded uncannily similar in pitch. But she waited until they were off the bridge and headed up the hill on the other side before speaking again.

"Looking back," she said, "I'm sure they wished they had done it differently. Done something to shut me up early on."

She could almost feel his gaze on her. What was it about this man that made her so aware?

"You might not have liked what they would have done." His tone was as grim as his expression had been, so there was no mistaking what he meant.

"You mean take me out? Oh, I'm sure they eventually wished they'd done that, too. Early."

"Before you became so well-known and they couldn't risk it."

She smiled. He really did get it. "I'm sure many of them saw that as an opportunity missed. They really didn't want it coming out that Jason and his whole team died because of them and their crooked scheme. Jason was going to go himself, alone—he would never ask his team to break discipline. But they insisted on going with him because they knew he was right. But those bastards wanted the world to think it was Jason's personal failure, when in truth it was political scum at the top."

"Scum," he said, "is too kind. And you are indeed a hero worth saluting."

She kept her eyes straight ahead, fighting the flush she felt rising in her cheeks. No matter how many times she told herself this wasn't personal, any of it, she couldn't seem to control her reactions around him.

...the first I've seen you react to.

Aunt Connie's words came back to her yet again. And she couldn't deny them, not anymore. Brett Dunbar was the first man she'd reacted to in years, the first to make her question if her heart truly had been buried along with Jason.

They'd talked about that just last night, she and her aunt.

"You loved Jason, deeply," she'd said. "But he's gone, Sloan. You fought that good fight, and he would be incredibly proud of you. But you know he wouldn't want you to stay alone forever."

She did in fact know that. At Jason's insistence, they'd had that discussion, given the nature of his work. Not out of any sense of foreboding or premonition, just the simple fact that it was entirely possible every time he left he might never come back.

"If it happens," Jason had said, "don't you dare forget me. But don't you dare spend the rest of your life mourning me either. Move on. Find somebody to love and who loves you the way you deserve. I will have died for nothing if you live alone and unhappy."

She hadn't been unhappy. The fight had gotten her through the worst of it, she supposed, in the way having children to look after got others through it. If she'd had nothing, no distraction, she didn't know what she would have done, how she would have handled it. But she'd had the fight, and that battle had driven her and left her no time to be unhappy.

But she hadn't been happy either. It was more a sort of numbness that evolved into a quiet routine that was soothing in its own way. And then one day she'd awakened and realized just how much time had passed.

"Sloan?"

She snapped back to reality, wondering how long she'd been driving in that sort of autopilot mode. "Sorry. I was just thinking how surprised I was every time I realized it had been another year since my husband was killed."

The moment the words were out she regretted them. She was sounding like a woman living in the past, unable to let go.

"The years go fast. It's the days that crawl."

Her breath caught in her throat at the simple accuracy of that observation. And with abrupt certainty, she knew that this man knew exactly whereof he spoke. He had lived it, just as she had.

"Who was it?" she asked, her voice quiet.

He didn't speak, and after a long silence she doubted he was going to. Cutter stirred in the back, making a noise that wasn't quite a whine, more of a sigh. Almost as if he was as frustrated as she was. Her past was, by its nature, an open book. Brett Dunbar was a mystery with a locked cover.

I know the feeling, my furry friend. He's a prickly one.

"Never mind," she said, careful to keep her tone even. "This isn't some therapy session, where I share my sad story and expect you to share yours."

In the instant she glanced at him anew, she saw surprise in his lifted brow and the tiniest quirk in one corner of his mouth.

She drove on for some time, enjoying the familiar yet long-untaken drive through the trees and rolling hills and glimpses of blue water, passing turnoffs to places she'd once enjoyed visiting. Perhaps she should do that again when all this with the property was settled. It would be hard. It always was, going places she had gone with Jason, but if she had cut all that out of her life, she indeed would never go anywhere or do anything.

"You don't mind silence, do you."

She flicked her gaze sideways at him. It hadn't really been a question, but she answered anyway. "Spend enough time with blowhards who never shut up, and you treasure silence."

He smiled at that.

Whether the snow at higher elevations had scared people off or it was simply the time of year and the fact it was a weekday, there was no one else there when they pulled into the parking lot near the ranger station that served as a visitors center. The lot was empty except for a blue sedan parked at one end of one of the drive-through double car spaces. She pulled up next to it.

Cutter was instantly on his feet and demanding to be let out. Sloan glanced at Brett, who nodded, indicating it was Rick's car. They got out, Cutter darting around them at a run as they walked toward it.

The dog sniffed at the car the way she'd seen the bomb-detection dogs do in line for the ferry. It was older but spotless. No dings or dents, and the paint was in good shape. What she could see of the inside was tidy—only a paper coffee cup in the cup holder to the right of the driver's seat and a blanket folded neatly in the backseat.

Brett tried the driver's door. Locked.

"Would he?" she asked. "Lock it, I mean. If he…" She let the words trail off. This was a friend of his, after all.

"If he wasn't planning on coming back?" Brett said. She should have known. Not as if he didn't have lots of practice facing the uglier facts of life.

"Might. People at that point aren't thinking straight anyway. He could have done it without even realizing it, force of habit. And I can't say it's impossible. But Rick adores his daughter, and I can't picture him leaving her alone after all they've been through."

"All right. I just wanted to be prepared." And she was speaking from an unpleasant wealth of experience. Too many she met in her current work couldn't endure what they went through. "Suicide is a particularly awful thing."

"I know."

There was an undertone in his voice, a grim-sounding thing that told her he did indeed know. Was that what was behind his understanding of grief? Had there been a suicide in his life? Or had he merely seen too many of them in his years on the job?

He was studying the car. After a moment he reached toward an inside pocket of his jacket. At that moment Cutter, who had been circling the vehicle, gave a sharp bark and took off at a run. He was headed toward the log building she could see set among the trees with a clear view down to the beautiful lake.

"Guess my car burglary will have to wait," Brett muttered, and started after the dog.

Sloan followed. The two-story log cabin that also served as a visitors center was clearly unoccupied. Beside the glass-paned door there was a rack with brochures and maps, affixed just below a bulletin board with an announcement that the center would be staffed starting June 1. She was too far away to read any farther, and apparently they weren't stopping; Cutter blasted past the station. And the sign that said pets were prohibited.

"Oops," she said. "Smart as he is, I guess he can't read."

"I'm not so sure," Brett said drily as they followed the dog. "He probably can—he just doesn't consider himself anybody's 'pet.'"

Sloan laughed. He seemed so bemused by his own observation, as if he was joking yet half believed it, she couldn't help herself. *The one Sloan likes...* Her uncle's words echoed in her head. Yes. Yes, she did like him. A lot. Too much. He was a cop, a man who put his life at risk on a regular basis, and that was not a place she was willing to go again.

Chapter 18

Brett noticed she hadn't asked about the part of that sign back there that said weapons were also prohibited.

"Hopefully," she said, as they kept after the dog, "since we're saving them a search, they'll forgive him."

"And us."

"Doesn't your badge usually keep you out of trouble?"

"Less often than it gets me in."

She gave him an odd look, almost troubled. As if the kind of trouble a cop could get into bothered her.

He caught glimpses of the lake as they went. It was quiet, peaceful and soothing. He should have made it out here before this, he thought. He'd been to the coast a few times after he'd first moved here, during storm season when the weather and the wildness matched his mood, but after he'd settled in, work had taken over.

Cutter, still several yards ahead of them, was clearly set on the trail to the falls. The dog didn't even bother to look back at them.

"We're headed back toward the highway," he said after another few moments.

"Yes," Sloan answered. "There's a tunnel. You should be able to see it right…about…now."

The narrow arched tunnel, formed by an intricately stacked swath of stones, passed just a few feet beneath the highway. Cutter was already, unhesitatingly, out the other side before they reached it.

The trail was well maintained and fairly level, and as the trees got thicker, some draped with moss, others with alien-looking exposed roots, it went from cool to chilly. But soon the thick canopy of trees showed a benefit: although it was still raining, and there were muddy spots along the trail, only a few of the drops made it all the way to the forest floor. Which was helpful, since he wasn't exactly dressed for this outing. He was glad that after he'd moved here, he'd given up dress shoes for something a little more rugged, with lug soles, but his suit coat and pants weren't very helpful in the chill.

Cutter never wavered, even when another trail would split off to one side. Brett wouldn't have minded, had the circumstances been different, taking it slower, appreciating the cool, mossy quiet. But Cutter was a dog on a mission, and he didn't want to lose sight of him. Given the wildlife that abounded, he was regretting not having put the dog on a leash. But he seemed uninterested— even the deer that darted away at his approach earned barely a glance.

"I've never seen a dog totally ignore other animals like that," she said.

"He's pretty focused," Brett agreed.

"Are you sure he isn't a runaway military canine or police dog or something?"

"The thought has occurred, since he acts like he's been trained. They're not really sure, since they don't know where he came from."

She wasn't, he noticed, even breathing hard, despite the fast pace they had to maintain to keep the dog in view. He wondered what she did to stay in shape. Because she was certainly that.

And the less he thought about her shape, the better, he told himself.

They reached the creek that Brett supposed was the source of the waterfall. A sturdy bridge that looked fairly new made for a quick crossing. Cutter didn't hesitate there either. The trail then curved and they came to an older bridge with rough-hewn wood railings and one big log split in half and laid flat-side up for the path itself. The sides were much more open, and Brett frowned until he realized Cutter was paying it no more attention than anything else. Definitely a dog on a mission.

Not far past the second bridge, the trail split.

"That's the loop," Sloan said. "It circles back and comes out here."

He nodded, keeping his eyes on Cutter, who had taken the left fork without pausing. They followed. It soon got rather steep, and Brett noticed the uptick in his heart rate and breathing.

"Four flights' worth," she said as they started the steps.

He let her take the lead as it became too narrow for them to walk side by side. He caught glimpses of the waterfall a couple of times as the trail curved around the side of the ravine. Nice, he thought. He'd like to come here under other circumstances.

With Sloan?

He slapped that idea down as soon as it hit. *Focus,* he ordered himself.

They came to the steps she'd told him about before and started up. Cutter was running now and quickly got out of sight. Before he could speak, Sloan had picked up the pace, trotting up the steps ahead of him. And damn him if he didn't enjoy the view; she was obviously in great shape.

And there he was again, his mind skittering off into places it had no business going.

She stopped suddenly just before the top. He nearly ran into her and grabbed her to steady them both. And denied to himself that he could have just as easily grabbed the railing.

Did he imagine there was a split second before she

spoke, an instant where she sucked in her breath at his touch?

She sucked in her breath because she just ran up about four flights of stairs, idiot.

"He's here. Or someone is. You should go first."

He agreed. If it was Rick, which seemed highly likely, better he see a friend than a stranger just now. There was only one problem. For him to go first, he was going to have to get past Sloan. And on this narrow trail there was only one way to do that. Squeeze past her.

He opened his mouth to tell her to take a few more steps into the viewing area, where it was wider. The words never came.

"Brett?" she whispered.

"Yeah. Right."

He started to ease past her. Felt the warmth of her, heat, really, in this chill. Wanted nothing more than to stop where he was and feel more. To lean into her, to feel the length of her.

She looked up at him, and he realized with a jolt that only the confusion in her eyes was keeping him from kissing her. He'd thought about kissing other women. But it had been more of an idle musing on what it would be like to really want to again.

Now he knew.

Rick. He needed to get to him. Now.

He made himself leave her. He barely gave the tall, picturesque waterfall a glance as he reached the viewing area, a fairly wide spot with a high railing. Rick wasn't over there, at least, contemplating the long drop. He was sitting on a downed log several feet back from the edge. Cutter seemed to realize in this case he should stay back. But he was sitting between Rick and the edge, Brett noticed. Somehow he doubted that was accidental.

Rick was dressed in a heavy jacket, a thick knit hat and hiking boots much better suited to this trail than his own clothes. A pair of gloves were beside him on the log. So he'd prepared, to some extent. But his shoulders were slumped, his head down, as if he hadn't even noticed the dog, as if not even the beauty around him could lighten his mental state. He looked as if he'd aged ten years since Brett had last seen him. His hair beneath the cap looked lank, lifeless. He looked thinner. And Brett was suddenly very glad they'd come.

"Rick," he said quietly.

The man jerked around, clearly startled. His brow furrowed. "Brett? What are you doing here?"

"Looking for you."

Rick blinked. "You came all the way here and hiked that trail looking for me?"

"Been worried, buddy."

For a moment the man looked puzzled. Then realization dawned in his troubled eyes. "You know."

"Yeah." He left it at that, hoping Rick would just feel the need to talk. He didn't want to have to coax it out of him. And after a moment of hesitation it came.

"I didn't do it. I'd never steal. What good would a couple hundred bucks do me anyway?"

"A couple hundred bucks from where?"

"The cash box in the office."

"Didn't even know there was one."

"They keep it there because sometimes people come in with cash to pay for copies, permits and things, and we need change."

"And somebody stole from it?"

"Not me!"

"I know, Rick. I'd sooner believe you could fly off this mountain."

Rick's eyes widened, and there was no mistaking the relief in them. Brett had seen it before, that expression, that look as if he'd gotten a reprieve. Sometimes just being believed was enough to turn the tide.

"Let's get out of here. You need to get warm, and so do I."

"I—"

"Come on. You've already been out here long enough. Let's figure out what we're going to do about all this."

That was what it took, that lifeline, that pronouncement that he wasn't alone. Rick closed his eyes for a moment, his relief palpable now.

"I am cold," he admitted, opening his eyes once more. "I've been just driving around for a couple of days. Sleeping in the car. Then I came here yesterday." He looked around. "Caro and I came here the day before she left for college. It's one of her favorite places. I was…trying to decide how to tell her."

"She'll just be glad you're all right. She's been worried, too."

Rick looked startled. "She knows?"

"Only that you dropped off the map. You're officially missing."

Rick lowered his gaze to the ground again.

"You've got people who care, Rick. You should have called me."

"I thought about it."

"Next time don't think. Do it."

Rick let out a long breath, then nodded. Cutter sensed the change. He got up, crossed to Rick, who looked at him warily.

"When did you get a dog?"

"Didn't. Dogsitting," he said.

"Oh. I—" He broke off as Cutter nudged his hand, then stepped closer and rested his chin on the man's leg. Slowly, as if underwater, Rick moved that hand. His fingers touched fur, and Cutter leaned into him. Looking utterly bemused, Rick stroked the dog, staring down at him. Brett could almost feel the pressure easing. That dog had…something.

"Meet Cutter."

He sensed Sloan approaching, guessed she'd realized things were under control now. He couldn't tell if it was his presence or the dog's—well, actually, he figured it was probably the dog—but Rick was steadier now.

"And this is Sloan Burke." Rick gave her a surprised and wary glance. It was the wariness that made him add, "She had a run-in with your boss recently."

Rick grimaced. "Charming, isn't he?"

"Not the word I'd use, no," Sloan said. "I'm very sorry you had to work for him."

Rick stood up at last, giving Cutter a last pat on the head, still looking a bit perplexed.

"I guess that's the bright side," Brett said. "You don't have to work for somebody stupid enough to think you were the one who stole the petty cash anymore."

"I don't think anybody stole it," Rick said. "I don't think it was that at all. I think he's just ticked I went into his files."

Brett frowned. "What?"

"He threatened to fire me then, that day I was looking for that application for you, when he found me in his office. But he didn't have grounds. I was only doing my job."

Sloan had gone very still.

"You think he faked the theft and accused you, because of that? To get rid of you?"

"I just know he spends most of his life annoyed about something or other, but I've never seen him mad like that day."

"Out of proportion to the situation?" Brett asked.

"Way out," Rick said. "It was just a misplaced file. It happens, although we have—had—a pretty good track record. But this one was practically hidden in his office, which he guards like a grizzly. No one's allowed in there if he's not there."

Brett's frown deepened. His gut had told him there was a connection, and he'd clearly been right.

"So it was his own fault?" Sloan asked. When Rick looked at her curiously, she gave him a small rueful smile. "I'm afraid I'm the one that got you into this mess."

Rick blinked. Brett quickly stepped in. "It wasn't your fault either."

"You did it for me."

Rick glanced from Sloan to him. "Oh." He looked at them both again and repeated, with a little more emphasis, "Oh. That's nice."

There was a whole lot of assumption in his words and tone. A denial leaped to Brett's lips, but he told himself this wasn't the time or place—that there never would be the right time or place—and held it back.

"I didn't tell him it was you who asked," Rick added. "If he was that mad, I didn't want to get you into my trouble."

Brett smiled, moved by the idea of his friend trying to protect him. And thankful that he had, so Franklin still didn't know who he was or that he was connected to Sloan. "We'll find the truth, Rick. I promise you that. Whatever or whoever's behind all this, we'll find out."

He meant it. He thought of Rafe's summation, of all the seemingly unrelated facets. If they were really all connected, if they were all one long tangled string of cause and effect, then there was one more question.

Just how far did that string go?

Chapter 19

Sloan's mind was racing so fast in so many different directions she had to force herself to pay close attention to the road ahead. All the things she'd learned from that short but heartfelt conversation she'd heard were caroming around in her head like a billiard ball run wild.

Was it really all connected? Had Brett's question on her behalf caused all this? Had Rick Alvarado been fired for simply finding some paperwork? Did that mean it had been intentionally hidden? Why? Was the water leak truly intentional, to provide another reason to deny their application? Was this all some political bombshell, ready to explode, or was that just her past experience coloring her view?

And again, and again, why? Possibilities battered at her until she wasn't sure of anything anymore.

No, there was one thing she was sure of.

She really liked Brett Dunbar. The way he'd handled Rick, the way he'd talked to him, shown such unhesitating faith in and loyalty to his friend, the promise of justice, that the truth would come out, endeared him to her. Those things were important to her, more than ever after her fight to vindicate Jason. Because they were the things Jason had fought for, died for. He had died because there weren't enough men like that at the top anymore. For a while she had doubted there were any at all.

But there was one here and now.

At the moment he was in the car ahead of her. When they had reached the trailhead again, this time with Rick, it was late afternoon. They'd paused by Rick's car, and Brett had turned to look at her. She'd realized he didn't want to leave Rick on his own just yet. Wisely, she thought.

"I'll follow you," she had said, and had headed for her own car before he could tell her to just leave—he'd handle it from here. She wasn't about to be cut out of this now, not when it appeared this really was all tied together. She'd suggested Cutter would be more comfortable in the back of her SUV, and when the dog followed her willingly, she was glad. More insurance that they weren't done yet. Brett had watched them go, and if he'd guessed her thoughts, it hadn't shown. But then, he had a pretty good poker face. She supposed he had to, as a detective.

She had watched as they pulled out. Brett was driving, while Rick rubbed his hands in front of the car's air vents. Brett had apparently turned on the heater. Since Rick had been better dressed for the chillier temperature up at the falls, Brett must have been even colder. But again he hadn't shown it if he was. And he certainly hadn't felt the least bit cold when he'd squeezed past her up on the trail. Nor had she when he'd gotten that close. And her body had fired up like a jet afterburner when he'd touched her.

And judging from the way Rick had looked at them both, it had shown.

"Damn!"

The curse burst from her aloud, echoing inside the vehicle, snapping her back to the present. Cutter woofed from the back.

"Sorry, dog," she muttered. "I don't usually do that."

And that told her how crazy things were getting. This was insane. That was all there was to it. She was not going to do anything stupid here. Maybe Aunt Connie was right, and it was time for her to think about meeting someone,

maybe dating. Maybe that was what her newly reawak-
ened senses were telling her. That it was time to move on.

But not Brett Dunbar, her brain was screaming. *He's
a cop! He goes into danger all the time, just like Jason
did. Stop it!*

She focused on the car ahead, wondering what was
going on inside. Wondered if at some point Brett would
explain the details of how she was the one who'd started
all this, however inadvertently.

Yeah, because it's all about you, right?

She chuckled aloud at herself. Cutter woofed again,
oddly sounding happier this time. Or perhaps not oddly;
clearly the dog was perceptive enough to understand the
lighter tone.

"You did good, Cutter," she called out to him. "You
knew he was there, didn't you?"

The short sharp bark that came then sounded for all
the world like a "Yep."

She laughed, feeling much better now. There truly was
something about that dog.

"Sorry it was so long," Brett said as he got into the
car. Cutter woofed softly from the back in greeting. "You
should have come in. It's getting cold."

He'd gone into the house with Rick, saying he would
stay only a few minutes to make sure everything was
truly all right, but it had stretched into nearly half an hour.

"He still needed to talk, I'm sure," Sloan said. "And
not in front of a stranger."

Brett nodded as he fastened his seat belt. "He wasn't
really thinking of doing anything drastic. Just stunned
and worried about what to do."

"You were right. He wouldn't abandon his daughter
that way."

"No. They've been through too much. He's feeling better now."

She glanced at the house, at the lit window in the nearest corner. Darkness shadowed the rest. She hoped the light would spread for that loving father. And wondered when she'd started thinking in corny metaphors.

"Now what?" she asked.

"I'm going to dig into that boss of his. Put on some official heat."

"Good." He glanced at her. She shrugged. "He's a nasty little man, the kind who likes making everybody under him miserable."

He leaned back, angled so that he could see her face. "Have I mentioned how much I admire what you did in DC?"

She blinked. Stared at him for a moment, then lowered her gaze. "Yes, I think you have."

She tried to swallow past the sudden lump in her throat. Somehow she had let this man, and his approval, mean too much to her. It was another step down that path she'd sworn never to walk again.

"And don't tell me anybody would have done it. You know that's not true."

"Thank you," she said, still not looking at him. Silence spun out between them. She tapped a thumb on the steering wheel, a small release for the nervous energy that was building up. "It's awkward sometimes," she finally said.

"What is?"

"Much of my life is out there, public knowledge, and so available for anybody to look up. It had to be to get the job done, but it puts me at a disadvantage sometimes."

She glanced at him as she spoke the last words, saw them register. He lowered his gaze, and she knew he knew exactly what she meant. He knew so much about her, while she knew next to nothing about him.

Except the most important things. The soul-deep character things that made him who he was.

Yes, she knew those. That was what had her in this tangled mess of emotions, wasn't it?

She waited, silently. He said nothing. And that, she supposed, said everything.

She smothered a sigh and ordered that inner voice that kept chewing at her to shut up.

"Back to the sheriff's office?" she asked neutrally.

"You don't have to do that. It's a long drive."

"But it's where your car is."

"I can get a ride in the morning. Just drop us at the bottom of the hill on the highway. That's on your way."

Because heaven forbid I should actually be allowed into a tiny corner of your personal life.

So much for shutting up that inner voice, she thought.

"Fine, Detective." It came out with an edge. Okay, shutting up the outer voice wasn't going real well either.

"Just trying to save you time," he said, sounding puzzled as well as stung, apparently at her tone. Or her use of the formal *Detective*.

"I said fine."

"You've already driven across three counties and hiked partway up a mountain, all for somebody you don't even know. You don't need to do any more."

When he put it that way, her earlier thoughts seemed a bit snarky.

"Besides, won't your aunt and uncle be worried?" he asked.

"No. I called them while you were inside."

She started the car and retraced their route back to the highway. He didn't speak until they were back on the main road and on their way to his requested drop-off point.

"One of the cops I worked with in LA once told me that the most frightening word in a woman's vocabulary is *fine*."

He said it so casually it took her a split second to get

there. "Yes, I suppose it can be," she said in the same tone, "since it often means exactly the opposite."

"Sloan—"

"It really is fine. The problem is mine. I'll drop you off wherever you want."

A sharp, short bark came from the back. Sloan glanced in the mirror. Cutter's head had popped up over the seat. Those dark amber-flecked eyes were fixed on them steadily.

"I swear your dog is glaring at us."

"Not my dog," he reminded her, turning his head to look. "And right now I think I'm grateful for that. Because he is glaring."

"Well, that's unsettling."

"Yes." He turned back to the front. "I'm told he prefers people to get along."

"Oh." One corner of her mouth turned downward. Honesty, she thought. He deserved that much. "My fault. I shouldn't expect to be welcome in your home just because you've been in mine. You were doing us a favor, in a semiprofessional capacity."

It sounded insufferably stuffy even to her, but he just gaped at her.

"Is that what this was about?"

He sounded so astonished she felt silly. And suspected they'd just been through one of those she-thinks/he-thinks situations men and women were famous for.

"Let's just say saving me maybe ninety seconds didn't seem like a big-enough deal for you to walk up that hill. Unless you had other reasons."

"I really was trying to save you the trouble. But there are other reasons," he said, his tone rueful. "It's not much to begin with, and when you add a huge pile of dirty laundry thanks to a dog that goes through towels like a Las Vegas pool, it loses what little charm it has."

She couldn't help it—she laughed.

"Just let me drop you both off. I won't invade your male space, either of you."

He gave her a look that seemed suddenly sharper. But he said nothing more, and when they got to the location he'd originally suggested, he gave her further directions up the hill.

The place, when they got there, wasn't anything like what she'd expected. They drove down a long gravel drive that cut through a wide grassy swath. There was a small dark brown cottage set back among some tall evergreens, cedars and spruce mostly, she thought. It faced east, with a large window that looked out over the grass and out to more trees in the distance.

"Doggy heaven," she said as she drove through the wide-open space.

"More like a tennis ball graveyard," he said. "I'm sure there's a couple dozen out there by now."

"He loses them?"

"Never. But his priorities change."

"This is a dog we're talking about, right?"

"Your guess is as good as mine."

She laughed again. She liked this Brett. The intense, focused detective was admirable, but this man, bemused by a dog, was...

"No more 'Detective'?"

She felt herself color slightly. "I'm sorry about that. Silly reaction."

"You," he said quietly, "are anything but silly."

He opened the car door and stepped out. She hit the button that unlatched the rear liftgate so he could retrieve his too-clever dog. She would stay in the car, she decided, to make it clear she didn't expect to be invited in. She didn't want to compound that mistake.

But when Cutter was out, he trotted around to the driver's door and sat, looking up at her expectantly. Not sure what else to do, she opened her door. She could at least say a proper goodbye to the animal, she supposed. She swung around in the seat and leaned down to scratch that spot below his right ear that Brett had told her he loved.

"You're such a smart boy," she crooned to him, lowering her head to nuzzle his soft fur. She felt a quick swipe across her jaw as he gave her a canine kiss. She laughed; she couldn't help herself. A memory flashed through her mind of a dark, shadowed man in pain and the way this same dog had somehow eased it with just a touch on the aching leg. She didn't doubt it now. There was just something about this dog that made you feel better.

Cutter started toward the house. But when she started to pivot back into the car, he stopped and came trotting back. He nudged at her. Puzzled, she reached out to pet him again. But that wasn't what he wanted.

At first she was startled when he caught her wrist in his teeth. But his hold was so delicate, so gentle she couldn't be scared at the odd action. But then he began to tug, still gently, until it seemed as though she had no choice but to stand up. The moment she did, the dog squeezed in behind her and nudged her forward, away from the car.

And toward the house.

"Dog," Brett said, almost warningly.

"What is he doing?" she asked, feeling a bit helpless when she stopped and the dog nudged her—firmly— again.

She felt a little better when the animal left her for a moment and proceeded to give Brett a similar nudge, although that one was a bit stronger. And then he was back to her, inching her along, then Brett again.

"Is he…herding us?" she asked, staring at the determined animal.

"It's in his blood, I'm told," Brett said. Then, with a sigh, he added, "I guess you'd better come in."

"Well, thank you for the warm invitation," she said

drily, and had the pleasure of seeing him look uncomfortable.

"I didn't mean it like that. It's just... I told you it's not much."

"Is it warm?" she asked. The night air was getting chillier by the minute.

"It can be," he said, and as if the words had jolted him out of whatever mental place he was in, he started to move quickly. "Come on. I'll get a fire started. It'll clear out the damp."

Cutter immediately stopped his nudging, as if he realized they'd given in to his wishes. Demands. Whatever they were. She admitted in some back corner of her mind that she hadn't really been resisting all that hard. She was ragingly curious. And if an invitation from a dog was all she was going to get, she'd take it. It wasn't as if she had to stay. She just wanted to see where he lived.

Just curious, she repeated. That was all it was. Nothing more.

And there was no cat for that curiosity to kill.

Just a wily, clever dog.

Chapter 20

Sloan was surprised the moment she stepped inside the place. The layout was intriguing and, given the traditional, almost cabin-like appearance of the outside, unexpected. The main space felt larger than seemed possible from the small size of the place, probably because the ceiling was vaulted. The wood floor held to the rustic feel, and the large stone fireplace on the far wall added to that. But the layout itself felt modern, open and appealing. Overall she thought the effect rather charming, if a bit rough.

While he built the promised fire in that big fireplace, she looked around more thoroughly. In one corner was a kitchen area, with small but up-to-date-looking appliances, set off by an island with two bar stools at one end. In the opposite corner an L-shaped wall blocked off what she guessed served as a bedroom, although it was open and doorless at the short end of the L. Next to that was a smaller walled-in space she assumed was the bathroom, and beside that a small alcove that held a desk, a laptop computer and a printer, along with a set of file racks that suggested he brought work home all too often.

The rest was all open space. In front of the fireplace was a dark blue sofa that looked a bit worn but comfortable. There was a pole lamp at one end, the kind with a reading light lower down, and a large, low, rough-hewn table. And to her delight, the wall space that wasn't taken up with windows was nearly all lined with books. There was a television on one of the bookcases, but it was fairly small and told her the man didn't live and die by the tube. She saw the remote for it on the table at the end of the couch, sitting next to a thick book with a bookmark about halfway through. A presidential biography, she noticed, one she'd read herself back in the dark days when she'd needed both inspiration and her faith restored.

Cutter had abandoned them for a station in front of the refrigerator. "Dinnertime for him?" she asked.

Brett glanced over, then chuckled and started that way. "Snack time, actually," he said. She followed, curious. "He doesn't eat until later, when a full stomach makes him thankfully sleepy."

She laughed, leaning her elbows on the counter as he opened the refrigerator. Her eyes widened as he pulled out a bag of what looked like baby carrots, the kind that were already peeled and shaped into neat, even pieces a couple of inches long.

"Carrots?"

"He loves them," Brett said with a shrug. "Told you, he's a different sort of dog."

He took a handful out of the bag, then tossed one to the dog. Cutter caught it neatly and chomped with gusto. It was quickly gone, and he tossed the dog another.

"If you'd told me he liked orange treats, I would have expected Cheetos."

Brett laughed. He gave Cutter the last carrot and then held up his hands palms out to indicate that was the end of the treats. The dog sighed audibly but seemed to accept the edict.

Brett put the bag away, then turned back to the dog. "You had a session this morning and then at Foxworth, and you've been up a mountain trail and down. Can we pass on the tennis ball marathon tonight?"

Apparently in answer, Cutter walked over to where the

fire was now going handily, starting to put out some nice heat, and plopped down in front of it looking contented.

Brett walked over and put another larger log on the fire. She wondered if there was any other heat in the place, remembering Ty's joke about the ranger station having only the fireplace. It must have, she thought. Otherwise it would get very cold in here at night, and you'd have to get up all the time to keep a fire going.

Or find some other way to keep warm in the dark hours.

A shiver that was all out of proportion to the rapidly fading chill of the room ran through her. She was obviously out of control. When Brett straightened from the fire and turned to face her, something in his expression made her speak hastily, before her unruly mind could career even further down a path she'd clearly marked off-limits.

"I'd better go. Let you get on with your evening." Maybe she should visualize that path blocked with some of that yellow plastic tape saying Danger. Maybe that would make her imagination behave.

Not while you're in the same room with this guy.

"You want to know the real reason I didn't want to invite you in here?"

No. "Yes," she said, nearly bloodying her lip in the attempt to not say it.

"You scare the hell out of me."

The very idea of Brett Dunbar being afraid of anything, let alone her, seemed absurd.

"I think you have that backward," she said softly.

He blinked. "I scare you? Why?" An expression that was an odd combination of wary and weary crossed his face. "Because of the badge?"

She wondered how often that happened, that people turned away from him for that reason. She supposed even if that meant they were likely the kind you wouldn't want as a friend anyway, it had to be wearing sometimes.

"No," she said, wishing she had a talent for dissembling. But she didn't, and she knew it, so she went with as much honesty as her tangled emotions would allow. "Because you make me think about paths I've sworn not to walk again."

She heard him suck in a quick breath, as if she'd sucker punched him. Perhaps that was how he felt. He'd probably had no idea of the crazy way she was reacting to him. And probably was happier not knowing, because now he likely thought he had to fend off another misguided female. Because she was sure there were others. She couldn't imagine a man like Brett Dunbar not having a trail of feminine admirers behind him.

For a long moment he just looked at her. Firelight flickered over his face, throwing the masculine angles into sharper relief and making him even more attractive, something she wouldn't have thought possible. And sending her mind into even crazier channels, engendering wilder imaginings about firelight flickering over him under other circumstances.

When he spoke at last, his voice was low and rough in a way that sent a jolt of sensation through her that was hotter than the fire and colder than the night all at the same time.

"I've got a few paths I've sworn never to walk again, too. One most of all, and that's the one you make me think of."

"Why?" she asked softly.

He let out a compressed breath. "Why do you scare me? Because you're an amazing woman. You're smart, brave, kind, generous and sexy as hell. For starters."

He took the breath right out of her. On some level she registered that she'd heard similar things before from other people, but never had it slammed into her as it just had when he had said it.

She stared at him for several seconds. He held her gaze, although she had the feeling he would much rather have looked away. It took her much longer than it should have to be able to speak.

"I meant…why did you swear not to walk that path again?"

He did look away then, and she wondered if he regretted what he'd said, what he'd betrayed by that unexpected barrage of compliments. She could almost feel him starting to pull back, to step away from the entangling emotions. But she could also feel the pain, his pain, and it was so strong, so awfully familiar, that she didn't, couldn't, do what she would likely have done under different circumstances.

Cutter's head came up, and the dog looked from Brett to her and back again. As if he'd somehow sensed a decision point and was waiting to step in again if necessary. She was just chastising herself for that silliness when she flicked a glance at Brett and saw him looking at the dog with an expression that matched her thought, as if he expected the dog to block the door if he had to.

"That," he muttered, "is one scary dog."

"You know my story," she said. "But I know nothing about yours. I realize you have the right to say it's none of my business. If that's how you feel, please just say so, and I'll leave."

Leaning on one arm resting on the hewn wood mantelpiece, he stared back at the fire. The silence stretched out until it became an answer in itself. She reached into the pocket of her jeans for her keys.

Five harsh words broke the silence.

"My story is your story."

She froze, holding her breath, afraid if she spoke, moved or even took that breath, he would stop.

"Minus the guts on my part," he added after a moment. "You faced it. I ran."

"Brett," she began, then stopped at the barest shake of his head. Finally, he lifted his head and looked at her. His gaze was dark, shadowed, with pain, grief and something she couldn't name.

"I was married. She was murdered."

Her breath caught. She'd sensed somehow that he understood where she lived more than most, that with him it hadn't been some platitude uttered by someone who had no idea what it meant to lose the person you loved most in the world.

She swallowed tightly. Managed to get the word out. "Murdered?"

"Because of me."

And there it was. That something she couldn't name. Guilt.

Chapter 21

He hadn't spoken those words in years. But now that he had, it was like uncapping a shaken beer: it bubbled up and overflowed.

"My first year as a detective in LA, I put away a high-level member of a street gang. He swore his people would make me pay. But they didn't have the guts to come after me."

She was looking at him steadily, a world of sympathy and empathy in her eyes. He was astonished at the relief just saying that much gave him. Because she understood, he thought. In the way only someone who's lost someone they loved in an unnatural, particularly cruel way could understand.

"Or," she said softly, "they knew how to hurt you even more."

Yes, she understood. And she could take it. She was strong. Stronger than he was. "They beat her. Burned her. Raped her. Shot her. And dumped her on our front porch for me to find."

He heard her smothered gasp, regretted having said it so bluntly. Regretted having said it at all. But it was too late, although he'd managed not to blurt all of it out. And now he waited for the platitudes, the insistence it wasn't his fault, all the things people said that made no difference at all. Nothing changed what was and whose fault it was.

"What was she like?"

His gaze shot to her face. She'd surprised him again. He struggled to find the words that best fit who Angie Dunbar had once been. "She was…happy. Innocent, in a way. She liked people. She had a…zest for life. She could find joy in the simplest things."

"She sounds wonderful," Sloan said.

"I would come home from a day of dealing with all the ugly, and the minute I saw her smile, I felt…clean again."

"Then she wasn't just your loss—she was the world's. There aren't enough people like that."

That easily, but impossibly, she spoke aloud what he had thought so many times. "Yes. The world needs people like her."

"I'm sorry for all of us, then." She gave him a sideways look. "Did you ever think of quitting?"

"Yes. But I couldn't."

"Because then they win," she said softly.

He nodded. But something about the shared moment was so intense he couldn't hold her gaze. He looked away, stared into the fire. How had she done this? How had she gotten him to talk about what he never talked about? How had she known exactly what to say, and more, exactly how he'd felt? Was it simply because she'd been through it herself? Was she just empathizing and doing it so well because she'd been there? Or was there more to it?

He made himself look at her, and it was much, much harder than it should have been. She was looking up at him, steadily, a world of gentle understanding in her eyes.

He was moving before he even realized it. It had been so long since he'd felt the urge he didn't even recognize it until his mouth was on hers.

He felt her little jump of surprise, and a tiny part of his mind suggested he should stop this before he regretted it. But that cause was lost the moment he felt her lips under his and turned to ash the moment he realized her mouth had softened, the surprise fading way.

She was kissing him back. She wasn't just allowing this, not just accepting it; she was kissing him back. Lighting a fire in him that made the one on the hearth seem no more than a flickering match.

She leaned into him, and a soft, quiet sound came from her, almost a moan. Need exploded in him, unlike anything he'd felt in longer than he could remember. It was hot, swift, consuming, and he wanted nothing more than to hit the floor and take this woman here and now. He wanted her naked, open and as frantic as he was feeling in this moment.

And he had no right.

The room seemed to rotate slightly, and he realized he'd forgotten how to breathe. He felt an odd tightness over his biceps, realized she was gripping them tightly, as if her hold on him was the only thing keeping her on her feet.

It took every bit of self-control he had to break the kiss. For a moment he just stood there, staring at her, feeling the quickness of his own breathing, wondering how this had overwhelmed him so fiercely when he'd been so on guard from the first moment he'd realized Sloan Burke got to him in a way no woman had for a very long time.

She was gazing up at him, lips parted, looking a little stunned. He saw her swallow, and his own throat felt almost unbearably tight. A bit of the heat faded from her eyes. She didn't step back, but he felt the withdrawal just the same. He opened his mouth, not sure exactly what he was going to say but feeling he needed to say something—

A slim finger touched his lips in a hushing motion. She gave a tiny shake of her head.

"If you apologize, I may slap you."

Since the hovering words would indeed likely have been some sort of "I'm sorry," he was startled into silence.

"I've been wondering for a long time what that would feel like," she said.

Damn. He'd told her he thought her brave, but that

wasn't the half of it. She had more guts, more outright nerve, than he'd ever thought of having. At least in this territory, where he was beyond uncomfortable—he was downright terrified.

And he was damned well going to forge ahead anyway.

"Maybe it was a fluke," he said.

For an instant something very much like his own fear flashed in her eyes. But then it faded, to be replaced with something warm and almost teasing. It took his breath away before she even spoke.

"Or maybe it's just that it's been so long for me."

"Me, too," he said, although that hadn't occurred to him yet. It had been a long time since he'd kissed a woman because he really wanted to. He felt out of his depth already.

"Then maybe we should try again," she said. "You know, test it."

Heat stabbed through him. He sucked in a breath. Had to steady himself before trying words. "Theories should always be properly tested," he finally said.

And this time she made the move, stretching up to him, and at the first brush of her lips the need he'd thought had ebbed erupted all over again, faster, as if it had learned the way now.

He grabbed her shoulders, pulled her hard against him. He deepened the kiss, savoring the taste of her. He felt the slight tentative brush of her tongue against his, and his body nearly cramped in response. He'd never felt it like this, so fierce, so immediate, so demanding that he truly wondered if he could back off this time.

Holding Angie had been like holding sunlight, warm, soothing, slowly reaching down deep. Kissing her had been, for him, healing, as if all the ugliness melted away and no longer mattered.

Kissing Sloan Burke was volcanic, and she was going to melt his very bones.

And then she pulled back, breaking the sweet, fiery

connection. She stared up at him. She looked flushed, shaken. He felt a little wobbly himself.

Something else flashed through her eyes then. It was too familiar for him not to recognize it.

Guilt.

The heat vanished. And suddenly there were four of them in the room, he and Sloan and a couple of ghosts.

She lowered her head with a sharp, jerky motion.

"Are you—?"

He stopped when she waved a hand. "Don't. Please. My fault."

Her voice was thick, husky, and he was afraid if he could see her eyes, he'd see tears. She stepped back, away from him. And despite the fire, he felt suddenly cold. And an entirely different kind of ache began inside him.

"Sloan," he said, then stopped himself this time because he didn't know what to say. Had the feeling saying anything would be wrong.

"You don't feel like you're betraying her? One minute we were talking about how wonderful she was, and the next you're kissing me?"

He hadn't thought about it like that, but when she put it into words, he realized that was pretty much how it had happened. And now at least he had a clue what was happening in her head.

"You feel like you're betraying Jason?"

She shivered. It was all he could do not to wrap his arms around her again, but he was afraid just now that would be like holding dynamite with the fuse lit.

"I didn't expect it to be like that. I thought I wouldn't feel anything, because of him."

He opened his mouth to speak, shut it again as something struck him about what she'd said, how she'd said it. "Are you saying there hasn't been anyone? Since Jason?"

"No one that made me even wonder," she said simply. And he couldn't find words for how that made him feel.

And again he had to fight the urge to pull her back into his arms.

"It probably sounds crazy," she said. "I know it's been a long time. People say I should be over it by now."

"People," he said, "are idiots. You never get over it."

Her gaze shot back to his face. He tried to find the right thing to say, realized there was no right thing, not for this. So he went with the truth.

"If you're lucky, you get past it. You learn to live with it, not let it control you. But there will still be times when it's all you can think of."

He saw her eyes widen, saw his words register, thought he sensed some of the tension leave her. So at least he hadn't said the wrong thing.

"Your wife," she began, then stopped. Maybe she felt the same way, that they were traversing a minefield. And again he went with the truth, since this was Sloan and nothing less would work.

"She truly was wonderful. But for me it's been eight years, and I already have enough to feel guilty about."

"You know it wasn't really your fault, don't you?"

"My job put her in harm's way."

"So only people with no family at all should be cops?"

He drew back. "Of course not. But they came at her because of me."

"If some insane terrorist had come here and killed me because Jason was fighting them, would it have been his fault?"

He grimaced. He wasn't liking how this was going. "That's different."

"How? You were both fighting a great evil to protect others."

"Sloan—"

"I understand, Brett. I get it. Really. Knowing in your head it wasn't your fault doesn't convince your emotions.

I don't know how many times I cursed myself for not trying harder to talk Jason out of enlisting."

Maybe she did get it, he thought. "Could you have?"

"Maybe. He loved me so much. But he might have always regretted it, and that would be at my door. Besides, he was who he was, and I loved who he was, so I didn't want to change him even if I could have."

"You were awfully wise for…what, twenty?"

She gave him a faint smile. "I was twenty-two when we got married. And I didn't feel at all wise. Maybe a little more now." She looked at him steadily. "For instance, I'm sure Angie didn't want to change you either. How could anyone?"

There were more implications in those last three words than he could deal with right now. This was more deep conversation than he'd had with anyone in years. Probably since the days when they'd sent him to the department shrink to work through what had happened. He hadn't liked it then either, because he knew nothing could change what had happened. The only reason he'd stuck with it as long as he had was Dr. Bickham had agreed with that, had said he couldn't change it, but he could help him learn to live with it.

He wondered if anyone had helped Sloan. Or if she was so rock-solid sane that she hadn't needed it.

Cutter stirred, shifting before the fire.

"Too warm, furry one?" Sloan asked, looking down at the dog as he rolled onto his side with a contented sigh. Whatever the emotional currents were in the room in the past few minutes, he obviously hadn't felt the need to interfere.

"Sometimes he doesn't move away for hours," Brett said. "I don't know how he doesn't fry his doggy brain."

That simply, the tenor shifted back to the normal, the mundane. The talk shifted to having to go and get back to the regular business of life. And he escaped responding to her question of how anyone could want to change him. A good thing, because he had quite a list.

After she'd gone, leaving him to the fire and a sleepy dog, he had to face the one reality he couldn't deny. Sloan Burke was reaching places in him he'd sworn he'd never let anyone near again. The price was too high.

But he couldn't quite silence the little voice in his head saying she would be worth any price. And that Jason Burke had known it.

Chapter 22

The set of headlights steady in her rearview mirror, even that far back, made Sloan think of that gold car again. She shook her head at herself. She couldn't even see what kind of vehicle it was, let alone the color. And again she told herself she wasn't being followed, although the headlights remained until she turned off onto her street.

She knew exactly what was going on. She was desperate for a distraction. Any distraction, to take her mind off that impossible kiss. So she seized on silly things like the idea of being followed.

She went through her routine and got into bed to read for a while. When she began to yawn, she turned out the light and put her head on the pillow. And snapped instantly wide-awake.

At 3:00 a.m. she finally admitted it was going to be a sleepless night and got up. The house was quiet save for the quiet patter of a gentle rain on the skylight in the stairwell as she went downstairs. She paused outside the room that had once been a study but was now serving as a bedroom to save her uncle the stairs. All was quiet and, she hoped, well. She felt a tug of sadness as she remembered how awful it had been for that strong, determined man to admit that while he would be better, he would never be completely well again.

In a way, Brett Dunbar reminded her of Uncle Chuck.

He, too, she was certain, would fight long and furiously before admitting defeat. If he ever would.

She didn't realize she was touching her lips until she came out of the haze of memory. That kiss. Kisses, she corrected. She was just as much to blame. More, perhaps, since hers had come second, indicating approval of the first.

To blame? Why those words? Hadn't she told him not to apologize? Where had the thought of blame come from? From guilt about kissing someone other than Jason?

And why don't you just stand here hanging on to the banister talking to yourself the rest of the night?

She shook her head sharply. Obviously how tired her eyes were didn't factor into ability to sleep. She should fix some hot chocolate, find something mindless on television, anything but what she found herself about to do.

She did it anyway. She booted up the laptop she'd left down on the kitchen table. And did what she'd sworn she wouldn't do: she ran a search on Brett Dunbar. She scanned the recent entries. Found no surprises. She'd already known he was good at his job, and the mentions of cases he'd broken were just further proof. She narrowed the search by date and location until she found what she was after, feeling a bit morbid even as she did it.

The stories were there even after all this time. It had been headline news in Los Angeles. She couldn't stomach the gruesome details. What Brett had told her had been more than enough. She couldn't imagine what it had taken for him to even say it.

She found a photo gallery and hesitated. But it was a publicly accessible site, so surely they wouldn't print anything gruesome, she figured. And clicked.

The first picture was a pair of mug shots, two hardened-looking men, one with deep scratches on the left side of his face. Her breath caught. Had Brett's wife done that? Had she fought them, gotten her licks in, as Jason used to say? Somehow that thought was almost as grim as an actual photo would have been.

She nearly quit but clicked once more. And a lovely, smiling woman was looking at her with warm brown eyes. She had blond hair in a short pixie style that suited her and a smile that fit everything Brett had said about her. Almost involuntarily she clicked again, needing to get away from that picture. And instead found herself looking at a shot of Brett himself, flanked by several others, coming out of the courthouse where the trial had taken place. For a moment she just stared, aching inside at the devastation so clear on his face. He looked not his lean, rangy self now but thin, hollowed out, as if he hadn't eaten for weeks.

She shut the browser, then shut down the computer, wishing she had never looked. As bad as Jason's death had been, she had still only had to read dry reports or hear it described. Brett had had it dropped on his doorstep, quite literally. And she didn't care how long he'd been a cop, how much he'd had to deal with in his work—there was nothing that could prepare someone for that.

And while he wasn't to blame for what had happened, she could see why he would feel that way. He wasn't a man who shirked responsibility. In fact, didn't she herself have firsthand proof he took it on when he didn't have to?

She went to the living room, curled up in the chair nearest the stairway, where she could hear the rain on the skylight. She tugged one of Aunt Connie's beautiful hand-knit throws around her, snuggling into the soft warmth. It was going to be one of those nights. She gave up trying not to think and just let it sweep over her. Let the thoughts, the images, careen around in her mind, hoping they would batter themselves to pieces and let her rest.

It didn't happen until the memory of Brett Dunbar's arms around her enveloped her. At that moment, with that memory of warmth and safety, she finally slept.

* * *

Brett got the text from Rafe as he was leaving Rick's house. He'd snagged a lift from the area graveyard-shift deputy back to the station. Since he'd already checked with the office to be sure nothing so critical he needed to come back from his personal time had cropped up, he'd picked up his car without even going inside.

Rick had been in a better place when he'd arrived. He'd talked to Caro, calmed her, in fact was heading east to see her. He was going to drive and work out what he would do next on the way. He had savings to hold them for a little while, and Brett had assured him he would be digging into the false charges and that it was probably best that he be away from it all for a while.

It was early yet, probably the reason for the text instead of a call, but Rafe was obviously up and functioning. And since Ty, the computer genius, was in Saint Louis, he'd probably been at it awhile already. Maybe something had turned up.

He stopped for Cutter, who had acted a bit miffed when they'd had to forego the tennis ball session this morning so he could catch that ride. The dog seemed to have forgiven him and greeted him at the door with wagging tail.

"Want to go see your buddy Rafe?" he asked.

Cutter barked, that same odd combination of long and short he'd heard before when the animal had greeted his friend.

It was curious enough that he asked about it when he arrived. Rafe smiled crookedly at the dog, who was dancing around him in evident happiness.

"He's got a bark for everyone."

"A different bark?"

Rafe nodded. "Well, Teague and Liam both had the same for a while until Teague met Laney. Now his is different. Or maybe it's hers. Dog doesn't explain."

Brett chuckled. "No, he doesn't."

"Funny thing is, apparently he used the same bark for Quinn as he did for Hayley right from the beginning. Like he knew they were going to end up together."

"Crazy. But yours was always different."

He nodded, then gave the dog a wry look. "And I try to ignore that if you put it into Morse code, that short-long-short he's doing is an *R*."

Brett's gaze snapped to the other man's face. "You're kidding."

"Nope. Wish I was."

Brett didn't know this man that well, but what he knew of him made this bit of fancy unexpected. Then again, hadn't he been witnessing this dog's quirks for days now, up close and personal? Why should this surprise him?

"Drew Kiley had some interesting things to say," Rafe said, back to business as they went up to the meeting room.

"Oh?"

"He said the original plan on those houses up the hill from the Days' was to guarantee new buyers nothing would ever be built to impinge on their view. But then Sloan's uncle wouldn't sell, so they couldn't. They could only say it was privately held and not built on for over a hundred years."

"Obviously that was enough for some people."

Rafe nodded. "Drew also said back at the time, there were rumors that the developer cut some corners getting approval for the project."

"What kind of corners?"

"He didn't know anything specific, just that there was a lot of talk about how it went through really fast, especially compared to others trying to get similar projects approved. It may be nothing."

"But it's another blip on the radar," Brett said.

"And that radar screen's getting pretty crowded," Rafe

said as he crossed to the table where the laptop was already open. "And Ty found something interesting."

"Is he always working?" Brett asked as they sat down.

"I don't think it's work to him. He lives for that stuff."

And indeed, when his image popped up on the monitor, he seemed excited. "Hey, guys. Got something. Somethings, actually."

"Go," Rafe said without preamble.

"I was poking around some more on our Mr. Franklin. Found something interesting. A regular monthly payment automatically transferred from his bank account to another in the name of some business. Same amount every time. Five hundred dollars."

"And?"

"I thought maybe it was a loan payment or something and that knowing who he owed might be useful."

"Good thinking," Brett said.

"Thanks. But one thing led to another and another, and turns out it's rent. The company he's paying owns the house he's living in."

"Five hundred dollars? Seems a bit low."

"Wait until you see this." Ty hit a couple of keys and an image popped up on the screen. It was of a large multi-gabled waterfront home. Brett recognized the area as only a couple of miles from the county offices.

"Are you saying he's paying five hundred dollars a month for that?" he asked, astonished.

"If you can get something like that for five hundred bucks, I'm moving out there," Ty said.

"That should be pushing three, maybe four grand," Brett said. He frowned. "Can you show me that location on a map?"

"You got it." An instant later the image was on the screen.

"That's what I thought," he said. "Same neighborhood

as Mead. He lives out on that point. No way somebody at Franklin's salary should be able to afford that."

"Can you dig into that company, Ty?" Rafe asked. "I'd like to know who's behind renting this guy that house for five hundred dollars."

"Give me a few minutes," Ty said, already typing again. The young man didn't say anything more, just reached out and shut off the cam without ever looking away from his other screen.

"He does get into it, doesn't he?" Brett said.

"That's why we're glad he's on our side."

"And I'm glad you're on the right side," Brett said, his tone wry.

Rafe shifted to look at him levelly. "If you need to claim no knowledge, we can take you out of the loop officially. Then we're just a source."

Brett smiled but shook his head. "Thanks, but I'm already hip deep. And I can't say I don't admire your efficiency."

"Fewer hoops."

"Indeed." Sometimes the system was way too unwieldy to really help the people it was supposed to.

He took advantage of a sun break to take Cutter out for a fetch session. The dog's energy seemed boundless, and his gymnastics as he bent double to catch several throws in midair made Brett wince. You were getting old when a dog could make you flinch just watching him.

As he threw and threw and threw, he pondered the situation. He wasn't sure where this anomaly would lead, but it was an odd blip involving the man who had both fired Rick and stymied Sloan's aunt and uncle. And if there was anything untoward in this arrangement, Ty would probably find it.

Cutter danced in front of him as he picked up the returned ball yet again. The dog had more energy than usual today, probably because he'd missed the morning run to go pick up the car.

And had missed the daily argument with himself about what route to take. Whether to avoid going by Sloan's or put himself in temptation's way.

Temptation.

He threw the ball with a new ferocity this time, reacting to the heat that blasted through him at the thought of last night. If he'd done anything stupider in recent memory than kissing Sloan Burke, he couldn't think of it. He'd paid the price for it all night long, tossing, turning and finally giving up on sleep around three. It had taken all his discipline to not go poke around the *Accountability Counts* website just to see her face. Then he told himself he should do just that and take another good long look at that wedding picture.

When Rafe came out and signaled him to come back, he was thankful for the interruption to his thoughts more than to the constant throwing. Ty was already up on screen when he came in.

"You'll want to hear this," Rafe said.

Brett turned to look at the young computer whiz. "What?"

"You're okay with this?" Ty asked.

It took him a moment to realize what he meant. And Brett didn't want to ask how he'd gone about finding whatever he was about to tell him.

"This whole thing started sideways. Why stop now?" he said.

Ty grinned. "I knew I liked you. For a cop, I mean."

"Yeah, yeah," Brett said, but made sure Ty saw he was smiling.

"Okay, so this company is just a shell, held by another shell, then a trust, then another shell, and on and on. Here's the list." A long column of names rolled by on half the screen. "I kept digging and went through some twists and turns and finally found one of the founding fathers of the whole labyrinth. This guy."

A photo popped up. Brett blinked, startled. Rafe leaned back in his chair.

"Well, well," Brett muttered, staring at the picture of Harcourt Mead.

Chapter 23

Brett wasn't at all sure what, if anything, this was going to accomplish. But he was here anyway, loitering just out of sight on the side of the Administrative Services Building across the street from the courthouse. He knew Mead was here. He'd seen the man's car—a sleek luxury sedan a decade newer than his own county vehicle—parked in the prime allocated spot next to his private entrance to the county offices, an addition he had insisted upon some time ago. Amazing how being the governor's frat brother got you things like that.

He also knew the guy would be leaving in the next twenty or thirty minutes. He knew this because Sloan, with some supporters in tow, was already on her way to the new waterfront boardwalk project Mead had spearheaded. The first section was to open in about an hour, and Mead wasn't going to miss the chance to trumpet his accomplishment. If the man saw anything silly about setting up a ribbon-cutting ceremony for a boardwalk that as of now was about fifty feet long, he didn't let it stop him.

His phone chirped an incoming text. Sloan, he thought, pulling it out. When he saw her name, he felt that odd tightness in his chest. And no amount of telling himself it was ridiculous to react like that, that he'd known she was going to contact him, made any difference.

Her message was short.

We're in place. Being obvious.

He texted back quickly.

Me too. Not being obvious.

She sent him back a smiley face that, ridiculously, made him smile.

Ridiculous was pretty much where he was living right now.

He toggled the phone screen to stay on, not wanting to have to swipe it in this situation. His position behind a large SUV put him out of the line of sight of the office and private door, but he could watch it easily. As long as nobody came out to get the big vehicle, he'd be okay. He didn't know who owned it, but it had a county parking sticker in the window, so he thought he could safely guess it would be there for the day, or at least until lunchtime.

He had nothing to do but stand there and wait. And try not to think about how on earth he'd ended up in this crazy place in his head. And especially try not to think about the other night and what kissing her—and her kissing him—had done to his equilibrium. Every warning his brain could muster went off every time he did think of it, and it got kind of noisy. And distracting. Sloan Burke was one very distracting woman. It was a good thing they'd worked this out on the phone last night, after she'd seen the notice that Mead was going to appear. If they'd met in person, who knew what would—?

The door opened. It was an upstairs office, and judging by the location, it probably had a view of the inlet just a few blocks away. He wondered if it had always been the admin's office or if Mead had demanded that, too.

Three men stepped out, deep in conversation. Or at least, two of them were—the smallest of the three seemed a step behind. The door closed behind them with an audible thump. The second man was tall, broad shouldered, with brush-cut blond hair, and he looked familiar in the way of someone he might have seen in passing before. He was wearing a suit, black like his own, but Brett guessed that one would cost about a month of his salary. The man was gesturing at Mead adamantly, not quite tapping his chest with a pointed finger, but almost.

And Mead was taking it, Brett noted with interest.

The third man hung back a little, watching the two in front of him with nervous concern. A name suddenly clicked into place. He'd not met the man, but his image was beside his name on the county roster. Rick's boss. The charming Al Franklin.

Brett realized he was still holding his phone, and he was about to slip it back into his pocket when it occurred to him to snap a photo. It wouldn't be great from here, but it might be enough to place the big guy. And, should it ever be necessary, prove they'd all been together. He had no reason to think this unknown man had anything to do with anything, but Mead was knee-deep in something, and better too much than not enough.

He took the shot, then a second at the last possible moment he could manage, when they were closer. He put the phone away, took the papers he'd stuffed into his inside pocket out and started walking toward the building on a course that would cross their path before they got to the parking area. His one concern, that Franklin might recognize his voice from the phone call he'd made, eased when the man made a hasty departure, as if he was glad to be away from the other two, and darted over toward the main parking lot. No special parking dispensation for him, apparently.

The big guy must explain the even more expensive coupe parked next to Mead's car, Brett thought as he picked up the pace. He tried to look intent on the papers in his hand while his peripheral vision tracked the pair as they reached the bottom of the stairs. He could see Mead's face now, and *unhappy* was a mild word for his expression. The man was seriously peeved.

"...put in my time—I want out of this backwater," he was saying vehemently. "He made certain promises. I've held up my end. He needs to hold up his."

If the big man answered, Brett couldn't hear him. He kept going. And sensed the moment Mead spotted him. He didn't look up but waited, still walking toward the pair, grimacing as if at the papers he held.

"Detective Dunbar!"

Mead's voice boomed out, and Brett let his head snap up as if he'd been startled. "Mr. Mead," he said, putting as much respect as he could manage to feign into his voice and demeanor. "Sorry, I was focused on paperwork," he said, as if he needed an excuse for not having noticed the man's presence.

"Over here?" Mead asked as he reached them.

Brett didn't think there was anything more than curiosity behind the question—he didn't sound at all suspicious—so he gave a slightly exaggerated grimace and waved the papers. "Beneficiary. Ex-wife problem."

He'd learned from Foxworth that Mead had a couple of those problems himself, and the comment made the man smile ruefully.

"Anything I can help with?" Mead's tone was pure politician now, making offers he knew he likely wouldn't be called on to fulfill.

"Oh, no, sir. You're way too busy for this kind of thing. But thank you." Brett didn't think he'd mistaken the look of satisfaction that flashed in the man's eyes. "And in fact, I was going to try to catch you while I was over here."

"You were?"

"I did a little research on your problem. That woman who's publicly harassing you, I mean."

"Oh?" Mead glanced at the second man, who had

neither introduced himself nor suggested Mead do so. Another note on that particular page, Brett thought. "Dunbar here helped me out with some woman who's making a severe nuisance of herself over some silly zoning situation."

Still the other man said nothing. He was nearly Brett's own height but bulkier, Brett cataloged even as he wondered why he was bothering. But the thoroughness was second nature, and more than once it had proved useful. He had this guy in the bully category based on body language alone.

That suit had been custom-tailored, he would bet. Maybe the guy could just afford it, as he could afford that car. Or maybe there were other reasons he needed a custom-fit suit. Concealing a weapon came to mind. And something about the man's demeanor made that thought not as far-fetched as it should have been.

"I talked to her, told her to back off, but I think she's going to show up this afternoon."

"Show up?"

"At your ceremony. I thought you should know."

Mead swore under his breath.

"I know," Brett said, trying for empathy in his tone. "You worked so hard to get that project through, and now she's going to try to spoil the big day."

The second man was looking more bored with every passing second. Mead was eyeing Brett, at first frowning at his news but then appearing thoughtful.

"Why don't you—"

He stopped as a buzzing sound issued from his breast pocket. Mead reached into his coat pocket and pulled out a phone. Brett couldn't hear the caller, but the administrator's expression and body language weren't hard to interpret. The man wasn't happy.

His own phone chirped again. He took it out for a quick glance.

Think it wkd. Asst just made a call. Lking at us.

"Exes," he muttered as cover as he quickly tapped out an answer.

Did. I'm a go.

Mead ordered the hapless Perkins to get the damned situation under control, then shoved the phone with some energy back into his pocket.

"I thought I was rid of that bitch," he snapped. Then he looked at Brett. "Thank you, Detective. You were absolutely right. She and her little band of miscreants are already there, causing trouble."

Brett shook his head as if in disgust. "Why doesn't she just give up?" he said, thinking all the while that if there was anyone less likely to give up than Sloan, he didn't know them.

The blond was getting impatient, Brett could sense. But he didn't shift his gaze, because Mead was looking at him more pensively now. Assessingly. For a moment Brett was on the edge of speaking, but his instincts told him to wait. Better if the idea came from Mead. His hunch paid off a moment later.

"You said you talked to her," Mead began.

"Perhaps I wasn't...forceful enough to make it permanent." His tone was purposely suggestive, and he saw Mead pick up on it.

"Perhaps," the man agreed. "It might take more."

"I'm on my own time at the moment." He poured on a little more oily eagerness and faux respect. "But I'd be happy to try again if you want, sir. I could push harder this time."

Mead pretended to consider it, but Brett saw in his eyes that he'd already decided. "I'd appreciate that, Detective. Would you like to ride down there with me now?"

Brett pretended to consider in turn, then shook his head. He wasn't sure he could tolerate being closed up in a car with this guy anyway.

"Let me go first, see if I can get her and her gang cleared out before you even arrive. Don't want you and protest signs in the same photograph plastered around."

"I like the way you think, Detective," Mead said with an easy, practiced smile that belied his earlier anger. "You get this Sloan Burke off my back, and we'll have to have a talk about your future."

Brett didn't miss the implied promise. Wondered what kind of future there would be for the man who latched on to these coattails. He wondered, but only with the tiny part of his mind that wasn't occupied with the other knowledge that had just blasted through him.

The tall silent man had reacted, unmistakably and strongly, the moment Mead had said her name. He knew who Sloan was. And had known before she had ever crashed onto Mead's radar.

And it sent a chill through Brett. He didn't know why, as she had said herself her identity and her past were no secret. But something about the way this man's eyes had gone cold, and about the size of his reaction, screamed a warning. Because for that instant, before he masked the response, Brett knew exactly what he was looking at.

A predator.

One who had just spotted potential prey.

Chapter 24

"Just trust me, please?" Sloan asked as her group gathered around her, puzzled by her seemingly meek capitulation. "It's all part of a bigger plan. And thank you so much for coming out. Coffee at The Mug is on me."

"Heads up," Brett said softly, low enough the others couldn't hear. "Perkins is headed this way."

She nodded as the small group began to scatter. They did trust her, so they were going, but they looked a bit doubtful. She hoped she could explain one day. She felt Brett's hand on her arm just above the elbow.

"If you don't want to talk here," he said in a tone that was not only louder but decidedly ominous, "then we can go to the county lockup and chat there."

His shift was so sudden, so smooth, that it took her aback for a moment. On some level she realized her expression was probably exactly what he'd hoped for, as Mead's pale, twitchy assistant reached them.

"You going to arrest her?" He sounded satisfied at the idea. "About time."

"She's going to come along quietly, isn't she?" Brett's tone was smooth, condescending. She resisted the urge to snap something back at him, knowing he was only playing a part.

"Do you have any idea how much I hate being referred to in the third person?"

"As much as anyone, I'd guess," he said in that same

tone, as if he were calming an upset child. He was so good at this, at being an entirely different kind of person, it was a little unnerving. "So don't make me use it."

"Make you!" She couldn't help it—her voice rose. "The problem is yours, mister, not mine." She made a show of trying to pull free. Brett pulled her back, but she noticed his fingers didn't dig in, merely wrapped around her arm and tugged. Caused no pain but looked as if he were jerking her around.

"Hush." He looked at Perkins. "Call your boss. Tell him it's all clear and that I'll talk to him later."

"Right away." A smirk crossed that pale face, as if the man was certain now what he was dealing with. He thought Brett was one of them, Sloan realized. Thought he would sell out his principles for whatever Mead could do for him. She was a little surprised at how certain she was that he would never even think about such a thing. Just as she'd been about Jason.

She muttered something under her breath for effect. It worked. Perkins smirked at her this time.

"My car this time," Brett said as they walked away. "It needs to look official. We'll get your car later."

"It's okay. I rode down with one of the others."

And so again she found herself sitting in that car with the shotgun above the windshield. It made her a little edgy until, when he pulled away from the waterfront, a tennis ball rolled out from under the seat. That made her smile, and she reached down to pick it up.

"How is he?" She glanced at the clock on the dash.

"No doubt waiting by the door for me to get home and put my shoulder out of whack throwing that ball for him."

His tone was wry, but she saw something in his face, a slight curve of one corner of his mouth, that made her say quietly, "Not so bad, having someone waiting for you."

"Different," he said.

That stirred up feelings she thought she'd managed to

tamp down. And again words she hadn't planned on saying slipped out. "Do you like it?"

He flicked her a sideways glance. "Not used to it."

"Why?"

The glance was longer this time, as if she'd startled him. "Pretty personal question."

"Yes," she admitted. "I have lots of them, it seems."

"Why?" he asked in turn.

"Because you tangle me up," she said in a tone that matched his earlier one for wryness.

"Sloan…"

"You should tend to Cutter."

"Yes. I'll take you home first."

"Don't. I'd like to see the rascal again."

There was a long moment of silence before he said, his voice low, "Are you asking to come home with me?"

She drew in a deep breath as she considered all the possible aspects of that question. She glanced at him, saw in the tightness of his jaw and the way he was staring at the road ahead as if it were a freeway in downtown LA that he'd meant just what she thought he had. A memory of that kiss suddenly rose up and nearly swamped her with heat and need. She hadn't felt like this in a very long time. Not since Jason.

I will have died for nothing if you live alone and unhappy.

She supposed it was strange to have her husband's words urging her toward another man. She doubted Brett would appreciate that she was thinking of him now. But she knew Jason had meant it, just as fiercely as he had loved her.

"Yes," she finally said. "I believe I am."

The silence was longer this time. She sensed his tension, wondered what he was thinking.

"Brett—"

"Are you saying what I think you're saying?"

His voice was harsh, tight. He wanted no misunderstanding, she thought. And who would know better how
people misunderstood, and turned their lives into chaos,
than a cop?

"Is your next question 'Are you sure?'"

"It should be. Because if the answer to that is no, then
the answer to everything is no."

It was like another check mark on a list she hadn't even
known she was keeping. He meant it. If she wasn't certain,
then as far as he was concerned, the answer was no. No
coaxing, no trying to get past her doubts with smooth talk.

"If I wasn't sure, you could fix that, you know."

He blinked. "I could?"

"Kiss me again. If it's anything like before…"

Her voice trailed off. She saw his hands tighten on the
steering wheel until his knuckles were white.

"Damn. It's all I've thought about since."

"Well, that's a relief," she said. "This would be really
embarrassing if it was just me."

"You've got about twenty minutes to change your
mind."

She wondered if he'd meant to sound so grim, but she
didn't ask. But she was curious. "Twenty?" They were at
least a half an hour from his place.

"Last drugstore," he said.

It took her a moment, but when she understood what
he meant, she decided silence was her best course. She'd
said more than enough. But she couldn't help feeling a
warmth inside her at this proof that he didn't make a habit
of this, and that he hadn't gone out and stocked up on protection just on the chance.

He was as unprepared as she was. She'd made a decision she'd had no intention of making, not now, not ever.
But somehow this man had changed all that. She was still
alive, and for the first time she truly understood what
Jason had said, that if she lived only in memories, if she

stayed withdrawn from the part of life that had given her so much joy, then he'd died for nothing. Because it was that life he'd fought for. Died for. Not just for her but for everyone.

And in his way, Brett fought that same battle on a smaller front.

She felt a twinge, a reminder that she'd sworn never to get involved with another protector, another warrior who risked his life for others. But what was she to do when that was the only kind of man who stirred her?

So have sex with him, enjoy it and keep your heart out of it.

She nearly laughed as the words went through her mind. That would be the way some women she knew would approach it and would be the advice they would give her. And had, a couple of times. But she knew herself, knew deep down that she wasn't made that way. She was incapable of keeping her heart out of it. She could guard it, protect it, limit its involvement, but letting a man into her body without giving him at least some tiny part of her heart? Not in her.

Maybe that was the answer to why this was the only kind of man who tempted her. The kind of man who would never abuse that gift, even if he couldn't—or wouldn't— give it in return.

She sat silently as he drove, pondering the oddity of learning something new about herself at a time when she would have thought she knew herself pretty well.

"Sloan?"

She snapped out of her reverie. Realized where they were. That last drugstore. "Haven't changed my mind," she said softly.

They had to break the momentum to give Cutter a necessary couple of minutes, but the dog was back so fast she had no time for second thoughts. But once inside, it was clearly Brett who was in a hurry. And from the moment he shut the door, grabbed her and kissed her, so was she. All the reasons she was here came flooding back on the tide of heat and want he roused in her. His mouth was hot, demanding, and when he pulled back for an instant, she heard a tiny sound of protest that she nearly didn't realize had come from her.

"You're su—"

"Yes." She cut him off before he got the word out. And then he took her breath away all over again by sweeping her up in his arms. At five-six she was not a small woman, but he did it easily.

It was more of the alcove she'd guessed at than a bedroom, and most of it was taken up by a closet and the large bed. He'd chosen sleeping space over walking space, and given his height, she understood. There was a book on a carved wooden chair that apparently served as both seat and nightstand, since there was no room for anything else. A pole lamp like the one in the main room arched over that side of the bed, telling her he read there. On the single free wall was a framed photograph of Mount Rainier at sunrise, the brilliant orange-and-pink sky made even more striking by the dramatic slash of dark shadow the mountain itself cast across the brightening sky. She wondered if he'd taken it and what it said about him if he had.

Beyond that, the room was utilitarian, tidy. No distractions from its intended purpose.

At least, its intended purpose until now. When he set her down next to the bed, she felt oddly as if she'd forgotten how to stand. He reached out to cup her face.

"I was going to apologize for the plainness of the room," he said softly. "But it's not plain at all anymore."

She felt the heat in her cheeks that he seemed to cause in her so easily. "I'll bet you say that to all the girls."

"There's never been one here."

That made her breath stop in her throat. This time she kissed him.

That quickly, she was frantic. She wasn't sure what she'd imagined the few times she'd dared to let her imagination go this far. But it wasn't the mad, heedless rush she was caught up in now. Now that it was here, she wanted no slow, gentle seduction, no slow build, no long slow caresses. Because in truth this had been building since the first day this man had stepped into her life. She'd waited so long to feel again that now that she was on fire with it, she didn't want to wait any longer. Couldn't wait. She wanted this man's skin against hers; she wanted her arms around him, wanted to be completely tangled up in him in a way she'd never been before.

The fumbling with clothes wasn't awkward; it only proved he'd been honest about how long it had been. And that heightened the need until she almost moaned aloud even before he pulled her, naked, into his arms. The thought flashed through her rapidly fogging mind that this could be life changing, and all her self-warnings about keeping her heart out of it were nothing more than the faint, distant foghorns she sometimes heard rolling up from the sound.

They went down to the bed together. Hands collided as they touched, stroked; heads bumped as they both tried to kiss every uncovered inch. Yet it wasn't awkward, at least not to her. She was far beyond feeling awkward. She was feeling consumed by the need that kept growing, surging inside her.

She traced the muscles of his back, marveling at the power there. His hands reached her breasts, cupped them. Helplessly she arched upward. His mouth followed, first teasing, then drawing her nipples into searing wet heat, and she nearly cried out as need cramped her.

Then something changed. She realized Brett seemed to be trying to slow down, and she shook her head. "No," she gasped. "Hurry."

"I'm getting a little crazy here," he warned, his voice thick.

"Good. Oh, good," she gasped out, trying to urge him on with her hands.

"Slow next time," he muttered.

Yes, next time. She liked the sound of that.

He was on top of her, a solid, strong weight that made her body ripple in anticipation. She reached to guide him, the hot, silken feel of him sending another ripple of heat through her. He groaned at her touch, as if he'd felt the same thing, and the harsh sound urged her on.

And then he was sliding into her, and she cried out. It was difficult at first; her body was unused to this. He hesitated, but she clutched at his back, then slid her hands down to the taut backside she'd so admired when he was running and pulled him forward. He made that sound again, and this time it escalated to a sharp groan of her name as he slid into her, filling the empty place she'd carried for so long. Her cry of his name blended with his voice, joining them in that way, too.

He was moving inside her, stroking with an urgency that answered her own. All thought of easing into it this first time was burned away as the heat built, flared. With every slam of his body into hers her mind screamed, "Yes, yes, yes," until it was no longer just her mind and the cries echoed in the small room.

He drove home one more time, and she felt it begin. She clutched at him, desperate to hang on. She was alive, so alive, and in this moment she let go all reservations, letting herself take the joy so long denied.

And then her body launched, exploding into a pulsing, searing flight that made her cry out his name again. And again it blended with his guttural shout of her name in turn, and she knew on some deep, long-buried level that *life changing* was definitely the term for this.

Chapter 25

He woke up alone and for a moment thought last night had been a vivid, searingly erotic dream. It certainly wouldn't have been the first one he'd had since a certain headstrong dog had led him up the proverbial garden path.

He blinked and raised himself up on one elbow. There was just enough light in the room to see the tangled bedcovers. And he didn't need the light to catch the lingering scent of her, that sweet aroma that reminded him of the purple flowers his mother used to grow on a windowsill.

That she'd managed to get up without waking him was surprising. Then again, maybe not. After last night, perhaps he should be surprised he woke up at all. Despite how many times he'd turned to her, or more gut slamming, she to him, in between he'd slept better than he had in years.

The air was a bit chilly, since he'd forgotten to set the old baseboard heater last night. He'd forgotten everything last night except the woman in his arms and, eventually, in his bed. Small wonder. He'd felt things last night that were incredible, more incredible than believing he'd lived better than forty years before finding out they were possible.

He listened for a moment, thinking he might hear the shower running. And regretting that the stall was far too small to share. He barely fit in it by himself. The gouge on the forehead he'd garnered the first week he'd lived here had taken a long time to heal and it had been a bit embarrassing to admit he'd been whacked by his own showerhead.

The cabin was silent.

No sounds even from the kitchen, so the coffeemaker hadn't drawn her. But her clothes, the ones he'd practically clawed off her, were gone. His own were now across the chair by the bed, not strewn across the great room along the path they'd followed to end up here. She must have picked them up. The thought made him edgy for reasons he couldn't explain.

She couldn't have just left—they'd come in his car. Not that walking five or so miles would stop Sloan Burke, not if she was determined. Did she want to avoid facing him this morning that much? He knew she had even less experience than he did in the proverbial morning after, but he also knew she had more nerve than he did. She must have; after all, she'd made the decision last night. And he knew on some deep level he couldn't doubt that there wasn't an ounce of run in her.

Belatedly it hit him that Sloan wasn't the only one missing.

Cutter.

He rolled out and dressed hurriedly in the jeans that were on the chair. The moment he cleared the alcove wall, he saw the cabin was indeed empty.

"So she ran off with Cutter?" he mused aloud, his mouth quirking. No sooner had he said it than he heard a faint light laugh coming from outside.

He hadn't really been worried, not deep down, so there was no explanation for the burst of relief he felt to hear her, to know that she was still here. But then, there was no explanation for a lot of things just now.

He went to the door and pulled it open. What he saw inexplicably tightened his chest. Sloan was throwing a ball for Cutter straight upward, and the nimble dog was catching it neatly, sometimes leaping high into the air as if the ball wasn't coming down fast enough to suit him.

He walked quietly out onto the porch, leaned a shoulder against one of the rough wood poles that supported the roof. And watched.

Her hair was dampened from the heavy mist this morning, her shoes were soaking, and the ball the dog brought her again and again had to be wet itself, but she didn't seem to care. She just laughed and crooned to the delighted animal and threw the now-more-gray-than-yellow ball again.

That she could be like this, after all she'd been through, was a testament to her character, he supposed. And in that moment he wanted nothing more than for this to go on forever. To stand here and watch woman and dog play with a sweet innocence he'd not seen in a very long time.

But the dog wasn't his.

And despite last night, neither was the woman. He wasn't fool enough to jump down that rabbit hole. She may have wanted, needed, the closeness, the joy they'd found last night, just as he had. But the bottom line hadn't changed. This was a woman who came with ties, and he was a man with a job that too often destroyed them.

On the next midair catch, Cutter spun even as he landed and headed for the cabin at a run, wet, muddy ball firmly gripped in his teeth. He ran past Sloan and straight for Brett. She turned, a wide smile on her face, clearly as delighted as the dog was at the play. But something changed when she spotted him; something softer yet more heated came into her eyes as she looked at him.

He should have put a shirt on, he thought as her eyes ran over his bare chest. Then again, maybe not, he amended quickly as she followed the dog toward him, looking at him almost hungrily. Involuntarily his gut tightened; that look was like a caress.

"Sorry if we woke you," she said as she came up beside him. "He just looked so hopeful holding that ball that I couldn't say no."

Cutter didn't seem the least bit sorry. In fact, if a dog could look smug as he glanced at the two of them, he did. As if he'd orchestrated everything himself. As perhaps he had, Brett thought, remembering that first day the dog had arbitrarily chosen to make the turn that had led them to her.

"Don't be. It was worth it to watch you two. Besides, I slept better than I have in ages."

"But not much," she said. Then color flooded her cheeks and she looked as if she regretted the words.

"Sometimes," he said, "it's not the quantity but the quality." He reached out then, lifting her chin with a gentle finger. "And sometimes it's both."

She smiled. Lifted a hand to cup his. The heat of her seared him.

"Sloan, I—"

"Don't."

He stopped, his brows furrowing.

"Look," she said, "I know this changes things. I know we're in a new place and we both need to figure out what it is and isn't. But not yet. Please?"

He drew back, feeling the oddest urge to grin at her as he said, "You're asking me, the guy, to dodge the morning-after talk?"

That color rose in her cheeks once more. He resisted the temptation to tease her, because he very much wanted to do exactly what he'd said, dodge the morning-after talk. Because he couldn't help thinking that as glorious as it had been, they'd only complicated things last night. Because they were both people with complicated lives and even more complicated pasts.

Not to mention that he suspected she was still very much in love with her husband. And that was something he understood too well. Even now he couldn't think of Angie without a pang of loss and sadness.

But at least she hadn't run. She hadn't vanished without a word this morning, swept away on a tide of second thoughts. Which he seemed to be full of. He guessed that meant he was a real adult now, past the stage where he could be just happy about a night of hot, unexpectedly spectacular sex and just be hoping for a repeat rather than thinking about all this.

At least he knew Sloan wasn't the type of woman who would make assumptions he wasn't ready to live up to. She'd said it herself, that they needed to figure out what this was. And, perhaps more important, wasn't. They had to—

The sound of his cell phone ringing cut off his thoughts. Probably just as well. He was getting damned close to having that morning-after talk with himself.

He went back inside, smothering a jolt of heat as he looked for his jacket, then found it where she had apparently hung it on the rack near the door. Sloan and Cutter followed him in, but she grabbed one of the towels he'd taken to keeping by the door and was drying the dripping dog off. She needed one herself, he thought, strangely pleased by the fact that she didn't seem concerned about her own appearance before the welfare of the dog.

He pulled out the phone and glanced at the screen. It was a new number he hadn't seen before, but it had his same prefix, so he tapped the talk button.

"Dunbar."

"Detective!" The bluster was unmistakable. Harcourt Mead.

He glanced at Sloan, then walked into the bedroom alcove to cut down on any background noise from Cutter. Tried not to notice how wildly tangled the bed was. Thinking about last night and the incredible things that had happened between them wasn't going to help, not when he needed to concentrate.

"Sir," he said, able to put more respect in his voice when he could openly frown without being seen.

"Sorry to call you on Saturday, but Perkins tells me you did a great job yesterday clearing out that nuisance of a woman and her cohorts."

It was all he could do to keep his tone steady as he fought the instant surge of protectiveness that hit him at the man's denigrating words. "Thank you, sir."

"I've gotten some new information on her. She could be a real problem. She's caused trouble before, a lot of trouble."

Brett felt a chill creeping over him. He'd discovered who she was. The big guy, he guessed. He'd known. He was more certain than ever now.

She's caused trouble before, a lot of trouble.

Those were the two sides in what Sloan had done, those who thought she had caused trouble and those who thought she had done something heroic. "Has she?"

"My friend the governor is all too familiar with her."

The governor? Not the big guy? Brett was getting that pit-of-the-stomach feeling that never boded well. And Sloan was right here now, looking at him. *Mead?* she mouthed. He nodded. He held up one finger, hoping she'd realize it meant he was fishing.

"She mentioned something about knowing the governor, even working with him."

"Oh, that's the front he has to put on, because she got some heavy hitters on her side somehow. The support of the military nut jobs."

"She seems harmless enough," he said. *Unless she's in bed with you, driving you crazier than you've ever been in your life.*

"Don't kid yourself. She's a malicious piece of work.

And I'd consider it a personal favor if you'd continue to keep an eye on her."

"My pleasure," Brett said, putting as much oil in his tone as he could manage. "Anything in particular you're concerned about?"

"Just keep her out of county business. If you can convince her—whatever you have to do—to give up on this silly zoning thing, I'd consider it an even larger favor. And believe me, Detective, I know how to repay a favor."

"Good to know, sir."

His mind was racing as he ended the call. Things were starting to happen. He'd obviously succeeded in earning the man's trust. He could use that. Mead had talked to the governor about Sloan. That made him uneasy.

But nothing made him more uneasy than the words that kept echoing in his mind repeatedly.

Whatever you have to do...

Sloan wasn't just on their radar now.

She was a target.

Chapter 26

"They can't do anything to me, not really. I'm too high profile, even after all this time." Sloan sat on the edge of the bed as Brett put away the clothes she'd helped him out of last night. She tried to keep her mind on the matter at hand. And tried to convince herself that getting him out of his clothes again wasn't the matter at hand.

"Even heroes die in ordinary accidents," Brett answered, tossing socks on top of the damp towel she'd used on Cutter, who was sitting quietly now, watching them. "Or at least, that's what we're told they are."

Lord, she even had him looking for conspiracies now. She felt ridiculous. But last night... She had no words for how she'd felt last night. She was afraid it must be showing in her face, afraid he'd read there that she'd like nothing more than to go right back to bed with him, and spoke hastily.

"You don't really think they'd—"

"I'm not positive they wouldn't," he said. "A fine line, but one I'm not willing to ignore when your safety's in question."

It sounded so much something Jason would have said that it took her aback for a moment. And her own thought came back to her.

The only kind of man who stirred her.

And stir her he did. In ways she'd never realized she was capable of being stirred. With Jason, sex had been a warm, rocking, home-at-last kind of thing. With Brett Dunbar, it was nothing less than explosive. And telling herself it was that way because they'd both been alone for so long wasn't very convincing. Maybe if they kept at it for a few weeks, took the edge off, then—

"Whatever you're thinking, hang on to it."

His voice was low, rough edged and sounded exactly as it had in the dark last night when he'd asked her to take the lead, to do whatever she wanted, whatever gave her pleasure. And she had, exploring his lean, rangy body until he was gasping under her hands and mouth.

She nearly moaned aloud at the memory.

"Damn," he muttered. And reached for her.

He'd never been much for lying in bed all day, but he could learn. With this woman in his arms, he could learn. Would happily learn.

Sloan snuggled against him and let out a long, relaxed breath. It brushed over the skin of his chest, not quite a tickle, almost another caress. Then she went still except for an odd motion with her right foot.

"I think I found your phone."

"Oh." He'd dropped it on the bed when he'd finished with Mead, feeling oddly as if it were burning his fingers. She reached down and fumbled for a moment, then came up with the phone. It still felt warm, but differently, this time from her, and it made all the difference.

"Don't look now, but you're being watched."

He drew his head back, giving her a puzzled look. Then he followed her gaze and saw Cutter, his chin resting on the edge of the bed, his eyes fixed on them intently. Ridiculously, he wondered what the dog thought of such human antics. At least he was sure human sex wasn't an oddity to him. After all, he belonged to Quinn and Hayley.

He put down the phone beside him and lifted a brow. "What do you want, dog?"

"You mean you can't read his mind?"

"That's his trick, not mine," he said, his mouth quirking. "And he's uncomfortably good at it."

"He shouldn't want out again so soon, should he?"

"It's not that look," Brett said.

"So you can read his expressions, then."

He glanced at Sloan, wondering if she was making fun. There wasn't a trace of teasing in her own expression, so he took her seriously.

"I'm learning."

Cutter reached out and nudged the phone with his nose. Sloan laughed. "He wants you to call someone?"

"I don't know. Rafe, maybe?"

At the name, Cutter let out a soft woof.

"Okay, now I get it," Sloan said, reaching out to ruffle the dog's fur. "You've gotten some message on the ether? Or you can hear the phone ring before it does? Your people are about to call?"

The dog took no offense at her teasing tone and gave her a quick nuzzling but went right back to the phone.

"Maybe it's the other way around," Brett said drily, "and I'm supposed to call them."

"Is there something you need to tell them?"

He started to shake his head but then remembered. "I do want to send them a photo. See if they can match it with a name."

"Who?"

"The guy who was with Mead and Franklin. He looked vaguely familiar, but I couldn't place him."

"And you think they can?"

"Tyler has some pretty amazing face-recognition capabilities." He gave her a sideways look. "And he doesn't need a case as an excuse to run it."

"And he doesn't have to worry about stirring up a hornet's nest in the process?" she asked.

"Exactly," he said to the woman who knew a little

something about stirring up more than just hornets. Dragons, maybe. And he wondered when he'd started thinking in such fanciful terms.

He called up the photos he'd taken of the men coming down the outside stairs from Mead's office. He selected the clearest, closest one of the tall blond. He was about to tap the mail option, figuring he'd send it to Rafe to forward to Tyler since he didn't have the kid's email or number, when Sloan shifted beside him to look. She went very still.

"You don't need to send it," she said, her voice low.

"What?"

"I know who it is."

He stopped the motion of his finger to stare at her. He angled the phone to give her a better look. "This guy?"

"Yes."

"Who is he?"

She shifted her gaze to his face. "Governor Ogilvie's bodyguard."

Brett blinked. "The guy who threatened you?"

She nodded. "Ramsey Emmet. Believe me, dear Rams is not a face I'd forget."

Brett looked back to the image on the small screen. He'd categorized him as a bully by body language and expression alone, so he supposed there was some satisfaction in learning he'd been right.

"So what would these guys have to talk about that's imperative enough the governor's consigliere comes to them?"

Sloan let out a sigh. "I'm trying not to fall prey to the idea that it's all about me."

He glanced at her. "As far as I'm concerned, it is, until I can prove differently."

She gave him a smile that had him thinking about postponing any thought at all for a while. Again. He made himself look back at the photo.

"Nice trio," he muttered. "Quite a power play we've got going here. One guy who knows he's not important so tries to make everyone think he is, another who's got a little power and uses it like a club, and a guy run by the most officially powerful man in the state."

"Officially?" she asked, apparently caught by the qualification.

He shrugged. "If you go by efficiency and connections and getting things done, I'm not sure Quinn Foxworth isn't really the most powerful guy around."

Cutter made a soft whuffing sound at the name, while Sloan studied him for a moment. "I'd like to meet them sometime."

Brett gently tugged at Cutter's ear. "Curious about his family?"

"Yes. But more about anyone you speak of with such admiration."

She caught him off guard with the tone of quiet regard but even more with the implied high valuation of his opinion.

"I…" His voice trailed away.

"You're a good man, Brett Dunbar, fighting the good fight. Are you surprised I respect you for it?"

He'd stared down hardened criminals with less effort than it was taking him now to meet her steady gaze. And something he saw in that gaze, in those eyes, something of her nerve and courage and, yes, the pain and anguish she'd been through, made a realization explode in his brain.

"You wouldn't be here if you didn't," he said.

"No, I wouldn't," she agreed softly.

She thought he was like her, brave and strong and good. He wasn't at all convinced he was all that, but she was, or she wouldn't be here, with him, like this. She never would have come home with him, never would have given herself to him. But she had; she'd given him everything.

And that kind of giving came with strings, whether he

wanted them or not. Whether he was ready for them or not. He might not be what she thought he was, but he wasn't the kind of man who took the kind of gift this woman— who was definitely what he thought she was—had given and tossed it aside as if it were just a meaningless, if pleasurable, encounter.

His stomach knotted, and he shied away from the sudden mess of feelings even as he grimaced at himself for doing so. All these years, he'd sworn he was done with caring on anything deeper than a casual level. He channeled what emotions he allowed himself into his work, helping people there.

He remembered reading something once, about how having people you cared about gave fate something to use against you.

He'd just given fate the biggest sledgehammer in existence to crush him with.

Chapter 27

Focus, Brett told himself. He couldn't let this emotional stuff derail him. There were other things to deal with now.

Like this guy in the photo.

The screen on his phone had blanked out, and he swiped it again. Looked at the image, remembered the man simply observing, saying nothing. Saying nothing because he'd already given Mead and Franklin their orders? Or because he didn't dare say anything in front of a deputy without checking with the man on the other end of his leash first?

Because for all his size and ominous presence, Brett had no doubt he was on a leash. What he didn't know was how far the man would go if he was ever let off that leash.

It hit him then, an image of this hulking bully turned loose. On Sloan.

A wave of nausea swept him, followed by a chilling anger deeper than anything he'd felt in years. The very thought of Sloan being threatened, of her being in any kind of danger from this kind of man, made him furious.

He rolled out of bed and yanked his jeans back on. Cutter jumped out of the way but stayed close, watching him with interest. He grabbed a lightweight sweater from a drawer and pulled it on. When his head cleared the neck, he thought he was calm enough to look at her.

She was looking at him much the way the dog was, curious but not wary.

"You're staying with me."

He hadn't meant to sound so sharp, but that image was beating at him.

"Am I?" she asked, her tone mild. Deceptively mild, he suspected. He'd started at the wrong end.

"I don't trust these people. And you're on their radar, not in a good way."

She frowned. "I thought that was the plan."

"It's not anymore. You just stay out of their way. No more demonstrations, no more showing up in Mead's way, no more fighting for the zoning approval."

"So because I slept with you, you now have the right to give me orders?"

Yes, deceptively mild, all right, Brett thought.

"That has nothing to do with this. I'm not giving you orders as...your lover," he said, unable to think of any other way to say it, since *the man you let do everything to you and who let you do everything to him* didn't have quite the ring he was going for. "I'm saying this as a cop. I don't want you going anywhere alone. If you're out, you're with me. If you're here and I can't be, you're with Cutter."

The dog barked, short and sharp. His entire demeanor had changed, and on that thought he walked over and stood in front of Sloan, squared up and alert, ready, looking for all the world as if he'd understood the words and that his charge was now to protect her.

"It got very male in here all of a sudden," she said, sounding more wryly amused than angry. "So let me get this straight. You want me to stay here, locked away, unless you're available to take the little woman wherever she might need to go?"

"You know that's not what I mean. I just want you safe."

"In case you've forgotten, I have responsibilities. Responsibilities that are as important to me as yours are to you. My family needs me."

He couldn't argue that. "We'll get them some help until this is over."

"The undesirability of having strangers come into their house aside, how am I supposed to agree to this when I don't even know what 'this' is, not to mention who gets to decide when it's 'over'?"

"I can't explain it," he said, feeling a little beleaguered. Odd how the very things he admired about her were a bit hard to deal with when turned on him. "I just don't want you in the middle of this."

"Seems to me I already am."

"You stirred it up, yes. But now you need to back off and let me deal with it. Whatever it is."

"I can't just go into hiding for no real reason."

"Sloan, I've been at this a long time. I've learned to trust my gut instincts because most times when I don't, I regret it. And right now they're screaming that there's something big and ugly going on here. Please. Give me a chance to find out what it is."

She stared at him for a long, silent moment. This had turned into a whole different kind of morning after. But he couldn't deny the urgency he was suddenly feeling.

"Could whatever 'this' is rebound on my aunt and uncle?"

He was tempted to just say a definite yes. It would be the easiest way to get her to do what he wanted. But he gave her the truth; Sloan Burke deserved nothing less.

"I don't know. But I can't say it wouldn't. They, or their property, are mixed up in this somehow."

"Then it's them you should be watching."

Cutter barked. And barked again. Short and sharp.

Sloan got there as fast as he did and in fact spoke first. "Call Foxworth. It's what they do, isn't it?"

"You'll trust Rafe to look after your folks?"

Her mouth quirked. "I think I'd trust him to storm the governor's mansion if that was what needed to be done."

Brett smiled then, feeling a little less knotted up inside. "Me, too." He glanced at Cutter, then back at her. "Then you'll stay with me? No arguing?"

Sloan tilted her head back slightly. In an affected drawl she said, "Why, Detective Dunbar, darling, if you wanted me to move in with you, all you had to do was ask."

When Cutter barked again at that, or at his no-doubt gaping expression, it sounded to Brett far too close to laughter.

"All set," Rafe said. "Charlie has trusted people everywhere. Including a cardiac care nurse. And I know a rehab therapist who'll come in and stay for as long as necessary."

"Foxworth has quite a resource list," Sloan said. She remembered what Brett had said about them not taking any payment and wondered just how this was all financed. This Charlie must be something special, she thought.

"Yes," Rafe said simply, "we do."

"And you?" Brett asked.

"I'll be on Mr. and Mrs. Day at night."

Brett's cell rang, and he nodded at Rafe before he walked across the room to answer it.

"I don't want them scared," Sloan said as she looked at the man she was trusting with her family.

"They'll never know I'm there," Rafe promised. "But not even the governor's going to get to their door."

She believed him. Something in his cool, steady gaze was more than reassuring. This was a man who would get the job done. As different as they were, Brett Dunbar and Rafe Crawford were cut from the same tough cloth.

"Thank you," she said.

"It's an honor."

The image of the salute he'd given her when they'd first met shot through her mind. Jason. She sucked in a breath, waiting for a rush of guilt to swamp her. It didn't come. The only thing she felt was a flood of heat at the memories from last night, a night unlike anything she'd ever thought to experience. Her pulse kicked up and she had to take another deep breath to steady herself.

She snapped back to the moment to find Rafe studying her silently. His gaze flicked across the room to Brett, then back to her.

"I think," he said softly, "he would approve. Brett Dunbar is a good man. The best."

She was sure she must be bright red by now. "It's that obvious?"

"To someone who doesn't deal in such things, yes."

There was no bitterness in his tone, just acceptance. And she found herself wondering even more about the enigma that was Rafe Crawford.

Reassured now that her aunt and uncle would be safe, Sloan sat quietly in Brett's car until they were back out on the main road.

"What am I supposed to tell them?" she asked then.

"Your aunt and uncle?"

"Yes. They'd never believe I'd just take off and go somewhere. I'm already going to have some explaining to do about last night."

Her breath caught on the last words as the images swept over her again. It took her a moment to recover, and she was thankful he said nothing.

"I don't like the idea of lying to them," she said before she let something really stupid out.

There was a long silence before Brett said, his voice a little rough, "You could tell them the truth. About where you are, I mean."

She looked at him out of the corner of her eye. "With you, you mean."

He nodded, and she couldn't help but notice he didn't look happy about it. He didn't even flick her a glance but was again driving as if he were back on an LA freeway at rush hour instead of out in the green countryside passing maybe one car every five minutes or so.

"They'll think…" Her words trailed off. She took a deep breath and tried again. "They'll think I've fallen in love or something."

"You're too smart for that," he said, his voice even rougher.

"Too late." The words came out barely above a whisper. But he heard her. Glanced at her at last. Something in that look made her realize there was more than one way to interpret her words.

"Sloan—"

"I'll have to let them think that," she said, thinking her voice sounded as ragged as his. "It's the only thing they'll accept. And I can't have them under any more stress, worrying about me."

He didn't answer that, just drove on in silence again, everything that had happened between them like another passenger, hovering, huge.

"I should warn you about something," he said abruptly. She wondered if he was that desperate to change the subject. Or maybe this was the same subject. Maybe he was going to warn her off, tell her not to assume anything because of all this. Or because of last night. Maybe he was afraid she was going to think he wanted more. Or more likely that she would, and he was going to warn her now so he didn't have to tell her later he wasn't interested in anything else.

The question she herself had to answer was, did she want more? He was everything she'd sworn to stay away from. He was also everything she was drawn to. And as Aunt Connie had said, he was also the only man who had stirred her, made her feel—although visions of last night made that tame description laughable—since Jason. Brett was—

"That was Mead on the phone back there," he said.

She gaped at him. "What?"

"At Foxworth, when my phone rang."

She nearly laughed aloud. Here she'd been, off on some emotional tangent that had nothing to do with what he'd been about to say. She'd built a scenario that didn't even stand on sand, let alone anything more solid.

"Oh," she said, feeling sillier than she had in a while. "What did he want?"

"To find out how I'd managed to get you to shut up and go away."

"What did you tell him?"

He gave her a sideways look. "Something he, being who and what he is, would understand. Probably even expects, if we've been seen together."

"Which is?"

His jaw tightened, as if he thought she wasn't going to like this. "That I took you to bed."

Her eyes widened. "What?"

"Sorry. It was the only thing I could think of that he'd believe had worked so fast, after all the trouble you caused him."

"You mean you told him you got me to back off by… seducing me?"

"He's that kind of guy," Brett said, sounding even more uncomfortable. "It's the way he works, so…I thought you should know I had to say that, in case he ever… I didn't want you to hear it and think… Oh, hell."

Sloan stared at him. Bit her lip, trying to hold back. But she couldn't. She burst out laughing.

He looked stunned.

"Do not ever put yourself in the same category as that pompous, overstuffed, phony windbag, Brett Dunbar. I'm not sure he's even the same species."

It was slow, but a smile eventually curved his lips.

"You are," he said, his tone heartfelt, "an amazing woman."

The explanation to her family was less difficult than she'd expected. In fact, she was more embarrassed by her aunt's delighted "Well, it's about time," and her eagerness to help her pack up some things.

"Shouldn't you be warning me?" she said, relieved.

"He's a good man, Sloan. I can feel it. You grab him and hang on."

She felt a twinge of guilt then, knowing the falsehood that lay behind this. But Connie rushed on, and the moment for confession was gone.

"I won't even tease him about not wanting to come in and face us," she said.

"He had to do an errand. He'll be back in a few minutes."

She didn't voice her suspicions that the "errand" Brett had gone off on was another visit to the drugstore. Yet again the memories rose up, and she hoped fervently she was right. No matter the reason, she wanted more nights like last night. In fact, she wanted an endless string of them.

And she stopped in the middle of zipping up the small suitcase she'd packed, realizing she had the answer to the question she'd avoided asking herself earlier. She did want more. She wanted everything.

She'd had the idea of keeping this isolated in her mind, of thinking of it as a sort of vacation, lovely while it lasted but with an end built into it. As she slid her laptop into the outside pocket of the bag, she told herself she'd better stick to that idea.

She was still telling herself that when she was back in the car with him, and they were headed back to his place. She was so busy lecturing herself that she only belatedly noticed he'd not made the turn to go up the hill. He kept going, then abruptly dodged across the outside lane and into the parking lot of, of all things, a lumber store. She looked at him, saw that his attention was on the rearview mirrors as they slowed.

But that wasn't the real difference.

It was like looking at a different man. This wasn't the quiet man with the mind that never stopped working; this wasn't the runner who laughed about the antics of a dog; this wasn't the passionate, giving lover of last night. This man was on alert, ready and wire taut. The very energy around him had changed.

This was the cop.

"Brett?" she said softly.

He didn't look at her. But he did answer her.

"We're being followed."

Chapter 28

He'd noticed the nondescript small gold sedan like hundreds of others on the road slide in behind them just before they'd reached his drive. It was the advantage of being in a semirural area, at least to the followee. Tailing someone surreptitiously was a lot harder when you didn't have many other vehicles to blend in with. On the other hand, it also made it harder to lose that tail when you didn't have a steady stream of other vehicles to use as a screen and an impediment.

He couldn't say what had really triggered his suspicions, other than he knew most of the cars in his small neighborhood of maybe a dozen houses, and this wasn't one of them. It was an occupational hazard, part of always knowing your surroundings, just something he automatically took note of. He knew it could be a car he just hadn't seen, but that little niggle of doubt, and the fact that it had been close to home when he'd spotted it, had been enough for him to make that first unexpected turn.

Sloan, thankfully, didn't pepper him with more questions. She also didn't do the instinctive thing of turning around to look. She simply waited. Trusted he knew what he was doing.

He pulled out his phone and put it to his ear, reaching out with the other hand to power up the terminal in the center console and masking that movement with the angle of his body. If he was wrong, it didn't matter, but if he was right about the tail, he hoped they would think he was just making or answering a call, not that he'd made them. He didn't want them vanishing just yet. He made sure the phone was visible in his hand and carefully didn't look back, just pretended to be listening as he waited, mentally counting down the time.

Sloan still said nothing. He silently blessed her for that as he took his one quick look at the passing sedan. The driver was the only occupant, unless someone was hiding as they passed. Then he zeroed in on the rear plate.

He reached for the console and typed in the license number, all the while keeping the phone to his ear, as if he were just idly looking around while he listened to someone talk.

By the time the answer popped up on the screen, the car was out of sight around a curve just ahead on the road. He put down the phone and read the registration data, which showed the vehicle as registered to a trust. He frowned. Why did that ring a bell?

"The Wallace Northwest Trust," he muttered, as if saying it aloud would jog his memory.

"It was the gold car?" Sloan asked, her first words since he'd said they were being followed.

"Yes."

She didn't say any more, but something about her silence made him look at her. "Sloan?"

"It's just that...the day we went down to reapply, after I called and asked for your friend, I thought maybe I was being followed. And then again the other night after we found Rick."

He went very still. "What? Why didn't you tell me?"

"It was just a feeling. I couldn't be sure, and there are a million gold cars like that."

He tried to keep his tone even. "You noticed a particular car? Like that one?"

She waved a hand, as if dismissing her own words. "I thought I was imagining it. A...flashback sort of thing."

He guessed that that and worse had happened when she'd been making nationwide noise.

"You should have told me."

"You were already doing so much, and—"

"You still should have told me."

She sighed. "In hindsight, obviously I should have."

She wasn't so determined to be right that she couldn't admit that. He liked that about her. Among the multitude of other things he liked about her, he thought wryly, heading his mind off before it could career down that road full of memories of last night.

She glanced at the screen, although it was harder to see from the passenger seat.

"That's who owns it?"

He nodded. "Registered and legal owner. It seems familiar, but I can't put my finger on from where."

She leaned over to see more clearly. "The Wallace Northwest Trust. Nice and vague. Could be anything or anyone. Could you run it? Or the Foxworth whiz kid?"

It snapped into place. "Tyler! This was on the list of companies and shells he came up with, backtracking to Harcourt Mead." He reached out to the keyboard once more. "I should check what other vehicles they own. Maybe this has been going on longer than we think. If—"

He stopped suddenly.

"What?" she asked.

"We don't know how high this really goes." She'd probably think he was crazy. Then again, she of all people might not. So he went on. "But we know how high it could go."

He'd been right. She got there immediately—he saw it in her face.

"But why? It's just a little piece of land that's been in my uncle's family for generations."

"I have no idea," he said. "But I think if we figure that out, we'll find all the answers."

He shut down the computer without making that next inquiry. His gut was saying don't leave a trail. Crazy when he wasn't sure of anything, but he'd learned the hard way to listen to that instinct.

She watched him, then shifted her gaze to his face. "You think they might…what?"

He glanced around before he answered. Confirmed what he'd caught with his peripheral vision: a gold sedan very much like the one that had followed them had pulled into the lot of the convenience store across the street. He couldn't see the plate from here, but he still knew.

"They could have a flag in the system," he said, "on names, plates, whatever, to let them know an inquiry was made."

She drew back slightly. "Would they know who made it?"

No one had gotten out of the car. Those instincts upped the volume.

"They'd know it was through the sheriff's office. And they could track it to this terminal eventually, although it would take some time. How much depends on how much juice the asker has."

"The car's back. Across the street."

He blinked at the sudden change. Not at the fact that she'd noticed it, though. She was on top of things, Sloan Burke. He smiled at her.

"Yes."

"He pulled in, parked, but hasn't gone into the store."

"You don't miss much, do you?"

She smiled briefly but said only, "So now what?"

He smiled back, held it. "Kiss me."

She blinked, clearly startled. "What?"

"For show, of course," he said, but couldn't stop his mouth from quirking upward.

"Oh. Of course. Mead probably put this guy on us."

"Exactly."

"Given what you told him, I think you should kiss me, then."

He grinned. Widely. And he didn't wince, even inwardly, when he realized that if he'd taken time to speak before doing just that, his words would have been something like "Damn, I love this woman."

The heat that flared the moment his mouth came down on hers rippled through him, banishing any thought of the cold outside, the follower across the street or the edge of the console digging into his ribs. She kissed him back, fiercely, eagerly, and within a split second his heart was hammering, sending his pulse racing and spreading the heat so quickly it took what little breath he had left away.

It took everything he had to pull away from her. For a moment all he could do was sit there, trying to convince his suddenly unruly body it wasn't going to get what it wanted—who it wanted—right now. And the way Sloan was looking at him, as if she was having the same problem, did not help at all.

"Well," she said after a moment, sounding as breathless as he felt, "that was convincing."

"It sure as hell was," he muttered, turning his head fractionally, just enough to see out of the corner of his eye the gold car was still there.

He heard her take in a breath, as if steadying herself. If her reaction was anywhere near as strong as his had been, he understood completely. And no matter how many times he told himself it was all too likely she was still in love with her dead husband, or that no woman in her right mind would want to deal with his own personal ghosts, he couldn't seem to stop his mind from roaring down roads he'd sworn never to travel again.

"I can see him," she said.

She was in a better position, he realized. "Anything?"

"I think he's on the phone. His hand's up to his ear."

"Maybe calling for instructions." He glanced at her. "Maybe we should give him something to really talk about."

Something glinted in those green eyes, something that reminded him—as if he needed anything to remind him—of last night. But one corner of her mouth twitched, as if she was suppressing a grin. That same flash of humor was in her voice when she spoke.

"If you want to have sex right here and now, in public, I think I should remind you that could be a career ender for you."

He was laughing before he even realized it was bubbling up inside him. It didn't feel quite so strange. He knew it had to be because she had made it happen more in almost two weeks than anyone had in the past eight years.

Still grinning, he reached for the key and turned the ignition. "Let's rattle his cage," he said.

Chapter 29

"We're going to Seattle?" Sloan asked as they slid into the lane for the ferry. It wasn't crowded at midday on Saturday. Most who were going over for the weekend had already gone, but later it would be jam-packed with people heading into the city for the evening.

They'd made the drive to the island terminal leisurely, as if they had no concerns and all the time in the world. Brett had made no dodging turns, no apparent effort to lose the gold car, which once out on the highway had dropped back behind a pickup and an electrician's van. So she had to assume he wanted the car to be able to follow.

"We're going through Seattle," he said.

"Because? I mean, besides that it would be easier to shed this guy?"

He flashed her a smile that made her pulse take a little leap. "Exactly. And of course, we're going on a romantic weekend getaway."

That leap shifted into a maintained race at his words. But something about the way he said them and that "of course" told her he hadn't really meant it. At least, not in the way she would have liked. Which told her more than she was ready to process about how far she'd fallen down this rabbit hole.

Fallen, heck. You dived in. Headfirst. No one to blame but yourself for this one, girl.

"You're assuming he's working for Mead, then?"

"Not completely. If he's not, it'll be easier to lose him in Seattle, and if he is…"

"We're playing to what Mead already thinks." With an effort, she kept her tone casual, joking. "Well, I'm packed, at least."

"Comes to that, my go bag's in the back."

Wait, this could really happen? "What would make it come to that?"

"If we can't shake him. That is, if he even follows us on. Looks like he's pulled off to the side. Probably calling the boss again."

"Not much for initiative, is he?"

Brett shot her that smile again, warming her even as she worked to quash the wish that they were really going away for that romantic weekend. "Or the boss is a micromanager."

"That sounds more like your friend's odious boss."

"Yes. And it could be him behind this."

"But why would he want to follow us?"

"Don't know." He was checking the rearview mirror again. "But he's in this somehow, so I'm keep all options open."

"What if he doesn't follow?"

"They we go straight north and take the other ferry back. And head to Foxworth."

Cutter sat up in the backseat and let out a muffled whuff of sound at the name. He'd been so quiet Sloan had nearly forgotten he was there.

"At least you don't have to pack for him," she said.

Brett chuckled as they moved up to the ticket booth. "Nope. His needs seem to be people he likes, tennis balls and food, in that order."

The woman working the booth recognized him. Sloan wasn't surprised. She supposed deputies were here often, since this was one of the main ways to get out of the county and to the city. Besides, any woman breathing would likely remember him.

"Nice dog," she said, glancing at the back window. Cutter politely endured the scrutiny, cocking his head at the angle that Sloan had noticed nearly always made people smile.

"Thank you," Brett said without further explanation.

"He'll have to stay there for the duration of the crossing, you know. Only walk-ons are allowed up top." Her voice held just the right amount of regret.

"I know. Thanks," he said as she handed him some change.

Sloan shifted her gaze back to the rearview mirror as the woman asked if he was on official business. Brett said no, but after he'd paid, the woman directed him to the first-on loading lane anyway.

"Nice," she said as they started moving again, cutting toward the lane reserved for special loading. Bikes went on first, for safety, then motorcycles, but they'd be next.

"I wouldn't have asked, but since she offered, it'll help," he said.

She realized he meant this would put them first on, first off, handy given what they were trying to do.

She turned her head as if she were merely looking out toward the water of the harbor but gave the rearview mirror a look as she did so. "He's still pulled to the side."

"Yes." He gave her another glance as they pulled to the front of the first-on lane, behind only an ambulance that appeared, thankfully, to be empty. "You're good at this."

"Haven't forgotten everything I learned in DC, I guess."

"I'm sorry. That you had to learn that way."

"Sometimes ignorance really is bliss. But foolish."

"A lot of people live that way."

She turned in her seat as he put the car in Park and

turned off the engine for the ten or so minutes they had before boarding began.

"And they're able to do that because of people like you," she said.

He gave a barely noticeable one-shouldered shrug. "And Jason," he said quietly.

It seemed so odd to hear her husband's name spoken by this man, the man she had spent such a long, passionate night with. It should have felt bad. Or she should have. Guilty or extremely awkward at the least.

But she felt none of that. Maybe because he'd spoken Jason's name with the utmost respect. Even with a note of understanding, as if he realized her feelings might well be conflicted. Brett Dunbar was a very perceptive man. Probably why he was so good at what he did.

"Yes," she finally answered, and left it at that because there really wasn't much more to say.

Cutter, still sitting up in the backseat, barked suddenly. Instinctively Sloan turned to look at him. He was glancing out the back window, and she realized the gold car had moved. It was now at one of the ticket booths and seconds later was driving toward the loading lanes.

"He's following," she said.

"Yes," Brett agreed, and she realized he'd already seen it. Amazing how he didn't appear to be looking around but was always so aware. Given his job, a good thing. She felt that twinge of warning again, but it was much more muted now. A night like last night could do that, she thought wryly.

Their line had started moving, and they were the second on after the ambulance. It put them in the center bay, near the open bow of the ferry. She glanced back.

"I can't see him," she said.

"He's back there."

"They really want to know where we're going."

"Or they want to make sure we really are going."

She frowned. "You mean they want to know where we are?"

"Or where we're not."

Her frown deepened, but before she could ask, he'd taken out his phone. He called up a number and hit the call icon.

"Dunbar," he said. "We seem to have picked up an appendage."

There was the briefest of pauses before he explained about the details on the vehicle. And why he hadn't pursued it.

Another pause. Then, "Thanks. We're about to board the ferry leaving the island. I'll try to lose him in Seattle. Then we'll head back."

He listened for a moment, then said a final "Right. Thanks."

He hung up and put the phone back into his pocket.

"Rafe," he explained. "Ty's on the car and looking for any others that trust might own." He seemed to hesitate before going on. "Your aunt and uncle are doing fine. Your uncle seems to have hit it off with the rehab therapist Foxworth arranged."

That surprised her a little. Uncle Chuck simply didn't like needing help, and he was openly grumpy about it, especially when he wasn't feeling well and needed it the most. But she was thankful for whatever small miracle Foxworth had worked.

"Thank you," she said.

"Thank Rafe. And Foxworth."

"It's amazing. What they do, I mean."

"Yes. I had my doubts when I first ran into them, but they're definitely the good guys."

"Like follows like," she said.

He drew back slightly. "Thanks. If that was a compliment."

"It was. One of many I could give, were you in the mood."

Something hot and primal flashed in his eyes for an instant. "Don't," he said. "We'll be back to ending my career."

Her cheeks heated as the words reminded her of her own comment. Actually doing what she'd teased him about would never even be on her radar, but she couldn't deny the thought was salaciously arousing. But then, that seemed to be a constant state at the moment.

And that was a place she had never expected to be again in her life. She wasn't sure she wanted to be there. But she was, and now she had to deal with it.

Chapter 30

Sloan kept silent through the ferry crossing, smiling only when Brett lowered a back window to let the fresh air of the crossing into the car despite the chill. Cutter leaned out, his nose twitching as he savored the smells.

"Why do I get the feeling he knows exactly what's going on and who's involved, and that if we let him out, he'd charge right back to wherever that car is?"

"Because you're getting to know him," Brett said, his mouth quirking.

Sloan smiled.

After a while Brett was tapping his finger restlessly on the steering wheel, and his expression wasn't happy.

"You don't like not knowing exactly where he is?" she asked.

"I don't like not knowing who he is and who he's working for," he said. "And I'm weighing the advantage of finding that out versus letting them continue to think we're blissfully unaware."

"Finding out?"

"We're on a boat. He can only run so far."

He was thinking about confronting the man? She didn't much like that idea. Then again, she had no doubt he could handle it.

"On the other hand," Brett said, "I don't want to make problems for the ferry crew. We need their help too often."

"And this isn't official."

"There's that," he agreed.

"We could take a casual walk. Cutter would be okay if we locked the car, wouldn't he?"

He looked at her, and something in his eyes made her feel that heat begin again. "Lovers would, wouldn't they?"

That quickly, he decided. He was out of the car and around to her side in an instant. It was a bit of a squeeze because a large work truck was beside them, but she didn't mind. It meant she had to get closer.

He reassured Cutter and locked the doors. They went up the steps to the passenger cabin. And at Sloan's suggestion, they went outside. She told herself it was because she always enjoyed the approach to the distinctive Seattle skyline, not because the wind of their passage would make it so chilly that they would need to cling to each other for warmth. That was just a side benefit.

"Did you see him?" she asked when, as the announcement of their approach to the dock came over the loudspeakers, they headed back to the car deck.

"I think he stayed put. Knew we had to come back."

She sighed. "Maybe Foxworth will have something by the time we get there."

"If it's there to have, they'll probably find it."

She thought about the odd relationship as they reached the Seattle dock. Brett was a cop to the bone, and yet he obviously appreciated that there were times when that was a hindrance as much as a help. Times when the kind of freedom Foxworth had was better.

"I think that I'd rather have Foxworth with that capability than some of the government types I've met," she said as she felt the gentle thump as the big ferry slid into the slip.

He gave her a look as the ferry workers went about readying things for off-loading. The familiar roar of motorcycle engines, firing in anticipation of the gate lifting, echoed around them.

"I'm sure I would," he said.

She lapsed into silence as they exited the ferry and Brett negotiated the city streets. He'd taken advantage of the lead they had by getting off the ferry second only to the ambulance and the bike riders. A short distance later—he obviously knew his way around the city—she couldn't tell whether their follower was still with them.

"He's there," he said, as if he'd read her mind. "He's not bad. So let's see—a hotel in town or head toward the mountains, maybe a casino…"

"You could just pull into the federal building," she said as she saw the sign in front of the Jackson Building, "and really rattle his cage."

Brett grinned at her. Whatever else might come of their time together, she'd seen more and more of that grin, and that pleased her. "I like the way you think. That would cause a bit of a jolt, I'm sure."

"But we're not sure we want to jolt him yet?"

"No. But I do want to get rid of him," Brett said. "Now."

A few blocks later, just past a large building, he turned into an underground parking structure. She'd been more focused on the man behind them, with occasional forays into petting Cutter simply because it soothed her, and didn't realize that to the right was a hotel until she saw the entrance, surprisingly grand for being underground. A good idea in rainy Seattle, she thought.

Brett pulled into an open parking space not far from the glass expanse of the front doors.

"Stay quiet, buddy. It won't be long," he said to Cutter, reaching back to scratch behind his right ear. The dog settled down in the backseat as if he'd understood perfectly.

They got out, and he walked to the back of the car and opened the trunk.

"Grab your bag. And give me the suitcase."

Sloan opened her mouth to speak, then stopped and did

as he'd said. This was his world, and she either trusted him or she didn't. She did.

She slung the tote bag she'd packed over one shoulder as he lifted out her small suitcase and closed the trunk. But he didn't move. He leaned against the car, watching the opening where they'd pulled in and the street out in front. For the gold car, she supposed. A couple of minutes passed with no sign of it.

But then Brett straightened. "He's on foot," he whispered.

She nodded, managed not to look.

"Remember your voice will echo in here at regular volume," he said, still whispering. She nodded again.

"Okay, we're on, sweetheart," he said, his voice even a bit louder than normal. The endearment rattled her a little until she realized he was setting the tone for the act. That they were just a couple here for a romantic getaway. That she found herself wishing it were true was her problem.

"I can't wait," she said sunnily.

"Neither can I," he said with sudden intensity.

He put his arm around her and they walked toward the hotel, acting as wrapped up in each other as they could. It wasn't difficult. On the edge of her vision Sloan saw a balding man in a tan jacket standing in the shadows just inside the entrance. She hadn't noticed much about him when he was in the car, but obviously Brett had.

She leaned into him. His arm tightened around her. "This was a brilliant idea, honey," she said with as delighted a laugh as she could manage. She thought she sensed a slight hitch in his step before he steadied it. She could almost feel the man in the shadows watching them.

"This is only the beginning," he said as they stepped into the light flooding out from inside the lobby. Her pulse took that little leap again, and she found herself wishing the words were true with a fierceness that shocked her.

And then he leaned down and kissed her.

For a moment, just for a moment, Sloan let it happen as if it were real. Not that she had much choice, not when the feel of his mouth on hers again sent that heat racing through her and made her knees a little wobbly. His tongue flicked over her lips and she opened for him. A delightful shiver, hot and cold, went through her and she sagged against him as her knees gave out completely.

It seemed an eternity and yet too soon when he broke the kiss.

"Damn," he muttered.

"That should have been a convincing act," she whispered, her voice sounded a bit shaky even to her own ears.

"Who was acting?" Brett whispered back.

He led her inside, nodding at the doorman but keeping his eyes on her all the way, just like any lovesick guy. With his head turned toward her, he could also watch the man from the gold car.

Once inside, his demeanor changed, abruptly enough that it gave her a bit of a chill. She shoved it aside. This was business, his kind of business, and no time for out-of-control emotions. "This way," he said, and headed to the right. He took wide, ornate staircase up one floor two steps at a time.

"You know this place," she said.

"Friend of mine runs security, and I've been to a couple of seminars here. In this room," he added, pushing open the door to a medium-sized room set up with rows of chairs and a lectern. Along the side of the room were wide windows.

He crossed to them nearly at a run. She followed, realizing the windows looked out on the street below. She got there just in time to see the bald man walking southbound on the sidewalk, his cell phone to his ear.

It took her a moment to spot the gold car—or at least its twin.

"There?" she asked. "Across the street in the next block?"

"We'll see," he said, never taking his eyes off the man.

When he got into the gold car and left, they knew the ruse had, at least for the moment, worked.

"Now what?" Sloan asked.

Brett gave her a sideways look, grimacing as he did so. "Not what I'd like," he said. He reached out, brushed the back of his fingers over her cheek and let out a compressed breath. It was enough to soothe her doubts, her unease, and vanquish the chill she'd felt at his quick change.

But not quite enough to banish the wish that this imaginary romantic getaway could have been real.

"Brett," she began.

"We'd better go. There's a dog in the car."

"Of course."

She wasn't sure if she should feel relieved or disappointed that he'd cut off whatever ridiculous thing she'd probably been going to say. She told herself she should be glad. Whatever was going on needed to be resolved before anything else could be addressed. If there really was anything else, and it wasn't just some crazy short-term emotional explosion between two people who had simply been alone too long.

And she was spending way too much time twisting and turning this around. Every word didn't have to have some deeper meaning; every action wasn't a declaration. She seemed to have forgotten everything she'd ever learned from Jason about how men think and was projecting her own confused emotions on to the situation.

A half-hour drive north and a short wait, and they were on a different ferry route heading back. Midcrossing Brett's phone rang. The conversation was brief, and he confirmed to the caller they were on their way, so she guessed it was Rafe.

By the time they pulled up at the Foxworth building, she had her emotions well in check. And she smiled again at Cutter's delighted greeting to Rafe as the dark-haired man met them at the door.

"Thank you," she said to him. "Brett tells me my uncle likes the guy you sent to help."

Rafe nodded. "Thought he might. Tim is a former military field medic."

Sloan blinked. "What?"

"He was injured, pretty badly, but he's come back. He's well trained, and he's armed just in case."

"So he works for Foxworth?"

Rafe shook his head. "This is his kind of payback. Foxworth helped him find the family of a guy in his unit who didn't come home. One he'd tried to save and couldn't. There were some last words that needed to be passed on in person."

For a moment she simply stared. Then she said softly, "You know, I think I quite like you Foxworth people."

Rafe smiled, and it transformed his usual grim expression. "Back at you," he said. "Besides, all I had to do was mention your name and he couldn't jump fast enough."

Sloan was saved from responding to that when Cutter suddenly spun and headed for the door. He rose up and batted the door button with a paw, then wiggled through before the door had even swung open all the way.

Rafe's mouth quirked, and he pulled out his phone. For a moment nothing happened, but then an alert tone sounded. "Knew it," he said with a shake of his head.

"Are you sure that's really a dog?" Brett asked.

"Not at all," Rafe said. "I'm just glad he's on our side."

They followed Cutter inside. Rafe walked to the computer and hit two keys. Tyler Hewitt's face appeared on the wall monitor.

"Hey," the young man said. "Mrs. Burke," he added specifically, respectfully.

"Sloan, please," she said, a little surprised at his tone, given they'd met, albeit virtually, before.

"I'd say he's done some homework on you," Rafe said, his tone rather dry. "Tyler tends to like people who go up against the 'big bad.'"

"And more so if they win?" Brett suggested as he rejoined them.

"Yep," Tyler said cheerfully. "So, that car you asked about. Or rather, the trust. It owns several properties and vehicles. I'm sending a list."

"Good," Brett said. "Thanks."

"Sure. And something else…" Tyler hesitated.

"Go on," Rafe said.

"I found another link, down deep. It's crazy, but I think it may be the one that pulls all this together. What happened to Sloan's folks and Brett's friend and why Mead's involved."

"What link?" Rafe asked.

"The guy whose company built those houses up the hill? He had a big investor who helped him get started way back in the day, some thirty years ago. It was buried in some investment fund, but this guy was the main holder, so it was mostly his money. And that fund is the one connected to the trust that owns Mead's house."

"And who is this guy?" Brett asked.

"He sold out a few years ago. Apparently to run for office."

The image on the screen split, and a moment later a photograph appeared on the other half.

Brett sucked in an audible breath. "Damn."

"Indeed," Rafe agreed.

Sloan couldn't speak at all. She felt as if she'd been standing on a curb waiting to step down onto the street when suddenly a bottomless chasm opened up inches from her feet. She didn't know where it had come from or what it meant. But she knew that face.

Governor Bradford Ogilvie smiled munificently down upon them.

"This," Brett said grimly, "just got really thick."

Chapter 31

"I don't understand." Sloan sounded beyond puzzled. "How and why on earth would Ogilvie be involved?"

"Maybe he's not," Rafe said. "Other than having the misfortune of being connected to Mead."

Brett said nothing, but his mind was racing, turning over possibilities, discarding some, accepting others and batting down a persistent one that was so out there he couldn't even take it seriously.

"Maybe," Rafe said, "he's just a generous guy who likes to help his friends."

Sloan made a harsh scoffing sound. "Generous is the last thing Ogilvie is. Unless you can do something for him."

"Personal experience?" Rafe asked.

"Let's just say what I could do for him wasn't on my list of prices I was willing to pay."

Brett's racing thoughts came to an abrupt halt. "What?"

"So," Rafe said, "he's one of those."

"Let me get this straight," Brett said, keeping his voice flat with an effort. "He offered to help you if you'd…what, sleep with him?"

"Nothing that formal," she said, staring at the photo. "Just a quick servicing in his office would do."

Brett shifted his gaze to the picture, afraid if he kept looking at her and thinking about what she'd gone through, he'd lose it completely. "You bastard," he said under his breath.

And suddenly that preposterous idea didn't seem so outlandish anymore.

"Interesting," Rafe said. "I've seen that same look on Quinn's face."

Brett looked at the other man. "Have you?"

"We call it his take-no-prisoners look."

Brett let out a breath he hadn't realized he was holding. He knew what Rafe meant. Angie had always called it his slaying-dragons look. And that was exactly how he felt right now.

He looked back at the monitor, at that face with the benign trust-me smile. "Oh, yes," he said.

"Just out of curiosity, what did you tell him?" Rafe asked Sloan.

"I told him to forget it, that I was used to a bigger man, in all ways," Sloan said.

Brett blinked.

Rafe laughed. "Talk about hitting them where they live."

"I thought then about going to the opposition party," she said, "but I didn't want anybody involved in this only because of politics. I needed somebody who really believed."

"You found him in Senator Bienvenido. He's a good man."

"Yes. He is. One of the few exceptions that proves the rule. And his wife is a treasure. She helped me so much when I got down about it all."

"I'm glad," Brett said softly, the first time he'd been able to look at her and speak without anger bubbling up inside him since she'd told them what Ogilvie had suggested. She smiled at him, and that old feeling welled up. He did want to slay her dragons. She'd fought them so long and hard; it wasn't fair she should have to do it again. And

Brett was big on fair, even as he admitted life generally wasn't. He couldn't change that, so he just did what he could to even things out in his little corner.

He looked at Rafe. "Quinn mean that, about a job here?"

"Yes," Rafe answered, one brow lifting in query.

"Good. Because I may be blowing my current job out of the water soon."

Sloan made a tiny sound. He looked at her, saw the touch of color in her cheeks. Realized she was thinking of the jokes they'd made about that today. His jaw tightened as he fought down the heat that answered that blush.

"Brett, no," Sloan finally said, her eyes fixed on him, concern darkening the vivid green.

"Yes," he said flatly. "I'm not sure what this is yet, but it's something. And I'm going to find out what."

He glanced at Rafe, who was watching them thoughtfully. Almost wistfully, Brett thought. He remembered the man's reaction to first meeting Sloan. And thought that even the hardened former Marine could fall for a woman like Sloan. Hell, any man could. If Rafe had been another kind of man, Brett would have thought of him as competition. But even though he didn't know him that well, Brett knew Rafe Crawford would never think about poaching. And Sloan was his.

It hit him then, hard and deep. Somewhere, somehow, he'd not just broken the rule he'd lived by since Angie was murdered, he'd blown it up. All his years of caution and avoidance might as well never have happened.

"What exactly are you planning that could have you losing the badge?" Rafe asked.

"Pulling out all the stops." He met the man's gaze levelly. "Or rather, asking Foxworth to. I want everything Ty can find, and I don't care how he does it."

Rafe drew back slightly. His gaze flicked to Sloan, then

back to Brett. Knowledge and understanding gleamed in his eyes. And then he nodded. "All right. On what?"

"Who. Mead. Franklin. Ogilvie. His muscle, the guy I sent the photo of. The guy following us today. All of them and anybody else whose name keeps cropping up."

Rafe nodded. He leaned forward, tapped some keys on the laptop keyboard. It took a bit longer this time, but after a couple of minutes Ty was back on screen, a large cup of something in his hand.

"Sorry—I was refilling the caffeine."

"I still think you need an IV," Rafe said wryly.

"A direct drip? Great idea, but I hate needles. Some help would be cool, though. We've got a lot on the platter right now. Southeast has that eminent-domain thing going on, and we've got that gun case here, and Charlie's mulling an outside-the-country case."

"I've got an idea about that help," Rafe said. "But right now I'm afraid I need to dump some more on you."

"Hit me."

"Remember how you always say you could find anything and everything if we turned you loose?"

Ty straightened up, looking a bit like Cutter when he homed in on something. "Yeah?"

"Consider yourself off leash," Rafe said, and gave him the list.

"Hot damn," Ty said, his grin so wide it nearly filled the screen.

"Periodic reports, please. And the usual caveats," Rafe warned. "The less trail, the better."

"How about no trail at all?" Ty said, still grinning. "I am so on it."

The screen went dark. For a long moment they all sat in silence, Brett feeling as if he'd launched a long-range missile. Restless, thinking he might have truly started something that could end his career, Brett stood up. He looked at Cutter, who had been lounging rather indifferently as the humans charted their course. Brett supposed they must still be on track in the dog's mind, or he'd make it known. And the thought barely seemed absurd to him anymore.

"How about we go outside," he said to the animal, "and I'll throw that ball for you for a while?"

Cutter was on his feet in an instant. He raced to the back door, grabbed a tennis ball that was still almost yellow out of the basket that sat just inside and waited for Brett to catch up.

"I'd say I'll give you a shout when Ty comes back, but I'm sure he'll tell you," Rafe said drily.

"Two weeks ago I would have laughed at that," Brett said just as drily.

He'd found watching the agile dog chase down the balls he threw was more enjoyable than he ever would have thought. He varied the power, the trajectory and the direction, but Cutter never missed a beat. It wasn't enough to take his mind off Sloan, however. He wondered what she was doing, if she and Rafe were talking. The usually laconic man certainly seemed to open up with her around.

He made himself focus on the next throw, sending it as far as he could toward the trees. He wondered if the reason he enjoyed this so much was in part that this was such a normal doglike thing, playing fetch. Watching Cutter just being a dog kind of made those moments when he did things that were practically uncanny recede a bit.

After a while he shifted to his left arm, something he'd started doing of late just to keep things even. He'd always been reasonably strong, but he hadn't thrown a ball this much since high school baseball. They'd told him then he had a decent chance to go pro, but he'd only ever wanted to be a cop. Much to his father's dismay, although eventually the old man had come around, and now, in their retirement in Palm Springs, his parents seemed almost proud of him.

He wasn't sure how long they'd been at it when Sloan

stepped out the back door. Cutter, who'd been on his way from the longest throw Brett had managed so far, changed course and raced over to her. He dropped the ball at her feet, then crouched down in front, tail up and wagging, in the universal canine "Wanna play?" signal.

Sloan laughed at him. It was a great sound. She deserved to laugh, and often. And getting involved with a guy with his job wasn't likely to make that happen.

They'll think I've fallen in love or something.

You're too smart for that.

Too late.

The exchange had been haunting him since it had happened. Had she meant simply that it was too late for her to ever fall in love again, after Jason? It had to be, because the only other meaning was one he couldn't believe. Just because he'd been fool enough to lose control of things and find himself neck deep in a place he'd never intended to go ever again didn't mean that she'd done the same.

And deep in his gut he was afraid to wish that she had. Because if a woman like Sloan ever did fall in love, it would come with everything. She wouldn't do it halfway—it just wasn't in her nature. No, if she fell in love, she would do it completely, no holds barred. And he might not be able to live up to that. Not anymore. Because giving her everything made him vulnerable, gave people, gave life itself, the biggest weapon of all to use against him. Hadn't he learned that lesson the hard way?

He watched her pick up the ball and start walking toward him, Cutter dancing around her feet. Need and want sucked the air out of his lungs. Not just for her body, although that had been the most incredible experience of his life, but for her herself, for the Sloan who had such nobility, such courage, the Sloan who had fought so hard, had stood fast in the face of huge obstacles, implacably closed minds and ugly threats.

It would be an honor to be loved by such a woman.

And the last woman who had loved him had died for it.

Angie had never felt so close as she did at this moment. Hovering, like some specter sent to remind him of the folly of following this path.

But Angie had never been like that. She had been ever the optimist, ever hopeful and always encouraging others to take a chance, to grab at happiness wherever they found it.

Would she encourage him now? People who had known her had often told him so, that she would want him to move on, to be happy again. His response had always been he wasn't ready, until they had finally stopped saying it.

He still wasn't ready. Was he?

"Is your arm tired yet?" Sloan asked as she reached him.

He shook off the odd mood. Or tried to. "Not yet. I must be getting used to it."

"He certainly enjoys it."

"Yes."

Brilliant, Dunbar.

"My dad used to tease our dog. Pretend to throw it and then hide it behind his back."

Brett glanced at Cutter, who was watching them intently. "I'm not sure he'd fall for it."

She laughed. And again it washed over him, soothing, as if nothing bad could possibly matter in a world where a sound like that was possible.

And you're losing your mind.

"Besides," he said, feeling he had to get back on track, "it would feel like disloyalty somehow. Like he would know I was cheating and never quite trust me again."

He's a dog, idiot. You're standing here talking about—

A smile curving her lips, full of sweetness, not amusement, stopped his thoughts midstream.

"I find the fact that a dog's trust matters so much to you

incredibly wonderful, Brett Dunbar," she said, her voice so soft and husky he nearly grabbed her right then and there.

"God, Sloan," he choked out. He wanted nothing more than to take her home and sink into her soft warmth, where nothing else mattered and everything seemed possible.

Instead he took the ball and threw it again. A little wildly. It went off to one side, into some thick brush. Cutter gave him a sideways look, and Brett had the strangest feeling the dog sensed his inner turmoil, and more, understood. But then the dog trotted amiably off toward where the ball had disappeared and the sensation was gone. And seemed beyond silly in retrospect.

When he looked at Sloan, all the craziness came flooding back. "I—"

He stopped, hovering on the edge of saying something he couldn't take back. She just looked at him, not prompting, not prodding, just waited, and he thought again how much he appreciated that about her.

There was a rustling as Cutter emerged from the brush, the ball successfully rescued. But the moment he cleared the tangle, his head came up sharply, and the ball dropped, apparently no longer important. He ran to the back door of the building. Looked back at them.

Brett sighed in resigned acceptance. "Why do I feel like I'm the one being trained by the dog?"

"Because it's true?" Sloan suggested. But her tone echoed with that wonderful laughter, and he couldn't help smiling at her as they followed Cutter inside.

"Ty's got a first report," Rafe said, gesturing to where the one-time hacker was already on the monitor.

Brett heard the steady hum and clicks of a printer, obviously processing several pages.

"Fast," he said as he sat down.

"Just the beginning," Ty said, sounding as excited as

he had—Brett glanced at the time stamp in the corner of the screen—nearly three hours ago.

With an effort, he pushed all else out of his mind and concentrated on the stream of data. There was an answer to all this somewhere, and he was determined to find it.

Chapter 32

"Aren't you going to have to go back to work sometime?" Sloan asked as they got back into his car. Cutter settled easily into the backseat, seeming content after the long fetch session. Brett didn't answer until they were out on the road again.

"Technically, I have enough leave time coming to take about six months off."

She blinked. "Maybe you should take a vacation now and then."

"Never wanted to. Before."

The last word hung in the air between them. She tried not to read too much into it, but...what if he did mean it in the way her mind had leaped to?

"How about now?" The words were out before she could stop them, and wishing she could call them back was pointless. All she could do was not look at him. But still she felt his sideways glance.

"Depends who's asking."

She wished she had the nerve to ask, "And if it was me?" She swallowed, wondering where the woman who had once faced down men who strode the highest halls of power had gone. This couldn't be any harder, could it?

Yes, apparently it could, because the words wouldn't come. Why? What was the difference?

The answer came to her, as it sometimes did, in Jason's clear, steady voice. *That was facing the past, Sloan. And nothing you did could change what was. But this, this is your future. Grab it.*

But you—

Are dead. Never coming back, girl. You know that.

She waited for the inevitable sadness to well up, to swamp every other feeling, to make the next few minutes a battle not to tear up. It didn't come. It was there—she could feel it, low and deep inside—but the rising tide that overtook her so often at any thought of Jason didn't come.

She knew it was crazy, knew she was merely having this conversation with herself, but in truth she had known Jason so well she was probably projecting what he would actually have said if he'd been here.

And what would he have said about Brett Dunbar? This time the voice was so clear, so…Jason it made her breath catch.

He's a good man. An honorable man. I'd trust him, to do what I can't anymore. Be there for you.

The question is, does he want to be?

Give him a chance. He's in the same place you are.

Her breath caught again. Why hadn't she thought of that before? She should have realized when he'd told her about his wife. Just because it had been longer ago didn't mean he didn't still feel the way she did. Sad, aching, alone, conflicted.

"Guess that answers that," Brett muttered.

She snapped back to reality. Was startled to see they were halfway back to his place. "Sorry. I was thinking."

She drew in a deep breath. *I love you, Jason. I will always love you.*

She saw his grin, his encouraging nod, as clearly as if he were here. And oddly, she heard a soft whuff from Cutter that sounded almost like encouragement.

"About vacations," she said.

She saw his hands tighten on the steering wheel. Plunged on.

"And what you would say if it was me asking. After this is all over, I mean."

"Yes."

She blinked.

"I would say yes," he clarified.

She let out the breath that had backed up in her throat. "Then consider it asked."

She saw his hands ease their grip. "Consider it answered."

She felt as if she'd scaled Hurricane Ridge and now had the expanse of miles spread out before her. Miles of possibilities, possibilities she'd thought lost to her. All because a dog had taken an unexpected turn.

She glanced back at the dog in question, saw that he was looking at her. Something gleamed for a moment in the amber-flecked dark eyes, something bright and alive and uncannily intelligent. And in that moment it all seemed perfectly logical, even reasonable. There had been nothing wrong about that turn.

Thank you, she thought. And that gleam brightened, fire bright, and she had the oddest feeling he'd understood. She reached back and scratched at that spot behind his right ear. He sighed happily. And suddenly he was just a dog again, leaning into her hand, urging her not to stop the delightful touch.

Eventually, when the dog seemed content, she turned back to the front. And saw they were in a left-turn lane, not the lane that would take them back to his place.

"Where?" she asked as he slowed to a stop at the signal.

"Your aunt and uncle's."

Instinctive concern kicked through her. Did he think something was wrong? "Why?"

"Three reasons. I want to meet the guy Foxworth called in."

He didn't say he wanted to check the man out, but she heard it in his tone. And the simple fact that he wanted to be sure the man was up to the tasks of both helping and protecting her family made her feel a warmth and safety she'd thought she'd never feel again. She hadn't realized how weary she was of carrying it all alone until this man had stepped in and shouldered part of the burden.

"Thank you." She went on without explaining. "Number two?"

"I want to walk the property. I have too many ideas and no proof of any of them. But it begins and ends there, so I want to look at every inch of it."

"All right. And three?"

He looked at her then, steadily. "I think it's time I met your folks again. On a different footing."

She couldn't even begin to put in words how that statement made her feel. *An honorable man.* Whether it had been her own thoughts manifested in Jason's voice or Jason himself somehow reaching out to her, it was the truth. Brett Dunbar was an honorable man. While that might not matter to many in today's culture, it mattered to her. A lot.

And when they arrived and she saw Tim Deford, the former medic who had responded to Rafe's call, she knew she was looking at another one. She seemed to be finding a lot more of them since Brett Dunbar and Foxworth had come into her life.

The stocky, muscular man was three or four inches taller than she herself and had brown eyes that were warm and gentle. He was standing by as Uncle Chuck got into his recliner, watching carefully, letting the older man do it but clearly ready to move quickly if necessary. When he was settled, the man turned, spotted Sloan and drew himself up straight.

"It's an honor, Mrs. Burke."

He didn't salute as Rafe had, but his voice sounded exactly the same. She didn't know what she'd expected, but she could see no outward sign of whatever injury had sent him home. She had seen a slight tenting of his shirt at the small of his back and guessed that covered the weapon Rafe had promised.

"The honor is mine, Mr. Deford," she said. "Thank you for your service."

She was surprised to see the young man color slightly before he turned to Brett. "You must be Detective Dunbar. Rafe called, said you'd probably be coming."

Brett lifted a brow. "Did he?"

"He said you'd want to check me out." He didn't sound in the least perturbed. "Make sure I'm up to the job here. All of it," he added, holding Brett's gaze levelly. She realized he meant the defend part of his mission here. And despite the gentle eyes, she had the feeling he would be more than capable if necessary.

"Rafe is wise."

"He is that. He and I met in rehab." He reached down and rapped his knuckles on what was clearly not a natural leg. "He kept his. I didn't."

"I'm sorry," Sloan said.

Deford shrugged. "Old news. Rafe and I still argue over who's better off."

Sloan smiled. "So you called Foxworth when you needed help?"

He shook his head. "I called Rafe because he helped me get my head on straight after this," he said, gesturing at his leg. "I didn't even know about Foxworth. But," he added, looking at Sloan, "I would have done this anyway, even if they hadn't helped me. I welcome the chance to pay you back a little for what you did."

She didn't know what to say. She honestly thought she'd done only what anyone would do. It was everyone else who kept acting as if it was some extraordinary thing.

"Don't minimize it," Brett said to her. "He's right."

"Taking a real personal interest here, aren't you, Detective?"

It was the first time her uncle had spoken since he'd settled into his chair. Aunt Connie was off running an errand, so obviously she already felt comfortable leaving things in Tim Deford's care. Sloan could see why.

"Yes, sir," Brett said, turning to face her uncle. "Real personal, and real interest." She felt that bit of heat in her cheeks yet again. Wondered if she'd ever get over it. "That all right with you, sir?" Brett asked.

"About time," Uncle Chuck said gruffly.

"Good. Now, I have to ask you something. Do you have a copy of the boundary map for your property?"

"Of course I do. It's in my file cabinet out in the garage. Sloan knows where it is."

"Let me change into boots. Then I'll show you," she said.

In the garage, with Cutter now out of the car and with them, she dug out the plot map. They spread it out on the hood of her uncle's big sedan. The boundary was, as Sloan had said, roughly in the shape of an L, with the house and yard at one end of the long leg, the street where the leak had been at the other and the shorter leg protruding some distance westward.

"I didn't realize it went that far over," he said, looking at the western boundary.

"It used to be a rectangular plot, but Uncle Chuck's grandfather sold a piece out of the side during the Great Depression. But he kept that top edge. Uncle Chuck said he thought the main highway was going to go in there, and he wanted the frontage."

"Sounds like a smart guy."

"Well, except for guessing where the state would put in roads, yes," Sloan said with a grin.

He chuckled. "So there's nothing up there?"

She shook her head. "They've left it natural. There are some beautiful old trees up there. It hasn't been logged in a very long time." Her brow furrowed. "I actually haven't been over in that part for quite a while. It's kind of difficult to get through. Lots of underbrush and a couple of blackberry thickets that are impassable."

Cutter barked. They both looked.

"Not impassable for you, huh?" Sloan asked the dog.

"Probably not," Brett agreed with a crooked smile. "Shall we?"

She would have much rather talked about what the future held for them, but by now she knew him well enough to know that in his own way, he was like the dog in his determination. He wanted the truth, and he'd pull every thread he came across to find it if he had to.

Chapter 33

"Damn." Brett yanked his hand back, knowing he'd gotten nailed again by one of the fierce blackberry thorns. He glanced at Sloan, who said nothing. She didn't have to. Her carefully neutral expression said it all.

"Okay, okay, you were right," he muttered. "I should have borrowed your uncle's gloves. Not that anything short of armor would stand up to these things."

"Well, you did find treasure," she said.

"What? The third old tire? Yeah, one more and I'll refit my car."

She laughed. His irritable mood vanished. That easily. At just the sound of that light, beautiful laugh. *You are a goner, Dunbar.*

They trekked onward. They'd spent three hours up behind the house, turning up nothing except the fact that his temporary repair had held and the puddle had been reduced to a barely wet spot. Sloan had shown him the old apple tree she used to climb as a kid and the cavelike place beneath a bent madrone tree she'd claimed as her own.

"I came here a lot in the beginning," she'd said, staring down at the place her adult self no longer fit. "I knew they hated to see me cry, so I came up here when I couldn't help it."

And he hadn't been able to help himself at the quiet, reflective words. He'd put his arms around her and simply held her for a long moment. She'd leaned against him as if she welcomed it, and the thought that he could actually give her comfort, even over an ache so long past, warmed him in a way he'd not felt in a very long time.

Although there was still ground to cover there, they had decided to move over and tackle the top of the upside-down L, where the trees were the thickest, while they still had good light.

"Can't even see the house from here," Brett said.

"We knew they couldn't build easily here because of the slope," she said. "But with the grading they did for the proposed highway, it would be the easiest way to bring in equipment and trucks."

"Starting with a bulldozer for these," Brett said, wincing as yet another thorn grabbed and tore at his arm.

So far they'd found the three old discarded tires, a rusted-out burn barrel overtaken by vegetation and, oddly, a flattened soccer ball in this section. They kept on, although Brett was beginning to feel this was one of his less brilliant ideas. It was rough going, and he figured he was slowly bleeding to death by droplets from all the thorn scratches he'd gathered. On his life list of thankless jobs, this was definitely a contender. Or would have been had it not been for the fact that simply being with Sloan moved it out of that category.

"Thank you," he said after a while longer.

She looked at him. "For what?"

"For not asking if I have the slightest idea what we're looking for," he answered with a wry grimace.

She lifted a brow. "I assumed we were looking for anything that doesn't fit. Doesn't belong. Isn't natural."

Just that easily, she put it into words that made sense. "Exactly," he said.

The trees were getting thicker as they went, some with a gap of only a yard or so between them. They brushed past a large fern, and he stopped. The explosion of feathers that lay on the ground told them some small gray bird had likely met its end here.

"Welcome to Mother Nature," Sloan said with a sigh.

"She is what she is. Emotionless. But she's also why it all works."

"Except for us," she said, sounding a bit wistful. "We fight it, get tangled up with emotions and our need to have reasons for everything."

He turned to look at her. "Are you saying you want to stop?"

She studied him for a moment. "If I was, what would you say?"

"Then stop. You don't need to get any deeper into this."

"But you won't stop."

"No."

"You're like Cutter with that ball—you'll chase it until you drop."

He glanced at the dog, who was nosing the scattered feathers with interest. "Ordinarily I might object to being compared to a dog. But in this case it just might be a compliment."

Cutter's head came up sharply. For a moment Brett thought it was because they'd been talking about him, but he wasn't looking at them. He was staring into the thickest stand of trees. His entire body was tense, his tail stood out straight behind him, and his ears were nearly flat to his head.

"Someone?" Sloan asked.

"I don't think so," Brett said. "He's not growling."

"But he's got something," she said as the dog suddenly bolted between two trees.

"I'd say," Brett agreed.

They followed, although it took a bit more effort on their part to work their way through the brush and ferns that grew across most of the floor of this grove. They lost sight of Cutter as he pushed farther up the hill.

"Is that still their property?" he asked when he finally caught sight of the dog again, digging at something up in the distance.

"I think so. But we're about as far as you can get from the house and still be on it." She pointed. "Up there is where they were originally going to put the road. They did the surveys, even cleared out some places, but something happened and they changed the route."

It took them another minute or two to get to where Cutter was, about midway between two tall evergreens. He didn't know what they were, only that they were very different kinds of trees, one with long draping branches trailing green that reminded him of juniper, the other bare of any foliage at all until its top burst out into the clear a good fifty-plus feet above them.

The dog didn't even glance at them. He was intently focused on whatever he was digging at.

"Well, at least it's not a puddle this time," Sloan said.

"Thank goodness for that. I don't relish the thought of another shower with a mud-caked dog."

She gave him a sideways glance, then looked quickly away. He wasn't sure what her expression meant, but it kept him from teasingly adding, "Now, with you, on the other hand…" He wondered if the same thought had occurred to her. He hoped so. But it was probably best he not say that just now.

They watched, Brett wondering if the dog was going to demand assistance again. But he seemed focused simply on his digging.

"Are you going to miss him? When they come back, I mean?"

He glanced at the dog. "Yeah," he admitted. "He's a… big personality."

She smiled. "It was nice of you to offer to watch him."

"It would have been," he agreed. "But I didn't." He nodded at the dog. "He decided."

He explained then about what had happened after the wedding. How Cutter himself had changed the plans. When he finished, she was staring at the dog. But she was smiling.

"I'm glad you didn't tell me that until now," she said. "I might not have believed it before."

"I know that feeling," he said. "There's a lot of things I wouldn't have believed about him before."

There was a rustle in the trees above them, and he glanced up. It took him a moment to spot the squirrel, who apparently wasn't happy about their presence. He wasn't actually chattering at them, but he looked as if he might start at any moment.

Probably start throwing things at us. He—

Sloan sucked in a sharply audible breath, almost a gasp. His attention snapped back to her.

"Brett," she whispered.

But she wasn't looking at him. She was staring at Cutter. Or rather, where he was digging. He shifted his gaze.

"Damn."

He took a step closer. Just to be sure, although he already was. He almost couldn't think, the pieces were crashing into place so swiftly in his head.

He crouched beside the hole. Pulled Cutter back.

"It's all right, boy. I've got it now. Don't dig anymore."

The dog, somewhat surprisingly given how he'd been going at it, obeyed. Which was a good thing, Brett thought grimly, since all of a sudden they were dealing with a crime scene.

Cutter had uncovered a hand.

Chapter 34

"This changes everything," Brett said, reaching for his phone.

"I know," Sloan answered, looking away from the hole. She reached down and stroked Cutter's head. The dog was sitting quietly, letting out only a brief whine, as if he was distressed by what he'd found. She'd heard search-and-rescue dogs suffered stress when they found only bodies and no survivors, so she supposed it was quite possible.

Sloan shivered, although she hadn't been cold up to now. The thought made her get out her own phone to look at her weather app. "It's supposed to rain tonight. Heavy."

He nodded. "I'll need to get the crime-scene guys out here fast."

"Brett?"

He paused before he could hit what was obviously a speed-dial number.

"Is this it? The reason for all this?"

He didn't pretend not to understand, nor did he put her off. But then, he never did. "No proof of that. Yet. But…"

She knew what he was saying. That his instincts were saying what hers were, that this indeed was the reason behind all of this. He turned back to his phone, which rang. He looked at the screen, then answered.

"Rafe. Things just got impossibly complicated." He listened for a moment. "Doesn't surprise me," he said then. "Especially right now. Your four-footed buddy just found a body."

He gave Rafe the basics, listened for a moment, then was done. Before he made his call, he looked at her.

"I take that back. There's one thin thread and a lot of circumstantial links."

"What doesn't surprise you?" she asked, guessing it was the thread.

"Mr. Muscle has a record."

"Rams Emmet?"

He nodded. "Manslaughter, ten years ago. Charges were dropped when the eyewitness disappeared. They investigated for a possible link but couldn't prove anything. Body was never found."

She stared back at him. Then, slowly, shifted her gaze to the makeshift grave.

She heard him calling out the necessary responders but wasn't really tuned in to what he was saying. She was too busy trying to keep her mind from getting ahead of the facts.

One thin thread, Brett had said. Not proof. But he thought like a cop. He had to, had to think about going to court and proving the case. Had to think about clever lawyers and judges with opinions that were supposed to be kept out of the system but too often weren't.

She only had to think like a person who knew from long, sad experience about smoke and fire and the lust for power that turned some people into dark and evil things.

"Who do you think it is?" she asked when he'd finished his calls.

"If we're really lucky, there will be ID in there."

"Would they really leave that?"

"Probably not. I said really lucky."

Something about the way he was staring at the body told her.

"You know," she whispered.

"I don't know anything," he said.

"You mean you can't prove it. Yet."

"For a cop that's just about the same thing."

She knew it was a jump, but she asked anyway. "Do you think it's that eyewitness?"

He looked up, then at her. "Careful," he said. "You get set on an idea, you end up fitting the facts to that theory instead of letting them lead you to the truth."

"But you have an idea," she said. She was certain of it.

"And I'm keeping it on a leash," he said. "For now. At least until we get an ID on this victim." He glanced back down the hill. "Call the house. Tell Tim we're probably dealing with a murder. Not a fresh one, by the looks of it, but still…"

Tell him so he can be on alert, to protect your family. He didn't say the words, but she heard them anyway. She made the call, half expecting to get questions she had no answer for. But it turned out she was worried for nothing. Deford listened to what Brett had said, answered simply, "Got it," and hung up.

Cutter growled. Sloan's breath caught as she felt an electric sort of shock jolt through her fingertips where she'd been stroking the dog. The dog had gone rigidly alert. He stretched his head out toward the area she'd pointed out earlier as the original site for the highway. She saw his nose flexing as he sucked in whatever scent had set him off. He looked at them, then back, as if he desperately wanted to break into a run but something was holding him back. As if he was torn between wanting to race toward whatever had caught his attention and putting himself between them and whatever it was.

Brett reached for Cutter, and the fingers of his free hand curled around the dog's collar.

"Easy, boy," he was saying softly as he stared in the direction the dog was looking. "I got the message. Stay with me now. I may need you."

Amazingly, the dog settled. The growls continued but lower. His head moved slightly, as if he could see what was out there, could see it moving. The growl became a snarl. All thought of Cutter being merely an exceptionally clever house pet vanished at the sight of those bared teeth. She glanced at Brett. He was reaching for his weapon. This man was, in his own way, as much a protector and a warrior as Jason had been.

You're doomed, girl. This is the only kind of man for you. Get used to it.

Cutter exploded into a fury of barking and snapping. The dog clearly wanted fervently to be free. Brett set himself against the pull. And then froze.

A tall blond man stepped out of the shadow of the trees. His own lethal-looking semiautomatic pistol was pointed at them. Suppressed, she thought, then gave herself an inward shake. What a ridiculous time to remember Jason's explanation that it was a suppressor, not a silencer, because silencing a weapon was impossible.

Ramsey Emmet. As if speaking of him had conjured him out of thin air.

Her gut contracted, and it took everything in her not to let her knees give way.

"Hands," the man ordered.

"Well, well," Brett said, ignoring the command and keeping his hand on the gun behind his back. "I was just talking to someone about your rap sheet."

The man frowned. "That's sealed." Then, clearly irritated, he ordered again. "Hands, Detective. One of them holding your weapon by the barrel."

"Manslaughter, eh? Short step from that to murder."

Sloan couldn't be positive from her angle, but she thought the man's gaze flicked to the grave for an instant. And he didn't protest or pretend he had no idea what Brett was talking about.

"He was in the way," he said dismissively.

Something suddenly occurred to her at his words. Brett had said the manslaughter case was ten years ago. He'd also said this wasn't fresh. But while she was no forensics expert, this body didn't look as if it had been in the ground for ten years.

"In whose way?" Brett asked. He sounded so calm, she thought, as if he had guns pointed at him every day. *Idiot. The possibility* is *there every day.*

"None of your business. Mead's a fool. And now you're in my way."

Was he saying the person in the grave had been in someone else's way? Her mind made a crazy leap. She had no love for politicians on any side of the aisle, not after her sojourn in DC, but this seemed out there even to her. But looking into this man's flat reptiiian eyes, she could believe it.

And he worked for the man who would likely not have been sitting in the governor's mansion had his surging opponent not quit and vanished.

Her mind raced, digging for memories of that election campaign. Had Evans ever really had a press conference or spoken to anyone? All she could recall was a published statement about his withdrawal from the race. As far as she could remember, he'd never been seen again.

She couldn't stop herself from looking at the body then. She barely suppressed a shudder. It was crazy, but her stomach was knotting, and that little voice in her mind was screaming this was it.

"Third and last time—hands where I can see them," Emmet said. "Now, Detective."

"I don't think so," Brett said. "Are you really stupid enough to kill a cop?"

"I know something about you, too, Dunbar. You're a man who was on the edge of cracking not so long ago. No one will be surprised that you finally worked up the nerve to end your miserable life."

Brett didn't react. Sloan wondered if it was true, if he'd been that lost after his wife's murder. If his understanding reaction to the possibility Rick was contemplating suicide had been because he'd once been close himself.

"Going to be hard to sell that if you shoot me from ten feet away," was all he said.

Emmet shifted his aim. To her. "How about this, then? This bitch has certainly made enough very important people angry that everyone will think she was vanished by them. Do you really want to be the reason another woman dies?"

Brett didn't wince outwardly, but Sloan knew him well enough now to know that Emmet couldn't have said anything worse. After a split second Brett shrugged. But he took his hand off the weapon at his back, leaving it still holstered.

"I'll still take you out," he said.

"So you care nothing about the woman you seduced?"

Brett flicked her a look. There was a warning in his glance, and she stayed put and stayed quiet. Jason had always told her the smartest thing anyone could ever do was let the people you trusted knew their jobs do them.

She trusted Brett Dunbar.

"That was just to keep her out of Mead's way," he said with a shrug, as if she'd been nothing more than a task at hand. "I could drop her like a hot rock and never care."

Something about the slight emphasis he put on the word *drop* snagged Sloan's attention. Followed, oddly, by Aunt Connie's words echoing in her mind. *Sometimes the only weapon you have is making people think you're less than you are.*

She was afraid. Not for herself but for him. And for Cutter, who was straining to get loose, no doubt to go for the man's throat. It went against the grain, against her very nature.

But she did it anyway.

She let out the most dramatic, heart-rending wail she could manage. "You can't mean that," she moaned. "You told me you loved me."

She staggered back a step, then another, then dropped to her knees, burying her face in her hands as if her heart were truly broken. And to hide the fact that she wasn't quite able to manufacture the tears to complete the image. She could still see between her fingers but thought she wouldn't hear a thing over the hammering of her heart.

Cutter erupted again into furious barking and snarling. He twisted and pulled forward. Brett stumbled, the dog pulling him off balance. She saw the instant when he let go of the dog's collar. Saw Emmet's aim shift to the dog, apparently fearing an attack.

Cutter raced right past him into the trees. Startled, Emmet's gaze tracked the dog's path. Brett lunged, so quickly she knew the stumble had been a feint. He took Emmet low and hard. As they hit the ground, Emmet's weapon fired. A little scream escaped her.

Sloan scrambled to her feet. The two men were rolling, twisting in the dirt. Emmet struggling to bring the weapon to bear. Brett struggling to stop him. Her heart skipped when she saw a wet red stain on Brett's shirt. For an instant all she could do was stare, all her old nightmares roaring back to life at the thought of a man she loved down and bleeding, maybe dying. She swore silently, looking around for something, anything, she could use as a weapon.

Brett was on top, his hands around Emmet's wrists. Trying to keep him from turning the weapon. Unable to reach for his own.

A weapon.

She darted over, fumbled at Brett's back for a moment. Then she had it, his pistol sliding out into her hands.

She dropped to her knees and jammed the barrel against Emmet's left ear. He hissed. "Bitch," he yelled.

"If you have any doubts about whether I'll shoot," she said through clenched teeth, "remember who and what my husband was. He taught me well."

"I'd believe her if I were you," Brett said, as casually as if he hadn't been wrestling for his life with a killer. "Drop the gun."

Emmet hesitated.

"I won't even blink when your brains splatter all over me," Sloan said.

Emmet went still.

And then Cutter was there, adding a warning snarl to the proceedings.

"Or maybe we'll just let him rip your throat out, as he's dying to do," Brett said.

It seemed to be that thought that tipped the scales. Brett wrested the weapon from Emmet's hand and got to his feet.

"Watch him," he ordered Cutter. The dog growled and took up a position within easy reach of that throat Brett had threatened. At his gesture, Sloan got to her feet as well, but she kept Brett's gun trained on him. Until Brett stepped over and took it out of her hands.

One of his hands was streaked with blood. Up close the blood was an ugly blotch on his white shirt. She stared at it. Felt a numbness start to creep over her. Was barely aware she was shaking, violently.

"It's his, not mine," Brett said gently.

She heard the words. Couldn't respond. Couldn't even react.

Because it could have just as easily gone the other way.

He reached out to her. Instinctively she jerked away, away from the blood, away from the possibilities.

This time when she went to her knees, the tears came freely.

Chapter 35

"Is she going to be all right?"

Brett glanced toward the closed door of the bathroom, where Sloan had retreated as soon as they'd arrived at Foxworth. It had been a long, exhausting process that had eaten the rest of the day, all night and into the morning, sorting things out.

"I don't know," he said honestly, looking back at Rafe.

The man had shown up at the scene within a few minutes, saying Deford had called him as soon as he'd heard the shot fired, since he knew his duty was to stay put and protect the Days. Although he had to be tired after essentially being on night watch, Rafe had been a strong presence, helping where he could but careful not to trespass on the official turf. He'd arranged for Sloan's aunt and uncle to escape to a hotel for a few days, knowing there would be a media storm coming. It was bad enough to have law enforcement tramping all over the place without adding reporters and photographers all on probably the biggest story of the century in the entire state. He'd also arranged for protection for the property after one of those zealous media types had turned burglar, breaking into the house apparently looking for some way to connect the innocent residents to the scandal.

Foxworth to the core, Brett had thought at the time. And had tried not to think about how Sloan had shied away from him but had leaned on Rafe as he took her from the scene back to the house.

"What about you?" Rafe asked.

"I'm fine. Emmet is the only one who got hurt, and that was his own fault."

"As it should be. Although I'm thinking the world would be a better place if you'd shot him."

"He would have shot Sloan. I could see it in his eyes. And I'm no sniper—no guarantee I could have prevented that trigger twitch."

Rafe held up a hand. "Not questioning your decision. You were obviously right. Just wishful thinking. Although it may be just as well if he's talking. I'm guessing the tremor is still rattling the halls of power down in the capitol."

"As it should be," Brett echoed.

"Indeed."

Brett looked toward the bathroom again. Sloan hadn't wanted to go home. She hadn't wanted to go to his place. In fact, she had barely spoken to him since the moment she'd gone to her knees in the dirt next to the body.

"I'm a little surprised the sight of a little blood rattled her so much," he said. "She's tougher than that."

"Maybe it's just reaction," Rafe said. "Nobody expects to find a body essentially in their backyard, let alone have the killer show up, ready to kill again."

"Maybe."

"Then again," Rafe said, "considering how you looked, maybe she was just rattled because she thought it was you that was hurt."

"But she knew almost immediately I wasn't."

"Women," Rafe said, "have some complicated thought patterns."

"I've noticed," Brett said with a grimace. He shifted his gaze to Cutter, who had taken up a station outside the bathroom door.

"He knows something's wrong," Rafe said. "He's been on her like glue."

"Yes. The minute the cavalry arrived and took custody of Emmet, he shifted to her."

"She'll be all right. She's a strong woman."

"Who's been through too much already in her life." Far too much, Brett thought.

"That's why she's tough," Rafe said.

"Yeah," Brett agreed glumly. On the word, Sloan finally opened the door. Cutter scrambled to his feet. She bent to greet him. The dog stayed with her, maintaining contact by leaning against her as they came back into the room. Brett remembered how soothing the dog's touch could be and hoped it was working for her the same way.

"Have you spoken to your folks?" Rafe asked her. She nodded. "How are they?"

"Now that it's over, they seem a little excited by it all." She sounded almost normal, Brett noted with no small amount of relief. Tired, yes, but her voice didn't have that distant sound, as if she'd retreated somewhere inside that he couldn't reach. "It helps that they never liked the governor to begin with," she added.

"Lot of that going around," Rafe said with a slight smile.

"Thanks for helping them get out of the chaos."

"What we do," Rafe said with a shrug. Then he eyed Brett curiously. "Have they ID'd the body?"

"Not officially yet." Rafe had been there when they'd eliminated the possibility it was the missing witness from Emmet's case ten years ago based on the simple fact that the witness had been female and this body was male. "But," Brett went on, aware on some level of just how much he'd come to trust this man by the slightness of the qualm he felt divulging what had not been made public yet, "the man had some metal pins in his right ankle, from a bad break at some point."

Rafe raised a brow. "That should narrow it down a bit."

"Yes. Especially since that detail matches Ken Evans."

Rafe straightened. "Wait a minute…the missing candidate? The one who supposedly had a mental breakdown?"

"And vanished. Yes."

"Son of a—" He stopped with a glance at Sloan, then looked back at Brett. "That's no tremor in the capitol—that's an off-the-scale earthquake."

"Exactly. The fallout's going to be thick and fast."

"How the hell did he end up buried there?" Rafe asked.

"Not sure," Brett said. "Except we think it might be because they were familiar with the spot from when the highway was originally planned and surveyed for."

"Hmm." Rafe rubbed a hand over his unshaven jaw. "And you figure he showed up now because you triggered something running that license plate?"

"I think the plan was to finally just move the body. I think they realized Sloan wasn't going to give up."

He looked at her then. She was focused on Cutter, who had jumped up on the sofa beside her and plopped his head in her lap. She was petting him slowly, gently, looking at the dog's dark head as he stared up at her intently.

Whatever magic you have, dog, work it on her, please. She needs it. Even if I don't know why, I know that.

"Even if they thought you had her under control?"

Brett glanced at Sloan. She didn't even look up. He smothered a sigh and answered Rafe.

"I don't think Emmet ever bought that I was looking to jump onto their bandwagon."

"Then he's a better judge of character than I gave him credit for," Rafe said.

Brett didn't know what to say to that, so instead he said, "Speaking of credit, your furry friend there managed the perfect distraction. If he hadn't dashed right past Emmet, drawing his attention, I never would have gotten the jump on him."

"He's right," Sloan crooned to the dog, still avoiding looking up. "You done good, Cutter-dog."

At least she was listening and acknowledged he was here, Brett thought. Even if it was indirectly. He considered trying to draw her in now that she'd spoken but somehow couldn't find the words. So he went back to Rafe.

"But I still don't get it. I would have sworn if he got loose he'd go right for the guy's throat. I know he wanted at him. I was afraid I'd have to explain to Hayley and Quinn how I let their dog get shot."

Rafe shrugged. "I've given up trying to explain how he always manages to do just the right thing."

Brett looked over at dog and woman. And wished silently he had a bit of Cutter's knack right now. Because he had no idea what the right thing was.

As he laced up his running shoes, Brett was seriously considering taking up another form of exercise. Something that required more concentration, that allowed less time for thinking. Because right now all this thinking was going to drive him insane.

He'd thought sticking to the alternate route would help, but it didn't. Every day it just made him more aware of why he was running here instead of…there.

I can't do this, Brett.

Do what?

I can't deal with loving a man who puts his life at risk every day. Not again.

The kick of joy at hearing her say she loved him had died a bitterly quick death. It had done no good to point out that in this quiet north-woods place what had happened was so rare as to be almost unheard of. Or that as a detective, he usually came in after the fact and rarely had to face the kind of thing that had happened that day.

And after that he had stopped. She was in such pain—it

was so clear on her face, in those beautiful eyes—that he couldn't bear putting any more pressure on her.

When she had decided she wanted to join her aunt and uncle at the resort hotel Foxworth had arranged, he'd been almost glad, hoping some time away with her beloved family out from under all this would somehow bring her back to herself. He missed her with an ache he could barely stand but kept telling himself it was for the best. It would give him time to think himself. To ponder life's oddities and the weight of difficult decisions.

He hadn't expected to not hear a word from her since.

He hadn't realized those last words had been goodbye.

Long days had dragged by, and all the chaos at work, all the huge mess that had come down after the positive ID on the body had come in, hadn't been enough to distract him from her absence.

Hell, they'd practically brought down the damned state government, and it still wasn't enough to distract him from her absence.

The embattled governor was still fighting, but he'd thrown Harcourt Mead under the bus the minute he realized the way the wind was blowing. And Mead had turned it all on the hapless Franklin, the lowest man on their twisted ladder and the only one with a witness against him, the bald-headed man he'd hired to follow them.

The only good thing Brett could see to come out of that was that Rick didn't just have his job back, he had Franklin's job. And Caro had an appointment to fly to Saint Louis and meet with Tyler Hewitt as soon as classes let out this term, and Brett had a feeling the Foxworth tech genius was going to have the help he needed soon.

So everybody's life was getting straightened out. The bad guys were in muck to their necks and still sinking, the good guys were getting their lives back, Hayley and Quinn would be back soon, retake custody of Cutter, and his own life would return to the quiet, isolated thing it had always been.

Because obviously Sloan wanted no part of him or his life. At least, not as it was.

And there he was, back to difficult decisions.

"Come on if you're coming, dog," he called out to Cutter.

The dog had, strangely, been standing at the window beside the front door all morning, staring out. Twice Brett had gone over to see if there was something there but had seen only the empty expanse of the front yard. He'd had to quash the sudden hope that it was Sloan, even though he knew if it had been, Cutter would have reacted differently.

Amazing how the dog seemed so easy to read now.

"Got me trained quick," he muttered to the dog as he trotted over and waited politely at the door. "Happy I always do what you want, are you?"

He remembered those words when they reached the bottom of the hill and Cutter turned right. The old route.

"Hold it, buddy. Not going that way."

The dog ignored him. And instead of stopping and waiting until Brett caught up, as he usually did, the dog just kept going. There was not, it seemed, going to be any discussion about this.

He had to hustle to catch up. He probably should have put the leash on at the door, but the dog had been so cooperative about the new route this week that he had quit worrying about it after the first few days and just focused on not collapsing during the extra mile he'd added.

It was soon clear where Cutter was headed. So clear that when he turned to head up the hill, Brett wasn't even surprised. It didn't matter, he told himself. They weren't there. Sloan wasn't there. Even the media had dwindled away, their focus now on the political fallout. Surely he could run past the damned empty house without losing it.

Refusing to admit he couldn't, he picked up the pace.

Going up the hill, he challenged himself not to slow, putting every bit of his concentration into holding steady, working hard to draw in enough oxygen to do it. It was tough, but he did it. Maybe adding that extra mile did it, he thought as he reached the turn at the top. It hadn't done what he'd hoped, helped him sleep better at night, but maybe it had upped his condition a little. Maybe yet another mile would—

Sloan's car was in the driveway.

He slowed. Stopped. Stared.

Cutter was already racing up onto the big covered porch. As if he'd known she was back. Brett remembered his odd behavior, the staring out the window this morning. The window that, as the crow flew, faced this direction.

Cutter started to bark. Loudly. Jolted out of his shock, Brett winced; it was early for a Saturday. This was not going to be appreciated by the neighbors.

"Damn it," he muttered, and started to run.

The door opened. Sloan stepped out and crouched beside Cutter, trying to quiet him. He stubbornly continued to bark. She straightened as Brett reached the porch steps. Brett knew she couldn't really have gotten more beautiful in less than a week, but he would have sworn she had.

Cutter finally quieted. "I'm sorry," Brett said, sounding stiff even to himself. "We've been going a different way, but this morning he got away from me and was dead set on coming this way. I don't know why he was barking. He never does that."

And you never babble. So shut up.

He did. He just stood there, staring at her, trying not to think. Sloan said nothing. What was there to say? he wondered.

I can't do this, Brett.

Hadn't that been clear enough? He should be glad, shouldn't he? Hadn't he sworn never to walk this path again? Never to give fate such a deadly weapon to use against him?

So walk away. She's doing what's best for both of you. Honor that.

"Come on, dog," he said. "Leave her in peace."

Cutter looked from him to Sloan. But the only move he made was to take two quick steps to stand behind her. Hiding? That didn't seem like the nervy dog at all. Wanting Brett to come get him? And thus end up within inches of the one woman he would throw away all that hard-earned wisdom for?

And then it hit him. He wasn't hiding. Or luring, at least not completely.

He was planted squarely in front of the door, cutting off her retreat.

"Cutter." The dog just looked at him. He let out a compressed breath, closed his eyes for an instant, reaching deep down for steadiness. "Excuse me," he said politely. "I'll get him out of your way."

He started up the steps. Cutter made a low sound, not a growl or a snarl but more a rumbling of warning.

"I think he just said, 'The hell you will.'"

Brett stopped. Her voice had that low, husky note that drove him wild. And he could smell her, that sweet, clean scent that was soap, shampoo and Sloan. His body reacted fiercely, quickly, and he wondered where the hell he'd gotten the idea he could be this close to her again and stand to walk away.

"Sloan," he breathed, unable to help himself.

"Brett, I—"

She lurched forward against his chest. Instinctively he caught her.

"You rat!" she exclaimed, and he let go, stung. He took a step back. Started to turn, ready to head down the steps, to get away. Realized that somehow Cutter had moved without him realizing, had gotten behind him. Cutting off his retreat.

"I meant him," Sloan said rather urgently. "He pushed me."

"Sorry," he said again, hating that he sounded as if he hadn't yet recovered from the push up the hill. "I know I'm all sweaty."

"I like you sweaty."

Her gaze darted away, as if she'd only realized after she'd said it just how that sounded. It did nothing to cool him down.

"I thought you didn't like me at all."

"Don't be stupid." She sounded exasperated now. "Sometimes you are such a guy."

"Guilty," he admitted.

A heavy sigh from Cutter made them both look at the dog. With an air so resigned it would have been comical had Brett been in a better mood, he nudged Sloan gently a step to her right. Then he walked over and nudged Brett in the same direction. Less gently, he noticed. And then he repeated the process. Herding them toward the porch bench.

"I guess we're supposed to sit down," she said.

Cutter woofed, sharply.

She gave in, went the rest of the way and sat down. Satisfied with her action, the dog turned to Brett. Feeling more than a little manipulated and fairly certain he wouldn't get past the dog without a fight, he followed. He sat at the other end of the bench, giving Sloan as much space as there was. Cutter plopped down on the porch between them, close enough that neither could move without having to get past him.

"I wonder just how far he'd go to get his way," he muttered.

"I've seen those fangs. They're pretty persuasive when he wants them to be."

"So Emmet found out."

"Yes. I heard they found the body of the witness."

He nodded. "He made a deal to take the death penalty off the table. Told them where he'd buried her. And admitted he'd buried Evans. Stopped short of saying he'd killed him, though."

"So he's turning on his boss?"

Brett nodded again. "His version is Evans's death was as much accident as anything when they tried to scare him into dropping out. After they buried him, Ogilvie and Mead made a devil's bargain. Mead was to stay put as administrator and make sure that property was never touched in return for Ogilvie's help later, when he launched his own political career. And he sucked Franklin in on it."

"With the house and who knows what else," Sloan said.

"Yes. They never wanted to move the body. They were afraid of getting caught. That's why all the stalling with the water leak and the fictitious land study. Besides, Mead wanted to handle it personally so he could tell Ogilvie it was dealt with."

"To show he was ready to be moved up?"

"Exactly. Bad guys often trip over their own ego." He studied her for a moment. She could take it, he thought. "But then Emmet realized you were involved."

"Me?"

"He didn't know it was you until Mead let your name slip that day. He and Ogilvie both knew you would never give up. And that you were too high profile to kill. So they knew they had to do it."

"So Emmet really was there to move the body." She let out an audible breath. "And he came then because they thought we were in Seattle."

He nodded. "We really did just get in his way. But the whole house of cards is coming down now."

"Good."

"How are your aunt and uncle?"

"Good. Uncle Chuck is feeling better. He wants to get home and into the garden. They'll be coming back tomorrow. I just came early to open up the house."

"Oh. Well. Good."

She nodded. And for a moment the silence just hung there like a dark cloud heavy with rain.

"Sloan—"

"Brett—"

When she stopped as they spoke simultaneously, he jumped in to cut off her starting again, before she said anything irrevocable.

"I'll quit," he said abruptly.

"What?"

"If the problem is my job, I'll quit."

She stared at him. "You can't quit."

"I can. I'll find something else. Foxworth maybe."

"But you're a cop. To the bone."

He turned, faced her. "I love you. To the bone."

If he'd wished for the vow immediately returned, he didn't get it. She colored, and he held his breath, hoping she wasn't about to tell him it had all been a mistake, that she hadn't meant it, that she'd just been off balance, that she could never love anyone after Jason.

It was another moment before she spoke. "After that day, all I could think of was how easily it could have gone a different way, that it could have been you that was hurt, or killed. I kept seeing that blood, and it was like it was happening all over again."

"Sloan—"

She shook her head and he lapsed into silence as she went on. "I told myself I just couldn't do it, couldn't take that risk again. But no matter what I told myself, I couldn't change one basic thing."

"What?"

"I love you, Brett Dunbar. As you are. Who you are."

He nearly gasped with relief. This time when he reached for her, he didn't care about anything except that she was in his arms again, that she had come willingly, even eagerly. She leaned against him, and he held her tighter.

"It took some time to work through it all," she said as she pulled her knees up to get closer. "Some time and some wise advice from my family. They made me realize that I fell in love with you because of who you are, not in spite of it. Aunt Connie said I would always be attracted to heroes. You're proof of that."

He told himself to thank Connie for the compliment. If he saw her again. Which he was almost afraid to believe. "But you said you couldn't live with my job."

"And it still scares me. I don't ever want to go through that again. But Connie also said I can't change what draws me, so I can live with it or live without it. And that living without it would be such a waste."

She took a deep breath. He didn't know what to say, was afraid to say anything. After a moment she went on.

"So I finally realized that there's something that scares me even more than what you do. And that's looking at my life ahead without you in it."

He was almost afraid to believe it. "Jason," he said.

"He will always be in my heart. And I will always fight for his brothers in arms." She leaned back to look up at him. "If I can live with your job, can you live with that?"

"I wouldn't have it any other way. I'll help, if I ever can. He deserves no less."

"And that's another reason I love you," she said.

Brett nearly laughed when Cutter echoed his long, contented sigh. And then he kissed her. Gently at first, but it caught fire with the ease of banked embers coming back to life. If he hadn't had to stop to catch his breath, he thought he could have happily gone on forever.

"Brett?"

"Mmm."

"I just realized."

"What?"

"You've never seen my bedroom."

He went still. "No, I haven't."

"Would you like to?"

Cutter didn't have to herd them this time.

Epilogue

"So let me get this straight," Hayley Foxworth said, staring at Rafe. "We leave for a month and Dunbar takes down about half the county and the governor?"

"And does it with the help of Sloan Burke? *The* Sloan Burke?" Quinn added.

"And this guy," Rafe said, nodding toward where Hayley was tugging gently on Cutter's right ear. The dog sighed happily, clearly overjoyed to have his first people home. "But yeah, that sounds about right. Oh, and we're building a house."

Quinn blinked. Hayley laughed. "We are?"

"Well, Drew is. For the Days. I already cleared it with Charlie. And we may be paying some college tuition, too."

Quinn laughed.

"Always glad to contribute to education," Hayley said breezily, secretly delighted at this evidence of how wholeheartedly Rafe had taken to the Foxworth mission.

"It's for a friend of Brett's," Rafe explained. "And an investment for us. His daughter may be the help Ty needs."

"Good enough. So I gather the dogsitting went well?" Quinn asked.

"You could say that." Rafe's voice took on an undertone that made Hayley stop laughing and focus on him. "Brett's got his own bark now."

Hayley laughed. "Guess that makes him officially one of us."

Rafe said, in that same tone, "And he and Sloan, they're…together."

"You mean together together?" she asked, brows rising.

"Damn," Quinn said, staring at Cutter. "He did it again."

Rafe nodded. "And it's good for Brett," he said, clearly anticipating Hayley's first question. "Really good. And for her. You'll see when you see them together."

"Well, well," Quinn said.

"I told you someday he'd find someone who'd lift that darkness," Hayley said, feeling like clapping her hands in happiness for her friend. She caught the glint of her wedding ring. She moved her little finger to touch it, savoring the feel of it and letting what it symbolized fill her up once more.

"Apparently it took someone who'd lived in darkness herself," Rafe said softly.

Hayley's glee faded a little, although she kept the smile on her face. *You, too, my dear friend. Someday.*

She dug her fingers into Cutter's thick coat. The dog sighed contentedly. She bent over him and whispered in that right ear. "Work on that, will you, my lad?"

Cutter whuffed softly in return.

Hayley chose to think of it as "Mission accepted."

She had no doubt this one would take a while, but she had utter faith in the uncannily clever dog that had changed her own life and the lives of so many others. But for now, she thought, she would take him outside with one of his beloved tennis balls and let him be just a dog for a while.

He could go back to saving lives and hearts later.

* * * * *

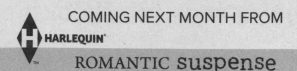

REQUEST YOUR FREE BOOKS!
2 FREE NOVELS PLUS 2 FREE GIFTS!

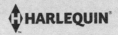

ROMANTIC suspense

Sparked by danger, fueled by passion

YES! Please send me 2 FREE Harlequin® Romantic Suspense novels and my 2 FREE gifts (gifts are worth about $10). After receiving them, if I don't wish to receive any more books, I can return the shipping statement marked "cancel." If I don't cancel, I will receive 4 brand-new novels every month and be billed just $4.74 per book in the U.S. or $5.24 per book in Canada. That's a savings of at least 14% off the cover price! It's quite a bargain! Shipping and handling is just 50¢ per book in the U.S. and 75¢ per book in Canada.* I understand that accepting the 2 free books and gifts places me under no obligation to buy anything. I can always return a shipment and cancel at any time. Even if I never buy another book, the two free books and gifts are mine to keep forever.

240/340 HDN F45N

Name	(PLEASE PRINT)	
Address		Apt. #
City	State/Prov.	Zip/Postal Code

Signature (if under 18, a parent or guardian must sign)

Mail to the **Harlequin® Reader Service:**
IN U.S.A.: P.O. Box 1867, Buffalo, NY 14240-1867
IN CANADA: P.O. Box 609, Fort Erie, Ontario L2A 5X3

Want to try two free books from another line?
Call 1-800-873-8635 or visit www.ReaderService.com.

* Terms and prices subject to change without notice. Prices do not include applicable taxes. Sales tax applicable in N.Y. Canadian residents will be charged applicable taxes. Offer not valid in Quebec. This offer is limited to one order per household. Not valid for current subscribers to Harlequin Romantic Suspense books. All orders subject to credit approval. Credit or debit balances in a customer's account(s) may be offset by any other outstanding balance owed by or to the customer. Please allow 4 to 6 weeks for delivery. Offer available while quantities last.

Your Privacy—The Harlequin® Reader Service is committed to protecting your privacy. Our Privacy Policy is available online at www.ReaderService.com or upon request from the Harlequin Reader Service.

We make a portion of our mailing list available to reputable third parties that offer products we believe may interest you. If you prefer that we not exchange your name with third parties, or if you wish to clarify or modify your communication preferences, please visit us at www.ReaderService.com/consumerschoice or write to us at Harlequin Reader Service Preference Service, P.O. Box 9062, Buffalo, NY 14269. Include your complete name and address.

HRS13R

SPECIAL EXCERPT FROM

H HARLEQUIN®

TM

ROMANTIC suspense

When a masked intruder appears in her son's window,
Nicolette Kendall needs help from reserved cowboy
Lucas Taylor. But even as his guarded heart begins to
crack, they must unravel secrets to save her child…

Read on for a sneak peek of
A REAL COWBOY, the first book in the
COWBOYS OF HOLIDAY RANCH *series*
by New York Times *bestselling author*
Carla Cassidy.

He stepped outside and looked around. "What are you doing out here all by yourself in the dark?"

"You told my son that cowboys only bathe once a week, and now Sammy won't get into the bathtub."

By the light of the room spilling out where they stood, she saw his amusement curve his lips upward. "Is that a fact?" he replied. "Sounds like a personal problem to me."

"It's all your fault," she said, at the same time trying not to notice the wonder of his broad shoulders, the slim hips that wore his jeans so well.

He raised a dark eyebrow. "The way I see it, you started it."

This time the heat that filled her cheeks was a new wave of pure embarrassment. "Look, I'm sorry. When I told my son those things, I'd never really met a cowboy before. The only cowboy I've ever even seen in my entire life is the naked singing cowboy in Times Square. I now have a little boy who refuses to take a bath. Can you please come back to the house with me and tell him differently?"

Amusement once again danced in his eyes as he gave her a smile that made her feel just a little bit breathless. "Basically you've come to say you're sorry about your preconceived notions about cowboys, because I think it would be nice if you apologized before asking for my help about anything."

"You're right. I am sorry," she replied, wondering if he wanted her to get down on her knees before him and grovel, as well.

"Okay, then, let's go." He pulled the door of his unit closed behind him and fell into step next to her.

"A naked singing cowboy...and you New Yorkers think we're strange." He laughed, a low, deep rumble that she found far too pleasant.

She realized at that moment that she wasn't afraid of cows or horses, that she wasn't worried about falling into the mud or getting her hands dirty.

The real danger came from the attraction she felt for the man who walked next to her, a man whose laughter warmed her and who smelled like spring wind and leather.

Don't miss A REAL COWBOY by Carla Cassidy,
available March 2015
wherever Harlequin® Romantic Suspense
books and ebooks are sold.

www.Harlequin.com

Love the Harlequin book you just read?

Your opinion matters.

Review this book on your favorite book site, review site, blog or your own social media properties and share your opinion with other readers!

Be sure to connect with us at:
Harlequin.com/Newsletters
Facebook.com/HarlequinBooks
Twitter.com/HarlequinBooks

JUST CAN'T GET ENOUGH?

Join our social communities
and talk to us online.

You will have access to the latest
news on upcoming titles and special
promotions, but most importantly,
you can talk to other fans about your
favorite Harlequin reads.

Harlequin.com/Community

Facebook.com/HarlequinBooks

Twitter.com/HarlequinBooks

Pinterest.com/HarlequinBooks

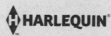